THE SEVEN CHAMPIONS
OF CHRISTENDOM

ST. GEORGE & THE DRAGON

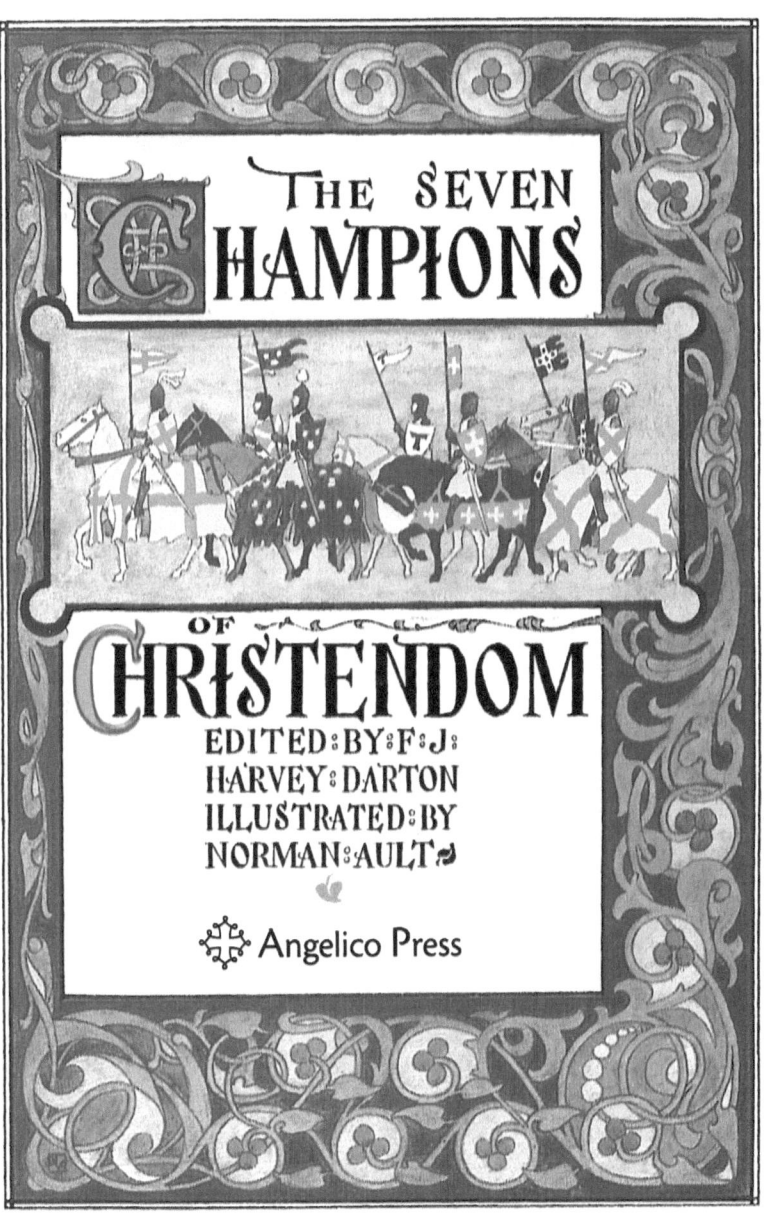

THE SEVEN CHAMPIONS OF CHRISTENDOM

EDITED BY F J
HARVEY DARTON
ILLUSTRATED BY
NORMAN AULT

Angelico Press

For information, address:
Angelico Press, Ltd.
169 Monitor St.
Brooklyn, NY 11222
www.angelicopress.com

Ppb: 979-8-88677-074-2
Cloth: 979-8-88677-075-9

Cover design
by Michael Schrauzer

INTRODUCTION

OF the man who produced the first version of "The Seven Champions of Christendom" practically nothing is known, except what the romance itself, and other works by the same author, suggest. He was baptized in May, 1573, by the name of Richard Johnson. He claims to have been first an apprentice, and afterwards a freeman, of the City of London; he may have had a court appointment in the reign of James I. It is not certainly known when he died. The British Museum Catalogue, with its impassive entries, is the chief obituary of many such another literary journeyman.

The derivation and promulgation of his best-known work, the romance here adapted, are no better certified. "The oldest known copy is dated 1597," says the "Dictionary of National Biography," with the addition that the book was entered at Stationers' Hall in 1596. The earliest copy in the British Museum Library is dated 1608. Lowndes, in

Introduction

" The Bibliographer's Manual," believes that " in all probability this work had been read by Shakespeare in some earlier edition not now known." Mr. Carr, of the New Shakespeare Society, points out some singular coincidences with Shakespeare's work— " numerous adumbrations, sometimes amounting to direct quotation." The general impression appears to be either that Johnson quotes Shakespeare, or that Shakespeare quotes Johnson (parts of the early editions of " The Seven Champions " being in blank verse—printed as prose—of more than respectable quality). I venture to suggest (as a guess, not as a hypothesis capable of proof) that both authors quote from an original now lost.

The only real proof of this suggestion would be the discovery of a MS. version—not an uncommon thing in the history of romance. The features which inspire such a guess are various. For one thing, the story itself, in Johnson's version, has very many of the constant factors of the medieval romance (to adopt a convenient term for what clearly survived the Middle Ages)—inconsequence, a wide range of desultory but often vigorous fantasy, a total neglect of practical detail and of chronological concordance (knights turn up when they are wanted, and with the necessary weapons, irrespective of their previous lawful occasions), and the fact that throughout the Saracen or Turk or pagan or Moor is regarded as the natural and permanent enemy of all decent people; whereas Queen Elizabeth and her merchant adventurers were much more keenly interested in the dyes and stuffs of the " Musulmanlike kingdom " than in ending, by means of Christian lances, the Grand Signor's alleged traffic with wizards and necromancers.

Shakespeare, again, knew the legend of St. George before 1596. He mentions in " King John," which is usually dated 1594, the hero who had " swinged the dragon," and so passed into the popularity of the tavern. And a famous reference in " King Lear " to " rats and mice and such small deer "—a literal quotation from the oldest version of the ancient romance of "Bevis of Hampton"—proves that, somehow or other, he knew something of these tales whose history is so baffling. We do not, indeed, in judging Shakespeare and lesser persons, allow enough for the strength of oral tradition before books became common. One of Johnson's editors points out that " Aubrey mentions. that his nurse could repeat the history of England, from the Conquest down to the time of Charles I., in ballads." Nursery

Introduction

rhymes never got into print till about 1740, but they are centuries older. Mr. Jacobs, in that delightful repository of fairy lore, "English Fairy Tales" (1890), gives a vernacular text of "Mr. Fox." Shakespeare, nearly three centuries earlier, uses the very same (then unprinted) words: "It is not so, and it was not so, and God forbid it should be so." There is no reason why a version of "The Seven Champions" should not have been floating about—able, like Ennius,".volitare vivus per ora virum"—for generations before either Shakespeare or Johnson heard of it. It is quite certain that such legends underwent secular changes. The "Guy of Warwick" of the fourteenth century Auchinleck Manuscript is a very different thing from the dismal chap-book versions of the eighteenth century. Nearly all the chap-book romance-stories have a larger, freer, and more artistic original. "The Seven Champions" itself suffered mutilation in its declension from Johnson's black-letter edition to the two-penny crudities of Aldermary Churchyard. Why should not Johnson have merely put into print ("by weary pen and painful author's toil," as his "Muse" is made to say) a familiar story of the day?

And it may also be urged that Johnson was

just the kind of man to do so. He collected, in this fashion, " The Pleasant Conceits of Old Hobson "—one of Shakespeare's jest-books, a " Percy Anecdotes " of the period. He did a prose version of " Tom Thumb." He wove a " Golden Garland of Princely Pleasures and Delicate Delights, being most pleasant songs and sonnets to sundry new tunes now most in use." He was plainly a busy writer, aiming not so much at expressing any ideals he had of life or literature, as at catching the public eye.

He caught it with " The Seven Champions." Whatever the *provenance* of the story, Johnson's version was immediately popular. It has been in print ever since. Many editors have rewritten it from time to time; among them W. H. G. Kingston, who introduced rather aggressive " morals " at intervals. The original is, to say the least, wordy and diffuse, euphuistic in its exuberance, but not always in its style. The present version is a very free one; I have simply considered the romance as a traditional story, not as what it certainly is not—a valuable piece of English literature. Johnson's text and that of the chap-books differ; I have used both as seemed most consistent with continuity and the reasonable divagations of romance.

Introduction

It is perhaps necessary to add that these "Champions of Christendom" have nothing whatever to do with the saints whose names they bear. Whoever St. George really was, he was most certainly not the kidnapped son of a Coventry knight. Johnson, or whoever first put the elements of the tale into a continuous whole, imposed a fictitious romance of chivalry upon the typical heroes of some European nations. Strictly, if one wished to be true to the romantic atmosphere, "Saint" should be read as "Sir," and Christendom would be better spelt "chivalry." On the other hand, the virtues of the knightly years are here at their best; and if the knights were warriors, and not saints, they were, in this venerable legend, fighting the battle of the Kingdom of God against the forces of evil—forces which, whether we call them giants or wizards or simply sins, are not yet wholly vanquished.

F. J. H. DARTON.

CONTENTS

Contents

LIST OF ILLUSTRATIONS

List of Illustrations

The PROPHECY

I

THE CAVE OF KALYB

LONG ago a certain knight of ancient lineage, akin to the royal line of Britain, lived at Coventry with his lady wife. He was High Steward of England, and his name was Albert. He had many men-at-arms and great possessions, and he ruled his lands well. He loved his lady truly, and she him. For many years they dwelt in honour and fame and happiness; but it was a sorrow to them that they had no son to inherit their wealth and power.

Now, one spring the lady began to be troubled with evil dreams. It seemed to her in these visions that terrible things befel her, and that from her came great woe (and also great good) to her husband and to England. Every night she dreamed thus, now one thing, now another, but always terrible and full of seeming truth. Her sleep was broken, and

3

she grew pale and timid, starting if anyone spoke to her, and seeing in any stranger or new thing some beginning of the unknown doom that she felt was to come upon her.

"Lady wife," said the Knight to her one day when they were alone, "what is amiss? Have you some secret sorrow? Tell me, that I may help you."

"It is nothing," she answered. "You cannot banish dreams."

"Dreams? They are nothing."

"They are real," she said sadly, "because they come unbidden, and make our minds a house for themselves, and we have no power over them. Soon they will have got possession of me altogether, and I shall have no thoughts of my own."

The Knight was sorely troubled. It seemed to him that something evil had laid hold of his wife. "We can conquer dreams," he said, to give her courage. "Look, if you sleep and dream, and I wake you, I drive the dreams away."

"Nevertheless, they come back," she replied. "They are signs of evil: they come in advance, so that I may be weakened and ready for what is to follow."

And she told him some of the terrors that she had seen in the night, when men and women can no longer choose what they will think.

The Knight, when he heard these fearful visions, sent forthwith to his wisest counsellors, old men who had grown grey in the art of ruling men, and had long forgotten how to dream. All that they could tell him was that dreams should be disregarded, for they had no truth and no meaning; and that was of little service, for they could not tell him how to set about making light of thoughts that come silently at night. And then the Knight sent for physicians; and one bled the lady, and another bade her take a decoction of certain herbs, to be plucked under a new moon, and a third said that to wear always next the heart a powdered mouse wrapped in a bag of lizard's skin would keep away visions, good or ill. But none of these remedies were of avail.

And lastly the Knight sent for magicians and astrologers, of whom there were known to be some in his domain, though they practised secretly, magic being unlawful in that region. These also, being promised a free conduct to Coventry and back again, came and exercised their arts. One would look into a crystal ball and see that the dreams had no meaning. Another cast a horoscope

The Prophecy

by means of the stars, and found that if under
one planet the lady did this, and under another
that, what was going to happen certainly
would happen; but he could not say what it
would be. Another one professed that he
knew the secret word that is written on the
Seal of Solomon the Wise; but all his knowledge did not cause the dreams to cease.

The Knight was in despair. By now he,
too, had come to believe that great and
terrible happenings were upon them. There
was but one person left of whom he might
seek aid with any hope of winning it, and
that was the enchantress Kalyb. For long
he dared not mention that terrible name to
his wife; he kept it hidden in his mind, and
spoke to no man of it. But every day his
wife grew more afraid, and all her strength
was wasted away. Kalyb might kill him by
wizardry; she might turn him into a block
of marble, to come to life again a thousand
years thence in a strange world; she might
strike him with a wand, so that he would
become a pig or a dog; but whatever doom
came upon him would be better than seeing
his wife die before his eyes of terror and
weakness.

For the truth is that Kalyb was an enchantress of grim power, prone to do evil upon

"THE KNIGHT SENT FOR MAGICIANS AND ASTROLOGERS"

no known cause, and very ready to vent her spite upon innocent persons. She dwelt many leagues from Coventry, in the far west, beyond the Wilderness of Wirral, and the Valley of Stones. Her cave—for the few who had been to her dwelling reported that her home was a great cavern—lay in the uttermost depths of the Dark Forest, where was always the sound of a wind moaning among dead boughs, and the roaring of beasts, and the twittering of unseen shapes. No man might walk there and not meet with fear.

All this Sir Albert knew, and pondered long. For himself he cared nothing; he was as brave as any man might be. But he dreaded that a journey of such peril might seem to his lady a worse evil than her dreams.

At length he told her his thoughts. " I can die but once," he said, simply. " It is plain that if no way out of these visions can be found for you, death is near you too; and if by giving my life I can save yours, I am content. Nor is it certain that I must die if I visit Kalyb. She has killed many, and many also have perished in trying to reach her cave. But some have succeeded, and who knows but that these very dreams, so terrible to you, are not meant to warn

9

me that I should consult her magic ? I
will go."

It was long before he persuaded his wife
that it was best for him to go. But at length
she yielded, and he set out, taking with him
but one attendant.

It was no great journey—but a day's ride—
from Coventry to the edge of the Wilderness
of Wirral. But that wilderness in those days
was a place of danger. In part it was a huge
stretch of heath-land, full of prickly bushes
and thick, low-growing shrubs, which bore
no fruit or flower to comfort men's sight or
satisfy their hunger. In the shrubs lay hid
serpents and venomous insects, and the soil,
grey and stony, gave no grass to soften the
road. And in part there was not even the
growth of bushes, but stones only, and barren
earth, and a few gnarled roots of trees that
had died long ages before. Here not so
much as a rabbit moved or had life, and the
few ill-favoured birds that flew overhead
seemed to pass the plain quickly, as if they,
too, were afraid. For two days and a night
the road ran thus.

Beyond that the land sloped upwards, till
the Knight came to high down lands, where
the green turf gave him ease, and the winds
blew from every quarter with a fresh and

lively breath. It was evening when he reached the heights, and he lay down and fell into a deep sleep.

In the morning he saw that the Valley of Stones lay before him. And here he sent his servant back, for he did not know what might be in front of him, and he would not take another man, it might be to death. The servant was loth to go, for he loved the good Knight dearly; but his master bade him return and say that thus far his journey was safely accomplished.

The sun had risen behind him, but was still low in the heaven. Sir Albert cast a long shadow before him as he left the green grass on the top of the hills, and began to descend into the valley. In a little time, so sharply did the path fall, he had outstripped the sun, and came below the range of its beams. Now there were no shadows, and the green of the grass seemed less bright. The hills appeared to stretch up and up at either side till they left but a straight strip of blue sky above and the long slopes in front to be seen. The track grew more uneven, and full of small stones. Then the stones became larger and more scattered, till they were great rocks, grey, and covered with grey and yellow moss. The track curved a little, and the Knight saw the whole valley open before him, now level for a long distance before it sloped upwards again. The rocks, still untouched by the sun, stood on either side of the path like cold ghosts. There was no sign of man in all that place; it seemed dead, and there was an utter loneliness and silence. Sometimes men fear because they can see terrible things, or hear them; sometimes they fear because there is nothing. In the Valley of Stones there was nothing; and chill and dread fell upon Sir Albert.

"My lady wife has feared greater terrors than this," he thought, and strode on up the hill. Presently, as he climbed, he came into the sunlight again. And now the stones seemed no longer dumb ghosts, but warm and sparkling; the turf shone, and he heard a lark rising with its song. In front the path mounted steadily upwards.

It was long past noon when at last he had crossed the whole valley, and came to its westernmost end, high up among endless hills. The path did not run right over the top, but cleaved a way in between two hillocks, their sides being cut away a little for it, so that the gleaming white chalk showed. In this pass the Knight stopped, and looked back at the long ghostly valley. "Thus far have

12

The Cave of Kalyb

I come in safety," he thought, "and have passed two dangers—the barren wilderness and the dreadful silence. Now must I meet the third."

The sun had begun to sink. He looked onwards. The path seemed to vanish a few yards away. He went on, and saw that it curved round a mound of earth. Beyond the mound lay a deep ditch, and above it yet another mound. The Knight went across the ditch, and found that he was in a maze of trenches and walls and paths, all of green turf, one after another. He followed first one path, then another, keeping always in front of him the direction whence the light came; but he seemed to get no farther among these grassy windings. The sun fell lower in the sky, and the cold shadows filled up the hollows, and still the path led nowhere but round and round upon its own track. Then, as twilight slid over the earth, and the birds' songs began to die into silence, the Knight left the path, and climbed, with great pain and labour, up a steep bank to westward. Twice he slipped on the short turf, for the slope was well-nigh upright, and he rolled down into the trench again. But the third time he flung his arm over the top of the earth wall, and so scrambled on top.

13

The Prophecy

There in front was a great green space, ending, as far as his eyes could see in the distance, in deep woodlands of a terrible dark green. Behind lay the ridges where he had been wandering, like a range of little mountains, with shadowy valleys between.

Sir Albert walked wearily across the green turf, which now gradually began to slope downwards again. At first the grass was fresh and thick, cropped short and powdered with little purple scabious, like amethysts upon a green table. But as the slope deepened and he drew near the Dark Forest— for it was Kalyb's lair that he now approached —the green became dulled and brown, like the dry growth of a barren common where gorse has been burnt.

On the edge of the forest the Knight halted. It would not be well to seek out the Enchantress by night, he thought, when the weariness of his journey was still upon him. So he ate a little of his store of food, and lay down by a great oak just outside the forest, and tried to sleep. Indeed, he slept, but it was a fitful and restless slumber, broken by dreams and sudden awakenings to terror. It seemed to him in one vision that he was being kept violently back from his lady wife, and that she looked on him with eyes of un-

14

speakable sadness and longing as he strove in vain to move; some force appeared to chain his limbs. He woke trembling; and all around him he heard the noises of dreadful night, when evil enchantments have more power—whisperings and squeakings, and hoarse, low voices full of fury.

Day came at last, and Sir Albert rose and ate. He loosened his sword in its sheath, and spoke silently a prayer, and turned into the forest. As he left the light and came into the shade of the dark trees, it seemed to him that thunder sounded, and the solid earth shook. In a little while there was no sky to be seen; nothing but black tree-trunks and twisted roots, and above a thick-woven canopy of gloomy branches and brown leaves. It was as if those trees had never in their lives seen Spring come upon the earth, or renewed their youth with fresh young leaves, but had stood there, unshaken by the winds of the world, growing old and yet older, till the sap in their veins ran thin and poisonous. The very creatures that lived in that place seemed of evil omen: birds of rusty black, with sunken, dim eyes and bald heads and fierce crooked beaks; lizards that had no green or blue radiance, but only a cold, brown skin with no light in it; snakes all black with never

15

a bright diamond of other hue; worms that
were pale and white and slow-moving. And
there were noises also: now a howling as of
beasts in pain; now a bellowing as of some
great monster, not loud only but threatening
and passionate; now a faint whimpering that
was almost weeping. Bats squeaked shrilly,
and brushed against the Knight with their
cold, leathery wings; the evil birds croaked
harshly at him. If ever fear walked abroad,
surely the Dark Forest was the place of its
marching.

Yet Sir Albert pressed on. The trees grew
denser; brambles and undergrowth choked
what faint semblance of a track he followed;
often he had to cut them away with his sword.
Hour after hour he struggled forward, until
his eyes had become so used to the dim light
that he no longer was desirous of the clear
day. Once he rested a while, and ate, and
went on refreshed. But it was not till late
in the afternoon that he perceived that the
darkness was growing a little less thick in
front of him, and the ground beginning to
slope a little upwards and to be more stony.

The change put new heart into him. He
hurried forward, stumbling hastily over loose
stones towards the light. And yet it was not
bright light in front of him, but only a cold,

pale light like that before dawn, a lessening of darkness.

The trees ended suddenly in a little clearing of grass and a few gorse and bramble bushes. The other side of the clearing rose a great rocky cliff, sheer and stern. In the middle of it, with pillars rudely shaped in the rock on either side, was a huge iron door, opening in the middle, with immense hinges and knobs upon it. There was no keyhole nor latch, nor knocker, but from one of the pillars at the side hung a carved brazen trumpet chained to the rock by iron links.

Sir Albert paused. Here plainly was the home of the Enchantress. Should he summon her by blowing the trumpet? Or would that command, as it might seem, rouse her to anger? He looked at the great door. There was no sound or sign of life behind it. There was an utter silence in the clearing; all the noises of the forest were stilled.

He walked boldly to the pillar, drew his sword, and held it ready in his right hand, took the trumpet in his left, and blew a strong blast.

For a second there was silence; then the sound of the brazen trumpet beat against the rock and was thrown back to the woods behind with a thousand echoes, as if from all

17

quarters unseen beings were blowing signals of tumult and war.

The echoes died in a jangling chorus. Then before Sir Albert's eyes the rock shook to and fro, and the ground beneath him quaked. There was a low rumbling, which grew louder and louder until it was a roar of rolling thunder. The iron gates, without moving, clanged as if they had been shut violently. When all the sound had ceased, a hollow voice boomed from behind them these words :

> " Return, Sir Knight, thy wife has borne a son ;
> But in that birth you both are quite undone.
> Fierce as a dragon shall he be in fight,
> Yet more than dragon's is St. George's might."

Sir Albert let the point of his sword sink to the ground, and his arm hung loosely, as he heard that strange saying. Every word was clear and distinct: yet he could find no meaning in them, except that his wife had borne a son and that he was bidden to return to her.

He stood in thought for a minute. Then he laid hold upon the trumpet again. And yet, as he seized it, he changed his mind, and let it fall. The voice had bidden him return. It may be that Kalyb herself had spoken. Here at least was certainly her lair. He had

"HERE PLAINLY WAS THE HOME OF THE ENCHANTRESS . . . HE
DREW HIS SWORD"

come to question her; he had had his answer before he asked the question. Who knew but that some terrible doom might come upon him if he pressed her further?

He turned and walked towards the dark forest, slowly and heavily at first, then more quickly, and at last desperately when his purpose to return grew strong in him and he thought upon those other words, "You both are quite undone."

II

THE BIRTH OF ST. GEORGE

It was more than a week since he first set out when Sir Albert, weary, haggard, travel-stained, came again to his castle at Coventry. The gates on either side the drawbridge were open, as was customary, and a guard saluted him as he passed. But though the news of his coming had gone before him, there were no signs of joyful welcome, no blowing of trumpets and assembling of men-at-arms. The very guards looked askance, as though they had some secret that they feared to tell him.

He came into his great hall. His boar-hound rose and met him, licking his hand in

21

welcome, and scattering the rushes on the floor with his leapings and caperings of joy. But that was the only joyful thing to be seen. The pages and serving-men wore dark garments of woe, the maids were red-eyed with weeping. A little group of attendants— the squire, the bailiff, and the seneschal and clerks and other officers—waited timidly till he spoke.

"What, Seneschal?" said Sir Albert. "Have I gone on a journey of peril and returned safely to be welcomed like this?"

"My lord——" said the Seneschal, and stopped.

"Sir," said the Squire, "what answer did you get from the Enchantress?"

"We marvel that you have returned safely, my lord," added a clerk. "Doubtless you have a strange tale to tell. Our tale is strange, too, and sad also."

The Knight looked at him steadily, feeling the burden of some new sorrow close upon him. "I do not know what the Enchantress meant by her answer," he said: "her words were without meaning, as it seemed. But I think they were words of doom." And he told them the rhymes he had heard.

"My lord," said the Seneschal slowly, "I can explain Kalyb's saying; but I fear that it

The Birth of St. George

has a sorrowful meaning. Let not your anger
fall upon me for my story."
"You know that I am just, Sir Seneschal,"
answered Sir Albert. "Say on."
"Listen, then, my lord. Trouble has come
upon you, close on the heels of joy, and all
the heavier because of that joy. Two days
after you had set out for the dark forest
your wife bore a son; and at his birth she
died."
He paused. Sir Albert could not speak.
But he made a sign to the Seneschal to
continue.

"'Thy wife has borne a son,
But in that birth you both are quite undone,'"

said the Seneschal gently. "The Enchantress
foresaw this, if, indeed, it is not of her con-
triving. There is worse to tell, my lord."
"Worse? What can be worse? Have I
not lost my dearest wife?" said the Knight
bitterly.
"That is not all you have lost, my lord.
The babe was a fine boy, and on him there
were curious signs which I do not doubt are
marks that one day he shall be great and
famous, as befits the High Steward of England's son. But perhaps we shall never know
of his fame. My lord, four nurses were set

23

to guard and tend him. They were chosen well, and no fault can be found with them. All the castle was on watch and ward as is customary in your absence. But what is all the caution in the world against magic? Two days after the boy was born, my lord, as he slept in the afternoon, two nurses being with him, he was stolen by black arts. They did not neglect their watch: one was busied with her needle, the other rocked the cradle and did but look aside out of the window for a moment. In that moment the babe vanished, with no sound or sign of any person, no, nor even of any evil spirit. We have searched everywhere, my lord. There is no explanation but the craft of some wizard, who, it may be, has a grudge against you."

Sir Albert was long silent. Then he questioned the men strictly about the guard that was set, and summoned the nurses, and questioned them also. But he could learn no more. The child had vanished in open daylight, and no cause seen.

"You said there were marks upon him," said Sir Albert presently. "What were they?"

"These, my lord," answered the Seneschal. "On his breast, in red, was the image of a dragon. In the palm of his right hand was a red cross. On his left leg was a band like a golden garter. Your lady wife, as she died, begged that he might be named George. I do not know——"

"Yes," said the Knight wonderingly. "It is as Kalyb prophesied, though I cannot tell how it will come true. She said he should be fierce as a dragon, and she spoke of St. George." And he fell into thought.

His servants and officers stood silent, with bowed heads. At last Sir Albert spoke. "It is plain to me," he said, "that my son has been stolen by magic arts; I do not know for what purpose. I do not know if the wicked Kalyb stole him, or if she had a hatred against me, who never wronged her in all my life. But she knew that great things were to come upon the boy; she knew of his birth before I came to her fortress. She bade me return; I have returned, to this sorrowful news. I think if she had desired me to ask her further, or to go back to the Dark Forest again, she would have said so. So I will not seek her again. But she said nothing of whether I should seek my son or not. And hear me now, my friends "—and he raised his voice till it rang through the hall—" I vow before you all that I will go forth from Coventry into every corner of the whole wide world in search of my son, and I will not come back here till I have found him—no, not if I have to end my days in a foreign land."

He strode from them to his chamber. When he had removed from him the dust of travel, he went to look upon his wife for the last time. Even on that day they were to bury her, with all due ceremony.

Messengers were sent into all parts of England—aye, and farther, for news of the boy St. George (for by that name he was ever afterwards called). They went and came back; they brought no tidings. Sir Albert had search made in all places where the child might be hid. But he learnt nothing. So he begged of the King that he might be freed from his office of High Steward, and the King graciously gave him his freedom. And then, having made all needful preparations, he set forth from Coventry to wander over the world till he found his son.

Never more did he set eyes upon his castle of Coventry. Never did he so much as hear of the son he had not yet seen. For ten years he was a knight-errant, taking up such adventures as came in his path, fighting with all the usages of chivalry and knighthood, and everywhere asking and hoping for the news

he never received. In the tenth year, worn
with travel and not far from despair, he came
to the Holy Land of Palestine, and there
joined in the wars against the pagan Saracens,
and was slain, fighting fearlessly for Christendom.

III

ST. GEORGE AND THE ENCHANTRESS

The son whom Sir Albert lost without ever
seeing him was destined to be the patron
saint of England, the slayer of the dragon.
The Enchantress Kalyb had indeed stolen
him, that she might work out his destiny by
giving him suitable arms and a chosen band
of companions. But he was not to set eyes
on other mortals for many a long year. The
only being in human form he saw till he came
almost to manhood was Kalyb herself; she
appeared to him always in the guise of a
lovely maiden, who had the gift of eternal
youth and beauty. For the rest, St. George's
comrades, or guardians, were none else than
twelve satyrs, hideous creatures, half men, half
goats, who waited on him, and taught him the
use of arms and all knightly arts, but would not
suffer him out of their sight for an instant.

So he dwelt in Kalyb's power for many a

long year, growing strong and wise and good to look upon, but ignorant of all that might be in the world of other men.

There came a day at length when Kalyb visited him, appearing more lovely than ever, and had serious speech with him.

" I will make you lord of all my magic realm," she said, looking longingly upon him, " if you will marry me and live with me for ever. By my power I will make you eternally young, even as I am. Am I not fair to look on ?"

" Even so, Enchantress," said St. George courteously, for it was true. " But I do not love you; I do not think well of your black arts. I think such powers are unlawful for men to use." For the champion, though he had never learnt anything of men's nature, had born in him, deep in his heart, a dread and hatred of all that was evil. " You are very fair, but you do wicked deeds."

" You do not know what wickedness is, poor youth," said Kalyb mockingly. " How should you ? And you do not know what power is. Look at this wand "—and she showed him a golden wand, curiously powdered with silver stars and signs in the ancient language of Arabia—" look at this wand. With it you may have dominion over the

solid earth. Strike the hard rock, and it will
fly open. Beat the ground with it, thus "—
and she struck the earth thrice in a singular
manner—" and the firm floor of the world
shall rock." And indeed there was a terrible
rumbling, and the earth quaked. " I can
give you all the wealth that there is now in
the whole globe; I can tell the secret places
where rubies and topazes are found, and
where diamonds hang on the trees. I can
change men's visages so that they appear
like beasts, or, again, transform the beasts
into the likeness of upright-walking men.
This wand and its spells are the least of my
powers."

The young man was strongly moved by
her promises. Yet he did not trust her.
" These are great wonders, lady," he said
simply. " But I have no liking for them.
Why have you bred me thus, so that I know
nothing of other men ? I have been told by
those ugly guards of mine that there is a world
outside your dominion, and that there men
strive for honour and justice, and live, and
love, and die; but what do I know of it, save
that I am well fitted for it, if their praise of
my skill be true ? What use should I make
of your powers when I do not even know
my own ? Who am I ? What is my lot ?

The Prophecy

What am I to do, I who am a man and no magician ?"

" Aye, who are you ?" laughed Kalyb bitterly, for by her magic arts she knew that St. George must one day leave her, and that soon ; but she did not know the manner of his going, and she was eager to prevent it if it were possible. " Who are you ? Who in this realm of mine are your parents ? Why have you been trained as a knight ? I could tell you. But that is mere human talk and knowledge; I can give you a better wisdom and a power far greater."

St. George pondered a moment. It came into his head that he would humour her, though what would be the issue of it, or how it would end, he could not guess. " Fair Enchantress," he said, " why should we not strike a bargain ? These powers that you speak of are without doubt greatly to be desired. But I am a man, and I desire yet more ardently to know what man I am, and for what purpose you have brought me hither and trained me in the knightly customs of mankind. If you will tell me that, and reveal to me the state and names of my parents, I will marry you, and you shall teach me this magic that you are so set upon giving me."

Kalyb wondered a little at his request.

St. George and the Enchantress

But she had fallen deeply in love with the splendour of his youth, and wished to defeat fate, and keep him always with her. But no enchantments can defeat the high purposes that rule the world for its good.

"Sir George," she answered, "it shall be a bargain. First I will tell you your lineage, and then I will show you certain marvels of my art, and then you shall marry me, and we will come into great happiness. Now, first, you are of the blood royal of England, the son of Sir Albert, High Steward, Lord of Coventry, and his lady wife. They have both left this life many years now. I can tell you afterwards the manner of their deaths. When you were born, I stole you by enchantments. Here in my kingdom you have been ever since."

"England!" said St. George. "That is a country of which my guards have told me much. Now reveal to me why I am here."

"Softly," said the Enchantress, for she knew that if she told him his destiny he would try to make it come true. "Let us first search out my other secrets, the wonders of my realm. They are things of the present; your fate is a matter for the future."

St. George made no bones about it. He felt, with this new knowledge, that he was

born for some great end which would come
to pass in the due time.

"Come," said Kalyb, taking her wand.
She waved it round and over his head
and shoulders, and muttered some words
that he did not understand; then she chanted
other words:

> "Hear, be awakened; see the unseen;
> Learn the wonders that have been."

He seemed, as she spoke, to become more a
man than before, less a prisoner in a strange
and mysterious land. Then, though he thought
he had wandered with his satyrs over all her
kingdom, Kalyb led him into a region close
at hand upon which he believed that he had
never before set eyes. They went by a
winding path among rocks, whereon grew
wallflower and stonecrop, for all the world
as if there was no evil influence in the place.
They came anon to a castle of lime and stone,
very well built, with many turrets, and upon
each a different gay flag. It was set upon a
hill, or great rock, so that any man approaching it could be easily seen from afar.

Kalyb struck the high portcullis with her
wand, and it rose above them with never a
sound of ropes or pulleys. Within were great
chambers marvellously decorated with rich

St. George and the Enchantress

tapestries, tall candles, and many-coloured glass. Beyond lay a garden full of sweet herbs and bushes cut into life-like shapes ; here was a unicorn in yew, there a peacock in box, there a whole file of horsemen in close-growing laurel. The garden ended in a great cliff of grey rock, covered in many places with yellow lichen; from cracks in the stone grew red valerian, and lean cats walked to and fro beneath, waving their thin tails at the smell of that strange plant.

" Here is your destiny," said Kalyb bitterly. " But it is better not to know it. It will bring you into great sorrows and through many hardships; there will be in it more sadness and toil than joy. Better to abide here, young knight; I can give you ease, and sweetness, and youth for ever, and power. What is the good of toil without end ?"

" Tell me my destiny," said St. George. " No man can be happy in ease that he has not earned; that much my manhood tells me."

Kalyb said no more. She made a pass with her wand. St. George was looking at the rock, and the red plant, and the cats. Suddenly he saw in their place, fast against the rock, motionless as if they too were rock, six comely knights fully armed. They appeared, as it were, asleep, and yet in a greater stillness than sleep gives.

"They will not wake until an appointed time," said Kalyb grimly. "These are to be your companions if you choose that life of hardship. Here is St. Denis, who shall be reverenced by France; he shall have the form of a beast, and shall marry a tree. This is James of Spain; his deeds shall be to kill a pig and change his skin. This is Anthony of Italy, who shall kill a foolish giant. St. Andrew, the next, will do no more than slay a magician. St. Patrick here shall set upon certain satyrs—you know their prowess. And, last of all, St. David will get his arms from a stone."

So she spoke, making at once a mockery and a mystery of these knights who were to be the champions of Christendom.

"Do not answer," she said, as St. George made as if to ask her questions. "I have not shown you all yet. You must not choose your destiny till you have seen all." For she still hoped vainly that St. George would choose to marry her, and so put himself into her power, to treat as she had treated the other champions.

She led him back to the castle, to the stables, which they had not yet visited.

St. George and the Enchantress

There were seven noble chargers, and by them all the trappings for the steeds of knights.

"These are for you and your comrades—if they are to be your comrades," she said. "This white horse is yours. He is named Bucephalus, after the horse of the great Alexander, who conquered all the world as far as Tartary. Now let us find armour for you."

They went to an armoury—a long chamber hung with swords and lances and shields. Here were gilt spurs, and steel morions, and surcoats blazoned with gold thread, halberds, sharp, thin daggers that would slit the life of a man out in a second, great two-handed swords, fine rapiers. There was not any weapon known to chivalry which was not in that gallery, each in order and bright for use.

Kalyb went to the end of the chamber, where hung by itself a great sword with a hilt in the shape of a cross. She took it down, and offered it to St. George. "Here is a sword which shall be the most famous in the world. No man save you has handled it; it shall be the sword of St. George. With it you shall be invincible, the champion of right against wrong, of good against evil. The name of this sword is Ascalon."

St. George took the sword. It lay in his

The Prophecy

hand as if it had been made to fit his grip ;
never had he held a weapon more easily.

Kalyb looked at him as he tested the sword.
She felt that her power over him was slipping
from her.

"Have I pleased you, dear knight ?" she
asked tenderly. "Have I armed you well ?"

"It is a good sword. I thank you, Kalyb,"
replied St. George. He knew his parentage
and his destiny now. It only remained to be
free of the Enchantress. And in a little while,
as she had promised, she would give him
magic powers. "Take me to my comrades,"
he said. "Will you not bring them to life
for me ?"

"Bring to life the men who shall take you
from me ?" said Kalyb. "I shall not let
you go so easily, Sir George. You shall see
how I might have served you had I willed;
then, perhaps, you will be grateful to me and
love me. Come."

They went back towards the garden and the
rocky cliff. When they came to the cliff, at
the end of it, where it sloped away towards
a dark wood, she gave him her wand.

"See, I give you my power," she cried.
"All that I have is now yours. Strike this
hard rock, and see how great is my gift, and
believe that I love you."

"ST. GEORGE STARTED BACK IN HORROR"

St. George and the Enchantress

He struck the rock. With a rending crash it burst asunder, and a narrow, dark way opened through it. St. George peered within. Then he started back in horror. On either side, in the rock itself, were the bodies of little children.

"What is this, foul wizard?" he cried, in dismay and anger. "What have you done to these innocent children that I see here dead in this cruel rock?"

Kalyb laughed savagely. "I told you that I had spared you," she answered. "I stole all these babes from their parents, and slew them, and placed them there. Even so I might have slain you had I not looked on you with favour. Do you see now what a gift of love and power it is that I offer you?"

"Never will I marry you, detestable witch!" cried St. George furiously.

"You will break your word?" said the Enchantress with malice. "You, a knight, promised to marry me if I would tell you your name and parentage. Can a knight break his promise?"

St. George was silent. He saw into what a horrible issue his promise had led him. He knew now that he was marked out to be the champion of England and right, and yet he was pledged, by the promise that had won that knowledge for him, to a wicked enchantress, whose every deed was hateful to him.

"Release me from my word, Kalyb," he said pitifully, at last.

"Never," she answered triumphantly. Then she saw how sorely he was stricken. "These were my enemies' children," she said more gently. "Come deep into the rock with me; bring the wand, and you shall see for yourself wonders that will give you pleasure, not sorrow."

She turned and entered the cleft in the rock. St. George made as if to follow her. But he saw that his opportunity had come. As she went forward into the darkness, he leapt lightly back, and struck the rock with the wand again. "Rock, be shut," he cried.

The rock clanged to with a noise as of beaten iron. There was a roaring in the cliffside, and the wood at a little distance bent and swayed as if a storm suddenly swept it. From the rock came shrieks and groans, and a rushing noise filled all the air. The earth trembled. Then there was a great stillness, for she who had enchanted that place was dead, and a thousand spirits had torn her body in pieces. All things returned again to their natural uses, for Kalyb's power was broken and gone.

St. George and the Enchantress

St. George stood speechless and aghast. He felt as if he were waking from a terrible dream. Then he remembered the wand in his hand and the sword at his side. He broke the wand across his knee, and threw the fragments from him.

"Lie there, evil thing," he said, as he cast it away, "and be a sign that thus shall all wickedness be broken and cast aside. Now for my comrades and the way of the champions."

He went to the place where he had seen the six knights bound in an enchanted silence. He found them there, but no longer still and dumb. They were rubbing their eyes and stretching themselves like men roused from deep sleep, and asking one another questions in amazement at their sudden freedom. At the sound of St. George's step they turned to him in wonder.

"Friends," he said, before they could find words to speak, "I am here to set you free, that we may seek adventure in the world together. I have slain Kalyb, the wicked Enchantress." And he told them all that had just come to pass. "Now it is for us to go forth in arms and right wrongs," he ended. "There are arms and steeds for us all here, and we will fare forth to seek our fortunes as knights must."

The Prophecy

They went to the stable where the horses were, and took each his charger. Then they chose such arms as they desired from the armoury, and having feasted together in the palace, and made such store of food as they could with ease carry, they left the realm of Kalyb for ever.

They knew not wither they were going, nor upon what quest. "We are to become knights by all due rites in reward of knightly deeds," said St. George. "The Enchantress told me that we should be the champions of Christendom. Let us seek Christendom, and do whatever tasks may come in our way; let us uphold the Christian faith against pagans, and our honour and right against all evil-doers."

There seemed to be but one path away from Kalyb's castle. It was not that by which Sir Albert had come thither many years before, for that had been created by magic arts, and so soon as Kalyb's power was destroyed, her wiles and snares were destroyed too. The path the champions followed led out into the wide world by lonely ways; fear of the Enchantress had driven men far from her dwelling. They journeyed many miles and met never another soul. At length they came to a place where there were seven cross-roads, and no signs of whither they led.

St. George and the Enchantress

" Here let us part," said St. George, when they had debated in vain which way they should take. " Here are seven roads, all unknown to us even as the world itself is unknown. Let us each take our own road, and find upon it the hidden things that life is to reveal to us. We shall come together again, be sure of that; the brotherhood of champions shall not be broken, even though we be apart for years."

They agreed to this with no more words; and so, with loving farewells, they parted, each upon a different road.

S͟T. GEORGE
OF
ENGLAND

I

ST. GEORGE AND THE DRAGON

THE road followed by St. George led him into many lands. It bore him first of all through England to the sea-board, where he took ship and sailed over the narrow seas to Europe. He journeyed through the Lowlands to Germany, and so across Hungary to where the Christians were fighting the Saracen Turks on the eastern edge of Europe. He took ship again, after many battles, and came at last to a city on the shores of Egypt, where was a lighthouse and a great castle of stone. Thence he set out to cross the desert to the court of the king of that country.

His good white horse bore him bravely through the burning sand. But with the heat and the long toil of his wanderings he was very weary. He longed to see again the city of Coventry and the woods of England and the faces of his own people. Here there

47

was nothing but glaring light and strange heathen folk, for whom he cared nothing.

As he thought thus, he looked about him sadly. Suddenly he saw a great way off a little hut by some palm-trees, and near it a man standing. He drew near quickly, and perceived that the man was a holy hermit, and the hut a rough shelter of leaves and branches, in which he lived.

The old man, his long beard shining in the sun, stood in his path, and held up his arms against St. George, motioning him to halt. "Come no farther, Sir Knight," he said, "whoever you may be."

"I stay for no man's bidding," answered St. George. "Why do you call me to halt?"

"This way lie sorrow and death, young man," replied the hermit solemnly. "Here is a land of mourning, and no mirth or entertainment for any man—no, not even if he is the bravest knight on earth."

"It would ill become me to claim that name," said St. George. "But it is my task to aid the sorrowful, and to dare all that a brave knight may."

"Many another has said that, in high hope," answered the hermit, looking narrowly upon him. "It may be that you are he who shall

48

carry out his hopes : such a one there may
be."

" You talk in riddles, holy man," said St.
George; " tell me what this sorrow is that
has fallen upon your land."

" The dragon," said the hermit. " There
is a loathly dragon here, who has his lair in
a cave in a fruitful valley that is one of the
green places in this waste of sand. This
dragon for twenty-four years has ravaged
the King's realm; and when he came hither
first (no man knew whence), he set up a
custom of taking one maiden every day to
devour. Many knights have gone out against
him, to kill him ; but with his poisonous
breath or his great claws he has slain every
one, so that none now dare assail him,
but we must offer him every day a maiden.
Now it has come to this : that there is only
one maiden of suitable age left in all the
kingdom, Sabra herself, the King's daughter.
To-morrow she must be bound and left in
the valley for the dragon; and he will devour
her, and after that I know not what will
come upon us. But if any knight can slay the
dragon, there is reward enough for him, for
the King will give him the Princess Sabra in
marriage, and make him his heir."

" I want no kingdoms," said St. George ;

" and as for your Princess, I know nothing of her. But if I can slay the dragon and save her, I will."

The hermit shook his head. " Many knights have said the like," he said. " You will see their bones in the valley if you are so rash as to venture there."

" Would you have a Christian knight fear to succour a lady in peril because others have failed ?" asked St. George. " I will fight the dragon. Let me rest here in your hut this night, and to-morrow you shall guide me to this valley."

The hermit tried again to turn him from his purpose, but to no avail. So he took the champion into his hut and refreshed him with his simple fare. That night St. George lay in the hut and rested, and the next morning early the hermit guided him to the entrance of the valley.

It was a deep ravine rather than a valley. At the bottom lay a little stream, whose waters so strengthened the soil that trees and flowers flourished abundantly. The entrance was by a rocky pass, on the side of which, stretching down the steep slope, grew a dark little wood of cypress-trees. Below, at the bottom of the valley, were rich meadows, and in the midst of the fairest and greenest

St. George and the Dragon

of them stood an orange-tree of surpassing beauty, the fruit whereof—for it was the season of ripe fruit—were larger and more splendid than any on earth. Beyond this meadow was the dark entrance to the dragon's cave.

St. George parted from the hermit at the entrance in the pass. The hermit gave him his blessing, and the champion set forth down the stony path, his horse picking its way carefully along the uneven track. The cypress-trees made the path dark and gloomy. But when he had passed them, St. George saw before him a princess so lovely that she seemed to light up the whole valley. She was clad all in pure white silk, with a golden circlet on her head, and she was bound to an outlying tree, looking pitifully down to the meadows, whence came at intervals a dull, low sound, as of a terrible threatening roar.

St. George halted for a second in wonder at her beauty. Then he spurred his horse and alighted by the tree. He drew his sword and cut the bonds. Then he knelt to her and saluted her.

" Who are you, Sir Knight ?" she said in surprise, and a little in fear.

" Princess," he answered, " I am not yet a knight; I have not won my spurs. But I desire to do all knightly deeds. I shall fight

51

this dragon, and, by God's aid, slay him. Meanwhile do you hasten back to the king your father, and say to him that a champion has been found for you, who will, if all go well with him, pay him his humble duty at his court when the dragon has been slain. Speed now, Princess, for the dragon grows impatient."

And, indeed, at that moment a roar sounded from the valley that made the branches of the tree rattle against one another, and set up an echo that rumbled like thunder in the hollow sides of the place.

The Princess looked long and earnestly at him, and he returned her look.

"I will go, brave Knight," she said at last. "But you do not know how great is the task you attempt."

"No task is too great if it will save you," he answered.

"If my prayers can bring you victory," said she, "you will win. Come back safe—to honour and to me."

With that she turned and fled up the path. At the top she turned and looked back at him, then she made what speed she could to her father's palace.

She found King Ptolemy sitting in great misery with his court. Not only had he, as

"ST. GEORGE DREW HIS SWORD, AND CUT THE BONDS"

he thought, lost his dearly loved daughter, but there was not left another suitable maiden in all Egypt, and none knew what mischief the dragon would do when the usual offering was not prepared for him.

" Let us all mount swift horses and camels," said Prince Almidor of Morocco, a suitor for Princess Sabra's hand, " and set forth at once for my kingdom. If the dragon follows, he can but take a few of us at first, and we shall soon reach Morocco, where an army of my bravest knights can deal with this monster."

" There is no need to flee," said Sabra, who had entered in time to hear this counsel. " A Christian knight has come to save me; even now he is doing battle with the dragon. He will overcome the monster; I am sure of it."

Prince Almidor laughed scornfully. " How many knights have been sure of victory ? How many has the dragon slain ?" he asked.

" This is no common knight," said the Princess. " He is not afraid; he does not flee to a far country."

Almidor winced. " Maybe this stranger knight is bolder than others," he said, more gently. " But for ourselves it is safer not to wait here. The knight may not prevail."

" Let us wait a little," said the King. " I do not think this knight, or any knight, can kill the dragon; but let us abide the issue. We shall be none the worse off an hour or two hence."

So they waited. But Almidor, seeing that Princess Sabra was not in the power of the dragon, renewed his hopes of winning her. He remembered the King's promise of her hand to any knight who might slay the dragon, and he set a plot in train to make sure that even if this Christian champion should overcome the monster, he should yet not win the Princess.

But St. George was even now in the midst of the hardest of all his fights. When the Princess left him, he rode swiftly down the rocky path, his armour jingling gaily, and flaming in the sun. The red cross of England blazoned on his shield seemed a very signal of triumph. He loosened his good sword in its sheath, but for the first onset set his spear in rest.

Down the path he went, down to the very bottom of the ravine, where, in spite of the hot sun of the desert, the air was cooler. All around lay the bones of dead knights, white and terrible, with here and there a dinted plate of armour or a rusty sword.

Bucephalus, the white charger, sniffed the air and snorted; he felt that some strange

St. George and the Dragon

beast was near. But the dragon had not yet
come out of his cave. From inside it came
low mutterings, harsh, deep growls that made
a man's blood run cold to hear.

St. George kept his eyes fixed on the black
entrance as he came into the meadow where
the fair orange-tree stood; its fruit glowed
like golden lamps. Suddenly the arch in the
rock seemed to be filled to the very top by
a rushing, glittering shape. Green and blue
and brown it seemed, and the colours changed
with every movement, like a lizard's skin.
It was the dragon coming forth for his prey.

The monster stood as high as a man upon
a horse. His body was covered all over
with shining scales ; his wings were stiff and
leathery. Two long tusks stuck out of his
mouth, and his tongue moved restlessly to
and fro round them, licking his red gums in
expectation of his feast. From his nostrils
came a hot and poisonous smoke, and the
beat of his huge wings, as he half ran, half
flew, towards the champion, made the orange-
tree leaves rustle like the clapping of hands.

St. George gripped his spear and spurred
his horse. The faithful beast was quivering
with terror, but, nevertheless, he galloped
forward. Every leap brought the knight
nearer; he could feel the hot breath and smell

the horrible odour of the creature. One more drive of his wings, and they met.

St. George felt as if his spear had run against a wall of stone, and was thrusting him violently back. The guard was forced back on to his shoulder, but he held to it firmly. But the spear was useless against the horny scales, and as St. George recoiled, drawing his horse up on his haunches, the shaft snapped, and the whole head dropped to the ground. Horse and rider reeled; the horse slipped as he tried to recover, and beast and man rolled over into the shade of the orange-tree. The dragon, with the force of the shock, had reared high into the air, so that when his fore-feet came down to ground again, the champion and his steed had fallen out of the way. But it seemed an escape only for a moment.

And then a wonder happened. As St. George and Bucephalus rolled under the orange-tree, dizzy and shaken, the dragon seemed to recoil. He roared terribly, but drew back from the tree, as a cat draws back from a dog. For though St. George knew it not, the tree was enchanted, and the dragon had no power over anything that lay in its shade. Moreover, its fruit had wonderful virtue, as the champion was soon to find.

St. George and the Dragon

St. George lay there a few seconds. Then he sprang up and mounted Bucephalus, and drew the sword from its sheath. "Now will I prove whether the Enchantress spoke truly of this good blade," he thought. "It can wound men—that I know—but can it pierce the dragon's skin?"

He urged the horse forward again, and made at the dragon. It reared on high, to bring its great fore-paws down the more heavily. For a moment there was an opening for a blow. St. George swung the sword across his left shoulder, swept it round, and smote fiercely across the monster's breast.

The shock of the blow numbed his arm; it was as if he had struck a column of brass. But, strong though the scales were, the good blade pierced them, though not deeply. Out of the wound spurted deadly venom (for dragon's blood is poisonous), so noxious that the touch of it split the champion's breast-plate from shoulder to waist, and its fumes in a moment took his senses away. He fainted, swayed in the saddle, and fell from the horse. But by great good fortune he fell once more into the shadow of the enchanted orange-tree; and Bucephalus, seeing where he lay, hurried to his side, and stood there by him in safety.

St. George of England

It was long before St. George came to his senses. The sun was high in the heavens when he opened his eyes again. Weary and sick, he felt its rays unbearable, and he reached up to a low-growing branch and plucked an orange. The cool touch of its skin itself refreshed him, and he had no sooner set his teeth in it than he felt his strength and vigour come back to him as if by a miracle.

In a few moments he had rid himself of the broken breastplate, and sallied out of shelter again. But now he was more wary. He saw that even his good sword could do little against the dragon's scales unless he could find some spot where they were thin or weak. He rode directly at the monster, but at the last moment turned aside, so that the great fore - paw crashed past him harmlessly. Quickly he wheeled Bucephalus, and swung his sword back-handedly at the beast's wing. cutting the skin, but doing no hurt that mattered. He pulled the horse up on to its haunches, and escaped the poison that issued from the wound. Enraged, the dragon turned on him in a flash, throwing up one of its great wings to steady itself as it swerved and heaved itself up. The scales gleamed dazzlingly, the hot breath of the creature was all round

St. George and the Dragon

him, the long talons in the fore-paw were so
close that he could see where they slid in
their curved, horny sheath, like a cat's; but
in that moment of peril St. George's eyes and
head were clear. He saw under the uplifted
wing a new colour, not the changing tones of
the brassy scales, but a golden yellow, as
of silk; it was soft and yielding in look, not
hard and stiff. He guessed what it was—the
weak place in the dragon's armour, the place
where thin skin was the only covering of the
dreadful body.

St. George used his sword by the point now,
not by the cutting edge. He thrust, deep
and hard and true, under the dragon's wing,
and drew the point out again, and thrust
again quickly as the monster reeled away
from him and the huge wing fell feebly. The
sword entered the dragon's heart. The creature roared once more, but now its roar was
like a hoarse rattling. The great legs suddenly grew weak, the body sank upon them,
and fell with a soft thud upon its side. The
dragon was dead.

St. George of England

II

ALMIDOR THE MOOR

The dragon lay dead. But St. George was sore wearied with the fight. He led his horse into the shade of the friendly orange-tree, where the grass was green and sweet, and the good beast cropped it gently, while the knight ate the fruit of the tree. So full of healing virtue were the oranges that in a little while he felt as if he was just going freshly into battle, instead of leaving a long and fierce encounter.

He went to the body of the dragon. It lay quite still. Some of the glistening brightness had faded from the hard scales, but the colour still glowed. He cut the great head off—no easy matter—and hung it at his saddle-bow. Then he mounted Bucephalus, and rode up the valley again, to go to the King's court and see once more the lovely Princess whom he had rescued.

His heart was gay at his victory; he had done a deed worthy of a Christian knight. The valley seemed more beautiful, the sunlight brighter, the grass greener, the way less rough. The trees at the mouth of the valley, as he drew nearer to them, looked as if they too gave a cool shade as consoling as the orange-tree's. A little breeze appeared to have sprung up; the boughs moved and flickered. There was a look of comfort and peace in the dark green.

But was it a breeze ? There was no motion in the air where St. George was. Why should the branches quiver ?

He looked more closely. Then he loosened his good sword in its sheath and drew himself up, erect and ready. He had seen that the movement was not of the trees only, but of men on horseback. The sun here and there caught little points of their armour and twinkled upon it.

Almidor, the Prince of Morocco, had sent twelve knights to waylay St. George, and these were they. He did not know whether the champion would overcome the dragon; he did not think it likely. But he felt a misgiving. He resolved not to lose the hand of the Princess, whether he won it by fair means or foul. He stationed these retainers of his, therefore, where they would entrap the Christian knight as he returned from the fray—if he did return—weary and unsuspecting. They were to slay him, and then Almidor would go forth and claim for himself the victory over the dragon. If, on the other hand, the champion had been vanquished by the monster, the knights would simply return to Almidor and say so.

That was his treacherous plan. It might have been successful if St. George had not been restored to strength by the enchanted orange-tree, and if he had not caught sight of the men in ambush in good time.

It was fortunate also for St. George that these traitorous knights were not well led. Perhaps they made light of their task, seeing that they were twelve to one. It may be that some sense of fairness at the last minute shamed them. But, whatever the cause, they did not set upon him in a body. Instead, two of them ranged themselves on either side of the track, and a third in the middle of it, fronting St. George. The rest stood apart in the trees, waiting their chance.

But St. George was not lacking in skill, if his enemies were. He saw that he must attack first, and at once. He let the dragon's head fall to the ground, that it might not encumber him. Then, putting spurs to Bucephalus, he galloped at full speed up the hill. The two knights on either side drew back a little as he approached, that they might swing downwards the more easily at the right moment. It was what St. George expected. He had kept a little turn of speed in Bucephalus for the last flash of onset. Just as he drew level with them he gave a sign to the good steed, who leapt suddenly forward with a great bound that took St. George past the first two knights and into the third. As the horse sprang forward the champion swung his sword up, and with the rush of the charge it came down—down upon the knight's helmet, clean and true, and shore through helmet and head down to the very shoulders.

In a flash St. George had tugged the sword free and wheeled Bucephalus almost upon his haunches to the right, swinging the good blade Ascalon blindly round with a wide sweep at the full length of his arm as he turned. The knight that side, as he had hoped, was within reach of the sword; it struck him, all unready for such a wild and sudden onslaught, at the joint of the neck armour, and he, too, toppled from his horse, dead as a stone.

By this the third knight, he on the left of the track, nearest the trees, had come to his wits again. He did not want for courage. He drove furiously down at the champion, who had hardly recovered from the second of his great blows. It was no time for defence; the knight was upon him. Bucephalus, after turning for the second encounter, was facing down the hill again, and not quite sure of his footing. Quick as thought, St. George gave him a touch with the spur. The good horse strained and scrambled, and took a slipping stride down the slope. It was but a little way, but it was enough. The Moorish knight had aimed full at St. George with a long lance, but with that quick motion of Bucephalus his aim was turned askew. The lance struck St. George upon the shoulder and glanced off, and as the Moor passed in his headlong rush the English champion swung Ascalon again back-handedly, so that the invincible sword smote the man upon the nape of his neck. He fell forward upon his horse's mane; the lance clattered upon the path as it fell from his dead hand, and the horse, unchecked, terrified, bore his body away into the valley.

So in hardly three minutes three of the twelve were slain. The nine were in a group, ten paces or so distant. They had hoped that their chance would come easily, at a moment when the English knight was engaged with their advance guard. But St. George had been too sudden and daring for them; and he knew that swiftness was still

"AS THE HORSE SPRANG FORWARD, THE CHAMPION SWUNG HIS
SWORD UP"

his best defence. He did not wait to see how his blow at the third knight had prospered, though the sound of the falling lance told him plainly enough. He set Bucephalus at a gallop again up the slope, and with a thunder of hoofs and rattle of steel, crying, " St. George for England ! St. George !" he clashed into the little knot of knights. Into their very midst he pierced, hardly striking a blow at first; but when he was among them, Ascalon played about their heads like forked lightning, and cracked their armour as a flash rives an oak. Most of them had not drawn their swords, deeming that a charge with the lance downhill would have served their treacherous end better. But at close quarters the lances were of no avail; they were so cumbrous that they prevented the horseman from getting free of one another, and one of them even wounded one of his fellows. St. George made what speed he could while he was in the midst of the enemy; right and left he slashed, and the blade clove armour and flesh and bones as if they had been paper. In a few minutes four more lay dead, while three were so sorely wounded that they fell from their horses and crawled painfully away to the trees, there to die.

The two last were more wary. They had

drawn out of the press of men quickly, not trying to reach St. George till they could fight more freely. He would be weary when he came to them, they thought, not knowing the powers of his sword Ascalon, or the strength he had gained from the orange-tree. They moved cautiously higher up the slope and waited the issue.

The last of the others fell from his saddle. St. George looked to see how many more there might be, for he did not know whether a whole army might not have been sent out against him. All round he turned his eye. There was no sound to give him warning of more besides those two. The sun burned and blazed; the dark trees stood motionless. Below lay the body of the dragon; already a vulture had sighted it, and was hovering before descending. There were no other men anywhere save those two.

For a moment the enemies stood in silence, looking narrowly upon each other. St. George pondered his best course of attack; the Moors wondered at the courage and fresh strength of this fierce stranger, and hesitated.

"Better to take to our swords," said one to his companion. "With that swift steed he is upon us before we can set our chargers in motion to shock him."

Almidor the Moor

"No sword for me," answered the other quickly, setting his lance in rest. "Did you not see how he used his sword ? No man could stand against it. I will not come within sweep of his blade. Give me my long lance; I'll gore him before he can reach me."

"If you miss with the lance, friend," said his comrade, "you are like to come nearer his sword than you hope, for you cannot recover so quickly as he. And if—— Hola ! On guard ! The man is upon us ! He is possessed by Djinns. By the beard of the Soldan, saw ever man such speed and fury——"

He spurred his horse. His companion urged his steed to charge. But St. George had gathered up all the strength of Bucephalus into a rush the like of which man never saw before. Up the hill the great white horse thundered, his nostrils wide, his huge chest fronting the breeze like the bows of a stately ship. There was a spirit in him that made him seem like a horse of more than mortal breed. And on his back his rider came exulting, his eyes alight with fierce adventure, the plume on his helmet streaming, his courage glowing in his face.

The Moors and their steeds seemed spellbound. Fear fell suddenly upon their hearts like an ice-cold hand. It was only for a moment : their pride and valour returned in an instant; but that instant was too long. St. George was upon them, with a huge shouting and a hammering of hoofs, his sword swung up over his left shoulder, his right arm all across his chest to get the fiercer sweep. He swerved Bucephalus as he came close to the knights, so that on his left he jostled the Moor with the sword; and then his arm swung across, the good blade Ascalon flashing over his horse's mane, and swooping with a downward glide upon the other knight's right shoulder. Through the armour and through the bone it clove, and deep into the Moor's breast; and he swayed and fell to the ground.

The sword was almost wrenched from St. George's hand by his fall, but the champion's grip was firm and true. He leant over in the saddle as the blade was dragged downwards and tore it free. Then he turned hastily to meet the other Moor. But he had fled; terror spoke in his ear, saying that the last of twelve was no match for the man who had slain eleven with his own hand.

He hastened back to Almidor, spreading, as he went, the news that the dragon was slain and its slayer on the way to the city.

Almidor the Moor

" The man is possessed by an evil spirit," he said to Almidor when he came into his presence in his private chamber. " Not a score of men, nor five score, could have over-come him. Never did mortal man fight with such bitter might. And his horse also is doubtless a gift of Shaitan, and powerful Djinns have given his sword magical power."

" Out of my sight, cowardly dog !" cried Al-midor in a fury, striking him upon the mouth with his hand. " What ! Twelve men not strong enough to kill one, and that one weary with dragon-slaying ? Go forth ! Let me never look upon your face again. I will have no cowards for servants."

" Coward ! No man shall——" and the unhappy knight put his hand to his sword enraged. But it came into his mind that he had indeed fled before St. George, and played a coward's part; and he was ashamed. He turned without a word and went from Al-midor's presence, his head bowed and his shoulders shrunken. He set out from Egypt that very day, and wandered hither and thither, fighting in causes he chose to espouse, and trying by brave deeds to win back his knightly honour. He was slain no long time afterwards in Palestine, warring against the army of Christendom.

St. George of England

But Almidor nursed his fury till it became a burning flame in his heart. He knew now that a Christian knight had truly slain the dragon, and would have the Princess Sabra for his wife, and he vowed to destroy the stranger by whatever means he could. But at that time he could do no more than hope and plot. He must go to the King and join in welcoming the conqueror, as though he bore him no ill-will.

St. George took no more heed of his enemies; he saw that the only one yet able to withstand him had fled. He sheathed Ascalon, and put Bucephalus to a slow pace to regain his breath. And so, with the dragon's head replaced at his saddle-bow, he left the valley, and came up into the desert track again.

He set forth patiently in the direction in which the old hermit had told him the chief city lay. He had not gone far before he saw a great crowd of folk coming to meet him. For a moment he thought he must encounter more enemies; but then he saw fair children in white among the multitude, and heard triumphal music sounding.

It was the King of Egypt marching forth to greet the conqueror of the dragon. He rode in a chariot of beaten gold, drawn by

Almidor the Moor

three pure white horses abreast, and by his side was the Princess Sabra, more beautiful, it seemed to St. George, even than when he first saw her awaiting the dragon in the valley. Behind the golden chariot rode thirty negroes in purple robes, mounted on camels, with scarlet harness. On either side were a hundred knights in rich armour. Men with all manner of musical instruments followed, and standard-bearers, and guards; and behind came the people of the city, bearing flowers and wreaths to strew before the champion.

St. George drew near and made an obeisance to the King. "Hail, King of Egypt!" he cried. "I bring you a gift." And he held up the dragon's head. So terrible was it even in death that the Princess turned pale and shuddered at the sight of it.

"You could bring no gift that will give greater happiness to my people," answered King Ptolemy. "Come with us to the city, Sir Knight, and let us feast. When we have made revelry you shall ask of me what boon you will."

With that he stepped down from the golden chariot, and, taking St. George by the hand, led him to the chariot again. "Tell me your name, Sir Knight," he said, "that I may proclaim it to my people."

75

St. George of England

"I am not yet a knight by full and due rites," said St. George; "but I seek to do knightly deeds wherever they may be found. My name is George, and I am of the royal line of England."

"Let his name, George of England, be cried to the people," said King Ptolemy; "and let the dragon's head be set upon a tall lance and bore before us."

It was done as he said, and so to the noise of joyful music they went back to the city, St. George in the chariot with the King and the Princess. But already there was a treacherous plot in the mind of Almidor the Moor.

When they came to the city, St. George was taken to rich chambers set apart for his use, and he washed the stains of travel and fight from him, and put on fair linen and new robes that the King sent him. Then they held a great feast, with song and minstrelsy. And when it was ended the King spoke thus:

"Sir George of England, you must know that I made a vow concerning the slaying of the dragon. I promised that whoever should do that deed should have my daughter to wife. Do you consent to that?"

St. George looked upon the Princess Sabra, and she upon him; and in that look their

76

Almidor the Moor

minds were made up. "If the Princess wills, but not against her will," said the champion, "I will wed her."

"I will be your wife," said the Princess gravely. "Take from me this ring in pledge of my love. It is of great power; it has such virtue that if any danger threaten you, the diamond in it turns dull."

"Be true to one another," said the King solemnly, as St. George took the ring. "You have plighted your troth before us all. Now let a loving-cup be brought."

"Sire," interrupted Prince Almidor, "grant that I may do a courtesy to your Majesty and to this brave knight. In my country we have the secret of a very delectable drink of Greek wine and certain spices, which we use upon such glad happenings as this. Let me prepare a bowl of it that we may all drink together, and I may have a share in the happiness of this day. I beg this boon as your guest."

"So be it," said Ptolemy graciously; and Almidor departed upon his errand. "Now, Sir Knight," added the King, "have you any other boon that you would ask?"

"There is a great boon, Sire, if you would but grant it me. I have done deeds of chivalry in many lands, but not yet have I

77

St. George of England

asked of any man the honour of knighthood
at his hands. I pray that you will dub me
Knight, so that I may be knight by lawful
title as well as by my deeds."

"That is a little thing, to give honour to
so brave a champion," answered the King.

He called for a sword, and bade St. George
kneel before him, and struck him lightly on
the shoulder with the flat of the sword's blade.
"Rise, Sir George of England," he said.

As St. George, now a full knight, rose from
his knee, the door of the banqueting-hall was
flung open, and the Moorish Prince appeared,
attended by black slaves. In his hands he
bore a great golden bowl, the handles whereof
were shaped like dolphins, with rubies for
their eyes.

"The loving-cup!" he cried, holding the
bowl aloft that all might see. "It holds a
precious draught of Greek wine, such as was
made for the great Iskander a thousand years
ago. The art of making it has descended
from father to son, from generation to generation, since the great Iskander died, far away
from here. The secret is kept warily; none
but I know it, and when I die only he shall
know it whom I tell. Come, Sir George of
England, pledge us first, and afterwards we
will pledge you."

Almidor the Moor

He stretched out his arms with the cup, and St. George lifted his hands to take it. But as he did so, three drops of blood fell from his nose, and the flaming lights of the diamond in the ring on his finger vanished from his sight. The ring had become dull; danger was near.

His arms fell to his side; he stepped back. The Princess Sabra, seeing the ring dimmed, started up with a cry.

Almidor saw that he was suspected; and rightly had the ring foretold danger, for the cup contained a poison so deadly that whosoever drank of it would fall dead as his lips touched the wine. The Moor feigned to stumble. In a moment the bowl fell from his hands, and every drop of wine was spilt upon the marble floor.

" Oh, my liege," he cried in a tone of the deepest sorrow, as one of the negroes picked up the bowl, " how uncouth am I ! Forgive me, and you, Sir George, grant me pardon also. My stumbling has cost you this precious draught, for it has no virtue if made a second time in the same moon. I crave your pardon most humbly."

" We grant it, Prince," answered Ptolemy, for Almidor was in high favour with him. " It is a slight mishap, the loss of a draught

79

so noble. We can pledge one another in wine less precious, but with a comradeship no less honest."

And they fell to feasting again. When the feast was ended, King Ptolemy proclaimed that the Princess would be wedded in two months' time, and each man went to his home with great rejoicing. A house and attendants were given to St. George, and he prepared to go thither. First, however, he spoke a few words apart to the Princess Sabra.

"Dear Princess," he said, "are you truly willing to wed me? You do not do this to the end that the King, your father, may keep his vow? I will not hold him to it if you wish otherwise."

"He is my father and my King, indeed," answered the Princess; "but you shall be my King also."

St. George kissed her hand and turned to go. As he turned, he saw that Almidor had been standing near—so near that he might have overheard the words. But he took no heed.

III

IN THE POWER OF THE SOLDAN

Almidor had indeed overheard, so well that he could make a treacherous tale of the words. He went without delay to Ptolemy, and sought private audience. It was granted at once, late though the time had grown.

"King Ptolemy," said Almidor gravely and solemnly, "I have grievous news for you. How did the stranger, this George of England, bear himself in your eyes?"

"Like a gallant knight," answered the King.

"He fought bravely, doubtless," said the Moor bitterly. "He is bold enough . . ." and he fell silent.

"What do you wish to say, Prince Almidor?" asked Ptolemy, wondering at his silence.

"Sire, I cannot say it. I know only one thing for certain."

"What is that?"

"He means to be King of Egypt," answered Almidor.

"What!" cried Ptolemy, starting up from his throne. "This Christian dares!" For Ptolemy was both weak-willed and hot-

St. George of England

tempered, as ready to believe rumours as to take offence at them.

"That is the truth, O King. He is a Christian, as you have said. And, alas! to my sorrow I must say it, he has conspired with the Princess your daughter. This night by chance I overheard them in talk together. 'You shall be King,' said the Princess to him, in such a voice that I could not but believe her. They mean to kill you and seize the power in Egypt and rule in your stead."

"They shall both die," said Ptolemy in a rage. "You are sure of those words? You cannot be mistaken?"

"I am sure, King Ptolemy," answered Almidor. "Our lives are not safe while this Christian is held in honour and beheld by all men as the betrothed of the Princess."

"Betrothed he may be, but never shall he wed her. They shall die together!"

"Nay, O King, be not harsh with the Princess. She has been led away by this persuasive fellow. Without doubt he has cast a spell upon her. Let me but have her for wife, and she will be rid of the spell. Let me renew my suit to you for her. Do not put her to death. Do as you will with Sir George, but spare the Princess."

In the Power of the Soldan

" As to that we will take further thought,"
said the King. " But the English Knight
must die. Would that I had never knighted
so vile a man ! Yet he is my guest. How
can I slay a guest ?"

" A traitor is no guest," said Almidor.

" But he slew the dragon, and he has eaten
my salt, and I have dubbed him knight. I
cannot put him to death. I will but drive
him hence, to return by the way he came.
Then if he sets foot in Egypt again I will
have no mercy upon him."

" There is a better way than that," said
Almidor, pondering. " Say that you wish to
test him, since you know no more of him than
that he slew the dragon, and that he says he
is of royal lineage. Then tell him that the
proof shall consist in an honourable journey
and a mission; he shall go as your Ambassador
to the Soldan of Persia, and if he returns in
safety and honour, that will have given him
renown in the eyes of Egypt and Persia, so
that he will not seem to be a stranger carrying
off the Princess. But you will so contrive
that he does not return, for you will give him
a crafty letter to the Soldan, which shall
entreat the Soldan to put the messenger to
death. So will your honour be saved, and
you be rid of this plotter."

St. George of England

"It is a good plan," said the King.

He lost little time in carrying it out. The next morning St. George came to pay his courteous respects to the King, and Ptolemy greeted him in a friendly manner. But after a little, "Sir George of England," said he, "I would speak privately with you."

He took him apart. "I find myself in a difficulty, brave Knight," he said. "I would gladly do you all the honour in the world; I have given you knighthood and my daughter's hand in proof of my esteem for him who slew the foul dragon. But you are a stranger to my people, and England is very far away. I am told that it is set in the midst of a great ocean, which no man of these regions has ever seen. Certain of my nobles take amiss that I should give the Princess Sabra to an unknown foreigner, though none says a word against your valour or your honour. They do but ask that you shall learn our ways and have some employment in our State. Now, it happens that I have need of an Ambassador to the mighty Soldan of Persia. He must be a man of noble bearing, and of courage and dignity, and of honest mind; and he must have also some skill in the courteous arts of peace, for weighty matters are afoot. Such a man I believe you to be. Now, if I send

you to the Soldan, and you accomplish this
mission honourably, you will be in the eyes
of my people as one of ourselves, and they
will see that the Princess is to wed one who
is a wise counsellor and a faithful servant as
well as a brave warrior. How say you ?
Shall I send you to the Soldan ?"

St. George saw that there was prudence in
what the King said; and when he had asked
certain questions, and learnt that if his
journey prospered well he could return by
the time appointed for his marriage to the
Princess, he consented very readily to go.

He was not long in making his preparations
for the mission. He said farewell very tenderly to the Princess, and was given a sealed
letter to the Soldan, and set forth.

His way lay across deserts, but it was not
hard to find, and he came in due time to
the capital of Persia. As he drew near the
city he saw a great procession. It was a
festival in honour of the heathen gods of that
country, and when the Persians saw the red
cross upon the shield of the champion, they
mocked him, and made light of the Christian
faith. At last he grew very wroth, and set
upon the procession, and broke down its
banners and trampled many men under foot,
so that they all fled in terror.

St. George of England

This was no good beginning for an embassy, and St. George was soon to be sorry that he had let his zeal for his Faith get the better of his prudence. The Persians hastened to the Soldan with the tale of the attack (leaving out the insults by which they had provoked it); and the Soldan, after he had beheaded the first of those who brought him such unwelcome news, sent out a hundred knights to seize the stranger and drag him before him.

The knights rode out gaily to their task. But it was in no gay mood that they returned, for St. George, seeing himself in desperate case, and being still filled with the fury that their insults to the Christian faith had roused, set upon them in a whirlwind of passion, and drove them before him as a storm drives dead leaves. And when, in a little time, the Soldan sent a thousand knights against him, these fared no better, but were driven hither and thither pell-mell.

But by now the whole countryside was roused, and such a multitude poured forth as no champion could withstand. They seized St. George and bound him, and if it had not been for certain officers of the Soldan they would have tortured him and put him to death there and then. But these officers caused him to be brought before the Soldan for judgment.

"Great Lord and King of Asia," cried St. George when he saw that he was in the presence of the Soldan himself, "I claim your protection. If you seek to kill me, I demand an honourable death, for I am of kingly lineage; I am of the blood-royal of England, no less proud than your own. But I demand also safe conduct out of your dominions with whatever answer you shall give me to bear to my master, the King of Egypt; for I am an ambassador, and by the laws of all mankind my person is sacred. If your servants will unbind me, I will give you my letter from King Ptolemy."

The Soldan signed to his guards to unbind him, but to keep close watch upon him. St. George drew out the letter, and it was handed to the Soldan.

" BROTHER " (the Soldan read silently),
    " These with all love and honour from us in Egypt. He who brings this is a terrible warrior, a Christian dog who has slain the dragon thou knowest of, and now plots against our Majesty, to drive us from Egypt, and take our Daughter to wife. He has eaten our salt, and we therefore cannot slay

him. Do thou slay him; and look well that
he doth no mischief to thy excellent Majesty
ere thou slay him, for he is a man of might.
Mayst thou prosper and live for ever !

"PTOLEMY, KING OF EGYPT."

The Soldan looked anxiously upon St.
George; there was bitter cruelty in his
eyes.

"Christian Knight, if knight you are," he
said at length, "do you know what is in this
letter ?"

"Mighty Soldan," answered St. George
bravely, "I know nothing but that I am to
be given an answer, and to bear it back to
King Ptolemy."

"You shall be given an answer," said the
Soldan. "Perhaps also an answer shall be
sent to our brother of Egypt and to his fair
daughter. But you will not bear the answer.
Dead men can go no journeys. You shall be
taken hence, and on the thirtieth day from
this day you shall die. You claimed an
honourable death, since you are of royal
blood. I do not know of what lineage you
are, nor whether you tell the truth. I have
never heard of this England you speak of; it
is not one of the ancient kingdoms I know of.
But you shall be killed by kings — kings of

beasts. Thirty days hence you shall be given to my lions."

He made a sign, and a host of guards seized St. George again, and set heavy fetters upon him, and threw him into a dark and horrible dungeon. No light came into it, and it was damp and noisome; rats and serpents visited him in the darkness, and when his guards—of whom there were at that time a hundred, all of knightly rank—brought him his poor allowance of bread and water each day, they came by lantern-light, which served but to be reflected in the pools of stagnant water in the huge dismal cell.

So he abode for thirty days, thinking sadly of Sabra. Ever and again he would remember also his six comrades, and wonder when it would come to pass that they should meet and do those deeds of which Kalyb had prophesied. Almost he wished to be back in her palace of vile enchantments.

The thirtieth day came, and that morning they brought him no food. He heard afar dull sounds, which seemed to him like the bellowings of wild beasts. But he hardly knew if he was awake, or if it was but an evil dream.

Presently a dim light appeared in one wall of the cell. A door had been opened which must lead into daylight at some little distance. But horrible sounds came through the door— the roaring of hungry beasts.

One of his guards entered by the usual door. "Christian," he said, "you hear the royal beasts who await you. For four days they have not tasted food. The Soldan, in his great mercy, commanded that they should be made fierce and hungry, so that they should make short work of you. You may go to meet them through yonder door, where there is a little light, or you may await them here in the dark. Doubtless they will not be long in finding you. The Soldan would prefer that you should go outside to meet them, for then he will be able to see your greeting; but he does not command this. You may die here if you please."

With this cruel speech the Persian withdrew.

St. George was filled with rage at the taunting words. All his old strength came back after the long night of despair in his cell. He lifted his chained arms, and brought the chain down with all his force upon his thigh, just above the knee. Such was the strength of the blow that the fetters snapped like thread, leaving a few links dangling from either wrist. With a great shout of " George for England!" he rushed out at the open doorway, through a narrow passage, and into the light.

He found himself in a kind of den, or pit, hollowed out of rock; a space nearly circular, with five doors in it, doubtless all leading to cells like his own. The floor was of crumbled stone and sand. The rocky walls rose thirty feet or more, and at the top was a parapet, over which the Soldan and some of his nobles were looking. At one point in the wall, on the level of the ground, was a large iron grating, now open, and by it, walking backwards and forwards, lashing their tails, and roaring terribly with hunger as they looked at the Persians above out of their reach, were two huge lions.

St. George remembered that speed had saved him against Almidor's ambushed knights. He tore his tunic and wrapped the pieces round his hands and wrists and arms, leaving the ends of chain free. In breathless haste he bandaged himself thus. The Persians were calling out taunts to the lions, and trying to show them the champion; but the beasts did not understand, and only gazed upwards and roared more terribly.

St. George crept across the soft sandy surface quietly, with quick strides. The lions were too hungry and too enraged to hear him. He came within two yards of them. Then he shouted suddenly.

They were close together, their backs turned towards him. At his shout they turned in a flash, with the silence and swiftness of cats. Together they crouched, their lips drawn back from their teeth, their mouths open. Together they sprang. But just as they sprang, almost as they left the ground, St. George sprang too. With true aim he thrust a fist and arm into each mouth, between the great jaws, the teeth meeting and tearing the bandage on his arms, the chain wounding the throats of the beasts and choking them. They writhed and swayed to and fro, pulling, pushing, turning, rearing up. All was of no avail. St. George thrust his arms the deeper, and stood his ground for all their endeavours, and in a few moments they were suffocated and fell dead.

But if St. George had saved his life, he had not won his freedom. There was no way of escape from the cell. He heard cries of wonder and rage in the gallery above. Orders were given, and the sound of men in haste came to his ears. He sank exhausted to the ground just as one of the doors in the den opened, and there came running in a hundred

" THE LIONS FELL DEAD "

or more Persian guards, who seized him and bore him unresisting back to his dismal cell.

The Soldan was afraid. He had heard of the dragon of Egypt, and he had thought that no man could slay the monster. But St. George had slain it. And now, unarmed and weakened by imprisonment, he had slain also two hungry lions. He seemed to be more than human. The Soldan resolved not to try to kill him. He would keep him a prisoner, walled up and bound, till he died.

So St. George was loaded with chains again and thrust into his cell. The very doors were closed with iron bars, and only a little shutter left, through which his food was pushed every day. He gave himself up to misery and almost to despair, and took little thought of escape. Not days, but months, passed before he looked again upon the sun and the faces of men.

ST.
DENIS OF FRANCE

III

THE ENCHANTED STAG

THE road taken by St. Denis of France when the seven champions parted from one another was a highway of adventure. Yet little adventure befell this noble knight, for from the very hour when Kalyb stole him (as she stole all the champions in their infancy), he had had another enemy besides the wicked Enchantress; and that was an enchanter no less powerful and cruel than Kalyb, the ill-famed Ormandine himself. Now, St. Denis did not at first come directly into Ormandine's power, but the wizard was able by his arts to throw misfortune in his way, and keep him from winning fame by deeds of chivalry. In every country he entered (and his road led him to the coast of England, and thence by sea to the mainland of Europe) such deeds were to be done and adventure to be found—but not by St. Denis, for Ormandine so guided his steps astray that he went by barren paths and lonely byways in the wilderness, so that he would have lost his skill in arms through lack of use unless he had felt in his heart that he was fated to do great things.

At length in his wanderings he came to the land of Thessaly, which in those days had a fair repute for chivalry; many knights were wont to come thither, and seek adventure against robbers in the high mountains, or in the wars of the Kings of Thessaly against the Saracens or in the splendid tournaments which the King often held. Here, thought St. Denis, he would at last meet some notable happening.

He stood late one afternoon on a mountain slope overlooking the great green plains of the country. Far off he could see the white towers of the capital city, almost a day's journey distant. The meadows beneath him were rich, and full of cattle and horses (for which, indeed, the land was famous). It seemed a region of happiness and prosperity, where doubtless honour might be won.

St. Denis resolved to rest where he was that night, and early next morning to ride to the King's Court, and offer himself for service in any way that might seem good. He looked round him for some resting-place. The grass was green and soft, and hard by was a fine mulberry-tree, whose shade looked cool and peaceful, and whose purple fruit glowed with refreshing juices. St. Denis led his horse to the tree, and unsaddled him; and he picked and ate some of the ripe mulberries to satisfy his thirst. Then he lay down under the tree, and in a moment fell into a deep sleep.

That was no ordinary sleep. St. Denis, indeed, had put himself into the power of his great enemy the enchanter, whose arts had more strength in Thessaly than elsewhere. That very tree under which he was sleeping and its fruit were enchanted.

When he awoke again he felt curiously active, and yet disinclined for warlike deeds. The moon had risen and set again while he slept, and already the sun was climbing the morning sky. He rose, and looked round him for a pool of water in which to bathe. He found one at a little distance—a deep, over-shadowed pool that reflected its banks as clearly as if it were glass.

He bent over it and peered into its depths. He started back in terror and amazement at what he saw. There in the water was not the form of a man, but the hairy skin and horned head of a fine hart. He looked down at his feet; they were hoofs, and his legs were slim and tapering. He tried to press his hands to his head, to drive away the terrible

101

vision; but he could not lift them as a man can; they too were hoofs. He had been wholly changed into a deer.

" Oh——" he groaned; and no words came from his lips—he could not speak. In a frenzy of fear and bewilderment, he fled swift as the wind up the mountain path down which he had gone the day before. On and on he ran like a mad thing, till at last he sank exhausted and panting on the ground.

Gradually his reason came back to him, and he grew calm. He saw that some terrible enemy of whom he knew nothing had in some mysterious way done this evil to him. Who that enemy might be, and why he had been so cruel, and how to be rid of the terrible spell, he could not guess.

When he had rested he went back more gently to the place where he had slept. There was his faithful steed still waiting by the mulberry-tree. The good beast knew him, in spite of his changed appearance. It came to him and rubbed its nose gently against his neck, and whinnied tenderly.

It was long before he could resolve what to do. He thought it best, in the end, to stay near the mulberry-tree, for that seemed to him to be the only thing that could have done him this harm—if, indeed, it came

The Enchanted Stag

from any visible thing, and not from an invisible spell chanted far off by some unseen magician. There he abode, cropping the grass, and drinking from the pool that had told him his fate. With him remained the faithful horse. And so for a long time, for more than a year, in truth, St. Denis was a hart, and lived the life of an animal.

But in the course of time he had one night a very strange dream. It seemed to him that he was walking in a very beautiful garden, in the midst whereof was a rose-tree of surpassing loveliness. Upon its branches grew at once roses white and roses red, and its scent was more delicate than that of any mortal flower. St. Denis, so his dream ran, went to the tree, and, since he was still a hart and desirous of leaves and green things to eat, ate some of the flowers; and immediately the spell fell from him, and he was changed into a man as before. Thereafter in his vision he appeared to meet a lovely Princess, but of that he was not sure, for he awoke before it was made clear to him.

When he awoke, his good steed was no longer by him, at which he marvelled, for it was wont to stay by his side always, day and night. But he had not been awake long when he heard far away the distant sound of hoofs in the mountains. It grew nearer and nearer, and presently the horse came in sight. But it had a singular appearance, as though it were pushing its way through trees and blossoms. A heavenly scent filled the air, and grew stronger as the horse approached. Soon the noble beast was close at hand, and the poor hart could see it clearly. In its mouth it bore leaves and blossoms, from which the scent issued. The blossoms were white and red rose-blooms in flower upon a great branch. The horse, by some strange means, had been led to wander into the mountains and find the enchanted tree, and bring a branch of it to the champion.

Immediately St. Denis remembered his dream, and he put his lips to the rose-blossoms and ate them. Hardly had he touched them when once again deep sleep fell upon him, and for many hours he lay almost as if dead. When he awoke he recalled all that had happened, and, mindful of his former grievous change, ran to the pool to see if he had been restored to man's shape.

This time he had no need to start back in horror. In the cool waters he saw himself exactly as he had been before he ate of the enchanted mulberry-tree. The spell was gone from him, and the power of Ormandine over

The Enchanted Stag

him had vanished. He fell upon his knees and thanked God for his deliverance.

Rejoicing, he ran back to his charger, and threw his arms round its neck. " Oh, my good steed, never will I forsake you," he cried. " We will go through life together, and when you are too old to come with me upon knightly adventures you shall rest in the greenest meadow in the world, and have the finest stable that man can build. But as for that accursed mulberry-tree, I will see that it does no more evil."

He hurried to the tree; drawing his sword and swinging it round with all his force, he clove the trunk at one blow of the sharp blade. But, instead of splintered bark and wood, he saw a wonderous sight. The tree fell asunder in two halves ; a sound as of thunder was heard, and out of the trunk stepped the most beautiful maiden St. Denis had ever seen.

" Princess—for such you must be," said St. Denis in astonishment—" how came you here ? What have I done that my strength should cleave this tree to the ground ? And why did I do you no harm in that stroke, if you were within this prison of wood ?"

" I was within it, and yet not within it," answered the maiden; and her voice sounded to St. Dennis like the chiming of silver bells. "You say truly that I am a Princess; I am Eglantine, daughter of the King of Thessaly. Many years ago—I know not how many—the vile enchanter Ormandine carried me off from my father the King, against whom he had a grudge because of the laws against witchcraft. He turned me into this mulberry-tree by his spells. But when you struck it with your sword his power over me was gone, and since the tree was wrought by magic, no harm to it could come upon me also. I could see through my leaves your sorry fate, and it was the whisperings they made at night that at length came to your good steed's ears, and bade him search for the magic rose-tree, and set us both free. Now let us go at once to my father the King, in his palace in the plain below."

Without more ado they went down from the hill together, the Princess riding on the champion's horse, and St. Denis walking at the bridle. With every step he took he thought her more lovely; and she was not backward in looking favourably upon him.

They came presently to the chief city. When the citizens saw the Princess—for it was but some ten years since she had been enchanted, and she lived in their loving

"THEY WENT DOWN FROM THE HILL TOGETHER"

The Enchanted Stag

memory—they ran out of their houses and shops and booths, and followed her with shoutings and joyful music; and so they arrived at the King's palace, the news of their coming flying before them, for rumour is swifter than the feet of men. The King was ready to receive them, and he ran down the marble steps of his palace door, and embraced her as she alighted from the horse. Then he greeted St. Denis honourably, and they entered the palace.

It was not long before the Princess Eglantine had told her tale, and marvellous it seemed to them.

" Sir Knight," said the King when she had ended, " I will grant whatsoever you ask of me."

" I could ask of you but one thing, Sire," answered the champion, " and that is the most precious thing you have."

" Whatever it is, you shall have it," said the King. " Ask."

" I ask your daughter in marriage, if she will deign to look upon me with favour. Though I am not yet dubbed knight, I am of the royal line of the ancient kingdom of France."

" Your lineage is high and proud, friend," said the King ; " but your boon I cannot grant. It is of my daughter that you must ask it. If she will give it, I will not say nay."

" Nor will I refuse to grant it," said Eglantine. " If you desire me for wife, fair sir, I will be your wife."

So gracious was the King and so well-disposed to the knight who had set his daughter free from Ormandine's enchantments, that he welcomed St. Denis the more joyfully for his bold request, and also he made him a knight, after the manner of chivalry. In a little time St. Denis and Eglantine were married amid great rejoicings, and afterwards a tournament was held, the news of which the King caused to be proclaimed through all Christian lands. In the tournament St. Denis held the lists against all comers, and overthrew every knight with whom he fought. When the tournament and all the revelry that followed it was ended, the champion and his bride set out to visit other courts, and seek out the six champions wherever they might be found. And first they journeyed to the court of the King of Greece. But whom they met there shall be told later.

S^T.. JAMES OF SPAIN

I

THE SLAYING OF THE BOAR

ST. JAMES OF SPAIN took a road which led him, after many perils and adventures, during which he won his spurs, to the Holy Land, and in course of time he found himself near Jerusalem. He was standing upon a hill looking at the domes and towers and gleaming walls of the city, when there broke upon his ears the sound of drums and trumpets, and the marching of a great company. He looked towards the sound which came from the city, and he saw the gates thrown open, and many people issuing through them. First was a troop of horsemen bravely apparelled in white and gold, with jewelled harness and jingling arms; there were more than a hundred of them. After them rode twelve knights on chargers, two by two. Each of these knights carried a long lance, from which floated a blood-red

113

banner embroidered with a picture of Adonai being wounded by a boar. Next came the King and his daughter, very richly clad. The King wore a gleaming circlet of gold on his head, and rode a white horse. The Princess rode a milk-white unicorn, whose long horn was covered with gold leaf. In her hand she bore a silver javelin, and she wore a breast-plate of beaten gold. Behind her rode a body-guard of a hundred Amazons. Last of all were men playing instruments of music and a crowd of humbler folk.

The cavalcade came near where St. James stood, and began to pass him. He spoke to a man who was close by him. " What does this gay expedition mean ?" he asked.

" You must come from a very far land, Sir Knight," said the man, " if you do not know that."

" I do not know so much as who that King and the fair lady by his side are," answered St. James.

" That is the King of Judah, our good monarch," said the man, " and the lady is his daughter, the Princess Celestine. This is the great hunting festival, when all the court goes a-hunting in honour of Adonai, whom we revere, and who was slain by a boar. Every year proclamation is made, and great

The Slaying of the Boar

prizes are given by the King. See, here is a herald about to make the proclamation."

As he spoke a herald halted near them. He was clad in cloth of gold, and bore a silver trumpet with a purple streamer hanging from it. He blew three blasts upon the trumpet, and cried in a loud voice: "In the name of the King and in honour of Adonai! To all men I cry. The King is pleased to offer a corselet of fine steel worth a thousand shekels of silver to any man soever who shall slay the first boar this day. Now set on, knights and squires. The hunt is up."

He blew three blasts again on his trumpet, and passed on.

St. James heard him out. As he listened his glance fell on the Princess Celestine, and he saw how fair she was. And she, too, saw him as he stood there, and thought him a knight of gallant looks and noble bearing.

"I will win the Princess," thought St. James to himself. "No other shall be my bride. For her I will dare anything."

With that he set spurs to his horse, and, making a little curve to avoid the more slowly moving cavalcade, he rode ahead over the plains to the forest to which he saw the hunt was going. He dismounted for greater ease of movement among the trees, and tethered his horse; then he entered the forest.

Hardly was he in the shade of the trees than he saw a huge boar in front of him, goring with its sharp tusks the body of some poor traveller it had overcome. The beast paid him no heed, so intent was it upon its task. He sounded his silver horn loudly, and the boar turned quickly. In a moment it saw the new enemy, and charged furiously. St. James awaited the attack with his lance in rest, meaning to leap aside himself at the last minute. The boar came on more swiftly than he had expected of so unwieldy a brute, and his lance did not strike it fair and full. It grazed its shoulder merely, and glanced off, and St. James had to leap very nimbly to avoid its tusks as it lunged sideways at him in passing.

The rush of its speed carried the boar some little way past the champion, who had time to throw aside his lance and loosen his battle-axe for use. The boar charged again as soon as it could turn. This time St. James was more wary, for he had gauged the speed of the monster's rush. He stepped aside again as it reached him, and swung the battle-axe down, across his body, on to the back of the boar's skull, with all his force behind the

The Slaying of the Boar

blow. The keen edge crashed through flesh and bone, and killed the beast instantly.

The champion cut off the boar's head, well pleased at his victory. He heard a noise of trampling and music close at hand, and looked round. The King and the Princess and their train had reached the forest.

St. James took his boar's head, and carried it to the King. Falling on one knee, he held it out before him. " Here is the first boar of the hunt, O King," he said. " Unless any man has slain another before me, I claim the reward your herald cried publicly but a little while ago."

" You are the first, Sir Knight," answered the King, perceiving that St. James was a man of rank and honourable position. " Yours is the reward. Let my armourer bring the corselet."

The armourer came forward with the corselet of fine steel. So wonderfully was it wrought that it fitted St. James instantly. Keen indeed must an edge have been to pierce it, and yet when the champion had it upon his body he felt no more weight from it than if it had been a shirt of fine linen.

" It beseems you well," said the King graciously. " Does it not, Celestine ?"

" Indeed it is a finely wrought corselet,"

answered the Princess; and she looked upon St. James with such admiration that he fell more deeply in love with her than ever.

"I am much beholden to Your Majesty for your gracious gift," said St. James courteously. "I came hither in search of knightly adventure, not thinking to win so worthy a prize as this."

"Whence do you come, Sir Knight?" asked the King; "and what is your name and lineage?"

"I am called James, and I am a Christian knight of Spain."

"What!" cried the King, all his graciousness gone from him in a moment. "A Christian! Then you die here and now, for I have vowed to put to death every Christian who comes into my realm. Ho there! Seize this dog and stone him to death!"

His attendants rushed forward in a body, and seized the champion, who, indeed, was too greatly surprised at this sudden change in the King to resist, even if resistance had been of use. And when they had bound him he regained his wits.

"Stop, O King," he cried boldly. "You may kill me if you will, though I have done no wrong to any man for which I deserve death. But remember that I slew this great

118

boar, and give me some respite for that deed. Let me at least have a time to pray and to prepare my soul for death, and grant me also that I may choose the manner of my death."

"I will never show mercy to a dog of a Christian," answered the King. "But such slight delay as you ask shall be granted you. And I will grant your other boon also. When you have had an hour for prayer you shall say in what way you choose to die. But let not this be a pretext to gain some means of escape; you shall surely die."

"So be it, King," said St. James. "But I tell you that you are doing ill, and one day you will repent of it."

"'One day' has yet to come," answered the King. "And what I will, I do. Now set about your prayers. We will continue our hunt. Forward, my friends."

And they plunged deep into the forest, their raiment shining, their harness making a merry noise. A hundred guards remained with St. James, who yet felt very lonely when he saw the Princess and all her attendants ride off into the cool, dark forest.

They unbound him and retired to a little distance, forming a circle round about him. For an hour he prayed steadfastly, and made

his peace with God, thinking indeed that the
time had come for him to lay down his life.

At the end of the hour the King and his
court came back, the Princess with them, her
eyes full of sadness.

"Bring that Christian dog before me," said
the King. "I have said that I would grant
his boon."

They bound St. James again, and set him
before the King. "Now, Sir James of Spain,
you are to look your last upon the sunlight,"
said the King cruelly. "Tell me, since I
have given you leave, in what way you will
close your eyes to it for ever."

A strange fancy had come into the champion's mind. He had a whim to die in a
certain way, if die he must. "Let me be
bound to a pine-tree, unguarded," he said,
"and then let me be shot by an arrow loosed
by a beautiful maiden."

"That is a new form of death, Christian,"
said the King; "but I doubt not it will serve
as well as any other. Let it be done as this
Spanish knight asks. The maiden to slay
him shall be chosen by lot from those who
are here."

They brought a helmet, and put in it a
bushel of white peas, and among them a
single black one. She who drew the black

The Slaying of the Boar

one (her eyes being blindfolded before the choice) was to kill St. James.

When all was ready they began to draw. And first of all the Princess Celestine was to put her hand into the helmet. She dismounted from her horse. A green scarf was tied round her eyes, and she stretched out her hand, fumbling at the edge of the helmet to be sure of reaching the peas.

There was a rattling sound as she put her hand among the dry, loose peas. Then she drew it forth again, and opened it, tearing off the scarf as she did so. On her white palm lay the black pea.

" Oh, I cannot !" she cried in distress. " I cannot slay an innocent man. My father "— and she fell on her knees before the King— " oh, my father, spare him ! What evil has he done ? He is a Christian, truly, but he was born and bred in that faith, and knew nought of ours. He knew nought of your vow against all Christians; else he would not have come here and told us his faith and lineage. He has done you a service by killing the boar."

" Bind him to a pine-tree," said the King sternly. " He must die; I have vowed it. Celestine, take your bow, aim truly, and kill him."

St. James of Spain

The guards seized the champion, and bound him to a pine-tree hard by. But Celestine did not cease to plead for his life.

"I will never kill him," she said. "I could not aim truly at a just man, who has done no wrong. Let him go, Sire; I dare swear he will leave your kingdom and never return, if you do but let him go. Bethink you that your vow was made because of the war that Christians have made upon us; you might well slay all who fought against you and sought to do you harm. But this knight has made no war. He came honourably in peace. Let him go in peace, even if you do not honour him as at first, before you knew him for a Christian, you seemed to wish. Remember that till he proclaimed his faith out of his own lips, you had not a hard word for him. O spare him, my father, for if you do not I too shall surely die!"

She clasped her father's foot with her hands as she knelt by his stirrup, and bowed her head upon it in tears.

The King hesitated. He knew that he was but killing the knight in order to keep to the letter of his vow, which, indeed, he had taken against his enemies rather than against peaceful strangers. But he hated all Christians bitterly, for they were trying always

The Slaying of the Boar

to drive him out of the Holy Land and make it part of Christendom. Yet he could not resist his daughter's pleadings.

"Have it as you will, Celestine," he said harshly. "Set him free yourself. But be sure that if ever again he sets foot in this land he shall be put to death, and no prayers shall save him, and it shall be no gentle hands like yours that shall cut him off from life. Tell him this, and bid him begone from Judah in a day's time. If he is found anywhere in my realm at this time on the morrow, he dies."

He turned away. Celestine ran to the pine-tree, and cut St. James's bonds with her hunting-knife.

"You are free, Sir James," she said eagerly. "I have begged your life of my father. But, alas! it is not better to me than if you were dead, for you must leave this land at once, and never return. If ever you come back, you will be slain—ay, and perhaps tortured into the bargain. Go; make what speed you can. Remember me. Take this ring from me, and wear it for my sake, and be sure that never will I forget you. Farewell."

"Farewell, Princess," said St. James; "I shall never forget you. I do not need this ring to keep your memory in my heart to my life's end. But I will treasure your gift, and

123

if ever we meet again it shall be a sign between us."

He said no more, but mounted his horse and rode away, the ring on his finger; and the Princess went back sadly to her father's court.

II

FLIGHT

St. James made the best speed he could to the borders of Judah. Often as he rode he looked at the ring the Princess had given him. On the inside of it were words engraved—" Fare well ever beloved"; and he thought that truly he had said farewell to all that he now held dear.

He looked back over the plains for the last time from a hill on the edge of the country. As he looked a plan suddenly came into his mind. Why should he not return in disguise ?

There was a wood not far off. Beyond that lay a little town of which he had heard from a chance traveller whom he had met not long before. He hastened on to the town, and bought in it a Moorish dress; then he returned to the wood, and, having dug a deep hole with his sword, buried the greater part of his

124

armour and his raiment, marking the place by certain signs that he might readily find it again. He sought out a tree with dark berries, of which there were many in the forest. He squeezed out their juice, until he had enough to stain his skin dark brown all over. When he had put on the dress he had bought, he looked every inch a Moor, and no one would have known him for the gallant knight who had slain the boar but a little while before. He stained also the white hide of his horse, and darkened the harness, so that there was nothing left for any man to recognise.

He resolved to feign to be deaf and dumb, so that his speech might not betray him. When he had satisfied himself that his appearance was suitable, he returned to Jerusalem, and went to the King's palace, and by signs indicated that he wished to be taken into the royal service.

It chanced that as he was making this silent request to the King's chamberlain, the Princess Celestine herself passed by. The chamberlain rose to greet her, and she acknowledged his obeisance; but her eyes were fixed in wonder on the Moor whom she saw. There seemed to her something familiar in him, she knew not what.

" Who is this man ?" she asked the chamberlain.

" He is a deaf and dumb man, Princess, a Moor who seems to wish to be taken into the King's household.

" He is goodly to look upon. Is he skilled in arms, and of courteous manner ?"

" For his courtesy I can only answer by what I have seen," said the chamberlain. "He seems to be of good demeanour. As for his skill in arms, I will try him."

He made passes in the air, as though handling a sword. St. James, who had heard very well all that was said, nodded his head joyfully. The chamberlain took a sword, and gave it to him, and took another himself, and they began to fence together. In a little while it was clear that the chamberlain, though a good swordsman, was no match for the stranger, who, indeed, suddenly sent his sword flying by a quick turn of the wrist.

The Princess smiled. " Let him be of my bodyguard," she said. " He is a stout fellow, and I need another good warrior just now." But though she felt that she knew his face, she did not guess who the Moor was.

So St. James was made one of Celestine's guards. In a little time he had shown himself so gentle in manner, so gallant in bearing, and

"PRINCESS CELESTINE HERSELF PASSED BY"

Flight

so expert in arms and courtesy, that he was made chief of the guard and special champion of the Princess. All day long he was near her, and had her under his charge, though he could not speak to her, and as yet dared not reveal himself to her.

There were many suitors for the fair Princess's hand in those days. Princes and nobles came from many distant countries to seek her: from Trebizond, and Bokhara, and Ethiopia; the King of Arabia came, and an Ambassador from the Emperor of Cathay, who had heard of her loveliness; and the Lord High Admiral of Babylon itself—all these and many more tried to win her hand. But she would have none of them, being true in heart to St. James.

It chanced presently that at one time there were a score or more of these suitors in Jerusalem together. Since, as they learnt, their suit was hopeless, they agreed well with one another; and they resolved that before they went away from Judah they would give a splendid entertainment in honour of the Princess. They planned to hold a banquet, and then a ball.

The Princess took with her her chief attendants, among them, of course, the champion of her guard. She had asked him by signs—

in which way by now they found it easy to converse—if he could dance for her a Moorish dance; and it happened that St. James was able to do this, and the Princess commanded that he should dance one with her at the ball.

St. James thought that this would be his opportunity. The revelry would continue far into the night, and when it was ended all the court would be weary, and heedless of anything but sleep. He made his preparations, which, as chief of the Princess's bodyguard, he could do without suspicion.

The banquet came and passed, and was followed by the ball. St. James, to give the Princess a message silently, had put her ring upon his finger; hitherto, while he was in her service, he had worn it on a fine gold chain round his neck, lest it should betray him at an inopportune time.

The time came for him to dance the Moorish dance with the Princess. He held out his hand to her to lead her. She saw the ring, and knew at once why she had seemed to find his face familiar to her. But she said never a word, for fear of discovery; only her hand pressed his, and their eyes met, and hope sprang up in their hearts.

They danced together, and then the Princess thanked him by signs for his courtesy;

Flight

but to her signs she added some that meant, " Remain here."

He stayed near her. Presently he heard her speaking to one of her ladies. " It is hot, and I am weary. I will walk upon the terrace for a little. I cannot choose one of my suitors for a companion, for fear of making the rest jealous. And, indeed, I am too weary for talk. I will go with my chief of guards, and take the air for a space, and return before long."

She made signs to St. James that he was to escort her to the terrace of the palace, and place guards in suitable positions. Then she went forth, St. James by her side.

They paced the terrace together at a little distance from the guards. She spoke to him in soft whispers, and he answered, and told her of his plans. She was to put on a Moorish dress, and meet him in the hall of her palace an hour after all the household had retired to rest, and he would take her thence by a back way, and through a private door in the city walls, of which he had been able to get a key made once when the real key was lent him for some special purpose. A little way outside the walls, in a clump of trees, he had two swift horses tethered. Once they reached the horses unseen and unheard, they would be safe.

131

St. James of Spain

All this he whispered to her, and she agreed to do exactly as he said. Then he led her back to the ball-room, and made an obeisance to her, and she pretended to dismiss him graciously. The walk upon the terrace had cooled her cheeks, and her joy made her eyes shine like stars, so that she seemed indeed to have gone from the ball-room to rest, and to have come back refreshed.

St. James left her and went to her palace. He made ready a little store of food, and saw that his sword and dagger were sharp, and loose in their scabbards; for he knew not when he might have to use them suddenly. Then he sat down, and waited as patiently as he could for the appointed hour.

The court came home from the ball; the palace for a little while was full of light and sound and confusion. Then one by one the lights died away, and silence slowly fell upon the place. St. James waited until well-nigh an hour had passed; then he stole softly out of his chamber and down to the great dark hall of the palace. Very huge and mysterious it seemed now, empty of all life. His light footsteps sounded to his anxious ears like the trampling of an army.

He sat down in a corner and waited again. The time passed, and the Princess did not

132

Flight

come. St. James rose and paced the hall quietly, in case by chance she was there already, and did not know of his presence, or thought him some enemy. But she was not there. His mind began to be filled with a thousand fears and hopes. He thought that she might have been discovered, and he dared not imagine what would then befall her. Then he fancied that she had been overcome by weariness, and had fallen asleep; and despair settled upon his heart, for he might not have such an opportunity of escape as this for many months to come.

He heard a step. He remained quite still. The sound came nearer, and he heard the noise of breath drawn quickly and anxiously. Then he knew that it was the Princess. " Celestine !" he whispered. She came to him, guided by the sound, and hand in hand they crept through the hall, out by the little door, and so at last out of the city. Not a soul saw or heard them; unperceived they reached the tethered horses, and in a few minutes were galloping across the dim, ghostly desert together, free and safe, never to return to Jerusalem while it was a pagan city.

S^T ANTHONY OF ITALY

V

BLANDERON'S CASTLE

ST. ANTHONY'S road led him afar without adventure. He, too, fared out of England, by sea and forest and desert. But nothing worthy note befell him till at length, at the end of a great plain, he saw before him a high hill. Round the lower slopes of the hill were fir-trees innumerable, so close set that their shade looked black rather than green. Above them were the white walls of a huge castle. It covered all the top of the hill, and stood four-square to every quarter; at each corner of the battlements was a round tower.

St. Anthony thought that here at last might lie some adventure of repute. He went boldly along the track he was following; it led him through the forest of fir-trees, and ended at the gate of the castle.

The gate was a lattice of stout iron bars, fast shut, nor was any warder to be seen, nor any horn, or means of summoning one. It seemed as if the gate were not meant to be

137

an entrance to the castle, but no more than a way to keep strangers out. Above it, in the stone wall, was carved in letters picked out in gold this rhyme:

"Within this castle lives the scourge of kings;
Death lights on him who bold defiance brings."

Here, indeed, lived a worthy foe for the champion of Italy, though he did not yet know it; none other than the giant Blanderon, a monstrous enchanter who was in league with many wizards and evil powers. Not only did he do foul deeds himself, and by his spells and his strength capture many innocent prisoners and shut them up in his castle, but he was wont to have in his charge also the victims of many other vile magicians.

But this St. Anthony had not yet learned. He sought to enter the castle and find in it whatever there might be to find. The great gate being shut, he rode all round the walls in search of another; it was more than a mile round the whole circuit. But there was no gate save the one he had come to first; the walls were as smooth as glass, and as high as a tall tree.

The champion went back to the gate, and peered through the bars. There was no sign of life within. He dismounted and tethered his horse, and took his sword, and beat with the handle of it upon the gate till the iron rang with the sound. For a moment he listened, and heard nothing. Then he struck the gate again, and the whole air in that still place was filled with the noise of beaten metal.

There was a deep roar within; a fierce voice shook the very air. Then came a rushing and a trampling, and the great voice roared again. St. Anthony saw through the bars of the gate, coming towards him in haste, a giant so huge and terrible that even his courage was aghast at the sight. He was as tall as four men, and in his hand he bore, instead of a club, an oak-tree that he had torn up by the roots. St. Anthony drew his sword hastily at the sight.

"Ah-h-h!" the giant roared; it was louder than the roar of a hungry lion. "Here comes another for my pantry!"

He gnashed his teeth, and twisted his lips up in a savage snarl. He kicked the bar that was across the gate on the inside, and it fell out, and the gates swung open. St. Anthony, undaunted, ran in; but he saw that it was of no avail to try to kill such a monster outright. He must weary him, or trick him into a false step, and must keep out of the reach of the tremendous club.

139

St. Anthony of Italy

The giant was already swinging the oak-
tree round in fury, missing the champion by
a hair's breadth. St. Anthony leapt aside,
and Blanderon struck at him again; but once
more the champion sprang away, and the tree
missed him; yet it came so close that an outlying branch struck his knee, and almost threw
him over. He recovered his balance, and
drew a little farther off.

And then began as strange a fight as was
ever seen, if that be a fight in which one is
for ever attacking and the other for ever
avoiding the attack. For full half an hour the
champion of Italy ran hither and thither, and
twisted, and leapt, and turned; and the giant
rushed at him again and again, roaring and
uttering terrible threats, and striking huge
blows with the oaken club in vain.

At length Blanderon began to grow weary;
and, indeed, St. Anthony was not so light-
footed or light-hearted as when first he beat
upon the castle gate with his sword. The
giant staggered a little in his gait, and lifted
his arm a little less vigorously when he had
struck a blow. At last he gathered up his
remaining strength, and swung the club up
above his head with both hands; down it
came, and if St. Anthony had been beneath
there would have been no fellowship of the

Seven Champions for him. But for the last time he sprang aside. The giant's arms seemed almost paralysed by the shock of the blow; his knees bent beneath him, and he stumbled forward and fell in a heap upon his club.

There was St. Anthony's opportunity. He ran in, and struck swiftly at the giant's right arm, which was nearest to him. The good sword smote Blanderon just above the wrist, and cut the hand clean off.

With a roar of pain and fury the giant struggled to his feet, and ran at St. Anthony, leaving his club lying on the ground, and trying to clutch the champion with his left hand. And now, if Blanderon had been unwearied and unwounded, St. Anthony might not have escaped, for it was not so easy to avoid the giant's grasp as the blows of his clumsy club. But the monster was weakened, and his legs tottered as he ran, and he was half blinded by sweat and anger. As he ran he tripped over his own oak-tree club, and fell sprawling, and lay helpless. Straightway St. Anthony ran in again with his sword, and with two swift blows cut off the monster's head.

Himself weary, he sank upon the ground, and stretched himself out. But the ground itself was enchanted, and no sooner had he lain down than he became cold and stiff, as though dead; all power of motion left him.

But meanwhile in the castle strange things had come to pass. The moment Blanderon was slain, his power over his prisoners was broken, though many there were in his prison who were not yet disenchanted, being under the spell of other magicians. It was wonderful to see those who had been set free coming to their senses, and wondering where they were, and recognising one another.

Among those from whom the spell had fallen was the fair Princess Rosalind. As soon as she was awakened, she looked round her, and remembered that the giant Blanderon had carried her off, she knew not how long before. She went to the castle battlements, and looked out to see if she could discover any cause of her new freedom. As soon as her eye fell on the courtyard, she beheld the giant stretched dead, with his head cut off, and close by him a gallant knight lying as if he, too, were dead.

She ran down to the courtyard, and felt the knight's heart; it still beat faintly, but he himself seemed to be in too deep a swoon to recover. The Princess went back into the castle, and searched all through the giant's

" SHE WENT TO THE BATTLEMENTS AND LOOKED OUT "

possessions for some draught or ointment which might be of avail. At last she came upon what seemed to be a suitable ointment, and this she took down to where St. Anthony lay. She began to rub his limbs with it, and to chafe his hands; and she took off his helmet gently, and rubbled his temples also. For a long while there was no result; but Princess Rosalind persevered. Nevertheless, she had almost given up hope, when the knight stirred a little, groaned, and awoke from his magic trance. She had broken the spell.

The Princess was the first thing he set eyes upon when he came to himself again, and he thought he had never seen anyone more lovely.

" What are you doing here, fair lady ?" he asked, struggling to his feet.

" That is what I would ask of you, Sir Knight," she answered gently, "for you must have a wondrous tale to tell if it is you who slew this wicked giant and enchanter."

" I slew him, in truth," said St. Anthony. " But it was not a wondrous deed. I did but let him weary himself, and so deliver himself into my hands. I think some spell must have been cast upon me when I had killed him, for I sank down to rest on the

St. Anthony of Italy

ground, and I knew no more till this moment, when I awoke to see you, fair lady."

And he looked at her with such love that she, too, felt that they were destined for one another.

"The ground, it may be, was enchanted, or was filled with a power of evil magic when the giant fell dead upon it; but now it seems that the power has passed, for you are whole and full of strength again. Tell me, Sir Knight, your name and estate."

"I am a Christian knight of Italy, by name Anthony," he answered. "But tell me, in turn, fair lady, who you may be?"

"I am the Princess Rosalind," she replied, "daughter of the King of Thrace. This cruel giant, whose name is Blanderon, carried me off once when I was hunting. I know not how long ago it was, for time itself is enchanted here, and not to be measured by mortal hours. This Blanderon was a magician, and in league with other wizards, all enemies of the human race. Many of their victims are shut up here, and I doubt whether they are all set free from their spells by this deed of yours. Belike you have only released those whom Blanderon himself enchanted. He told me there were many others. Come with me, Sir Anthony, and I will show you the saddest of them all, unless it has been their happy fate to be set free also."

She led him to the other side of the castle, where was a garden full of sweet flowers, surrounded by a dark yew hedge. In one corner of it was a wide pool, or little lake, bordered by yew-trees cut into the shape of beasts and birds. On its waters swam six pure white swans, and upon the head of each was a little crown of gold.

" Alas, dear sisters !" cried Rosalind, when she saw them; and at the sound of her voice the swans swam towards her to the edge of the lake, and stretched out their long white necks to her piteously. " Oh, dearly loved ones, the time is not yet come for you to be free. This valiant knight has slain Blanderon, and broken the spell that is upon me; but we do not know who it is that has enchanted you, since it was not Blanderon. But we will discover the secret. With this knight's aid, all things are possible."

" What is this strange thing you say, Princess ?" asked Sir Anthony. " You called these swans your sisters. How can that be ?"

" They are indeed my dear sisters, Sir Anthony. Some vile magician whom we do not know did them this harm, and turned them into swans, and gave them into Blan-

deron's keeping. I pray you, come with me
to the King my father in Thrace, and give
him the good news of my freedom, and afterwards devise some way to free these poor
birds of the spell."

They went back into the castle, and made
provision for the journey. There were many
good horses in the stables, and abundance of
food, and arms, and raiment in the proper
chambers. The other prisoners who had been
set free by the death of Blanderon were likewise
preparing to leave the castle. They thanked
St. Anthony for his prowess, and bade him
farewell and departed; and with the Princess
on a white horse beside him he set out with
good hope for Thrace, taking with him the
keys of the castle.

It was a long journey to Thrace, but they
accomplished it with light hearts, so glad
were they to be together. They came at last
within sight of the chief city. But before
they reached it they heard far off the tolling
of many bells mournfully, as if for a great
funeral or a season of universal sorrow. St.
Anthony asked a peasant whom they passed
what it meant.

" It is the day of mourning for the King's
daughters, my lord," said the man courteously. " On this day seven years ago they

all vanished, and no man knows how, or where they are to be found, or if they still walk this earth alive. It is said that some wicked magician stole them, but this is not known for certain. All we know is that they are gone from us, and that they were dearly beloved by the King and by us his subjects. He appointed this day to be kept always as a day of mourning until they are found, and very ready to mourn we are for such gentle ladies."

St. Anthony turned to the Princess, who had her face almost wholly veiled, because of the sun. "Show this good poor man who you are, Princess Rosalind," he said.

She uncovered her face. "Do you know me, friend?" she asked, looking at the peasant.

He fell on his knees with a cry of joy. "Oh, Princess! do I know you?" he said. "Do you not live in all our hearts, our Princess Rosalind? Tell me, if you will be so gracious, whence do you come? Where are your sisters? How have you been hid from us so long?"

"I am alone, but for this brave knight," answered Rosalind. "My sisters are under a spell, and I am but now freed from one." And she told him all that had happened.

"Princess, this is a day of wonder, of sad-

149

ness and rejoicing together," he said, when she ended. "Let me go before you swiftly to my lord the King, and tell him this news."

He hurried away to the city, while they went more slowly on their weary horses. Presently the tolling bells ceased. "He has given his message to the King," said St. Anthony. "Soon we shall be in your Sire's presence, and it may be that I must leave you and seek other adventures."

"No, no, dear Knight; do not leave me!" said the Princess. "I will go with you to the end of the world."

At that St. Anthony knew that they loved one another, and he was filled with joy. "Dear lady," he answered, "I am your servant always. If we cannot save your sisters, will you go into the world seeking fortune with me?"

"I will," she replied. And so they came into the chief city.

The King's palace was set in a great semi-circle. Marble steps, with pedestals on either side on which were lions in stone, led up to the audience-chamber. But the King did not wait therein to receive his daughter. He hurried down the steps to greet her and St. Anthony; then he led them within, and was told all that had happened.

Blanderon's Castle

He could not guess who had enchanted the six Princesses; but he resolved to go instantly to them, taking with him many knights, to see if haply he might find some means to break the spell. From St. Anthony he obtained the keys of the castle, and in a few days' time he set out with a great company of knights, and ladies also to serve the Princesses if they should be restored to human form.

St. Anthony and Princess Rosalind did not go with him. They were fatigued by their journey, and they had heard, also, of a great tournament to be held in honour of the wedding of the King of Greece's daughter, at which St. Anthony wished to joust. All the bravest knights of Christendom were to be at this tournament, and the champion had a hope that there he might meet once more his fellow-knights. He had taken counsel, moreover, with the King of Thrace and his Princess, and they believed that at such a great gathering of knights, if anywhere, news might be heard of the enchanter who had bewitched the six Princesses. So St. Anthony and Rosalind were married, with no splendour or festival, because of the lamentations for the swan-Princesses, and in due time they set out for the tournament in Greece.

S^T. ANDREW ^{OF} SCOTLAND

I

THE VALLEY OF EVIL SPIRITS

ST. ANDREW'S road led him through England to a seaport, where he took ship and sailed to Europe. When his wanderings on land continued, he found himself at length upon a very lonely path that grew narrower and more winding at every step. It took him through what seemed to be the greenest of meadows, going zigzag across the long, rich grass without, as it appeared, rhyme or reason. But the reason was made clear when St. Andrew left the path in order to take a shorter way across a bend in the track. The moment he was off the path he sank in the ground almost up to his waist, and only by throwing his head and shoulders violently backward and clinging to the track he had left did he reach dry ground safely. The whole green meadow was a treacherous quaking bog, with only this one way through it.

Presently the meadow sloped away to one side, the path running along the upper edge of it. Soon there was no marshland left by the path at all. The grass ceased, the way became dry and barren, with a gaunt, windswept, leafless hedge on one side, and rocky slopes on the other. Hardly a living plant or flower grew in that place. The green things were thin and wan, of a sickly yellow hue, as though no cheerful sunlight ever fell on them. Such flowers as there were had blooms of a dull threatening purple, and livid pale berries, and ragged thorny leaves, as if they were meant to offend and not to delight the eyes of mankind. The air grew colder, and a fine white mist seemed to be approaching at a little distance.

Again the path sloped, now very steeply. St. Andrew found himself in the mist. It was of a strange thinness, and hardly shut out the prospect from his eyes, but only served to make it unreal and ghostly. And, indeed, that was a ghostly place, for it was a haunted valley, full of evil spirits. The hedge had ceased. In its place were a few gnarled roots with little hold upon the ground. There were deep, dark holes in the grey soil, like

The Valley of Evil Spirits

foxes' earths, but larger. Stones and great boulders bestrewed the way.

A hand plucked St. Andrew by the arm. He turned quickly. There was no one near him. " It was but fancy," he said to himself; but in his heart he knew that it was no fancy. He went on boldly. Suddenly there was a whispering in his ear of strange words in a tongue which he could not understand. The words seemed evil, for they sounded full of anger and threatenings. But there was no being in sight who could have spoken them.

St. Andrew perceived that there was some spell at work in the valley which he could not understand. He feared lest he should fall under its power. But he kept a stout heart, and rode on, drawing his sword and holding it in readiness.

The moment he had drawn the sword the spirits seemed to take it as a challenge. On every side unseen hands caught at him. One would seize his reins and try to draw them from his hand; others struck him lightly in the face, or pulled his foot out of the stirrup, or strove to clutch his throat. All round him he heard whisperings and faint, shrill cries. He waved his sword fiercely in every direction, but it met with no resistance. He grew

St. Andrew of Scotland

confused, and his good horse snorted and whinnied in fear.

St. Andrew murmured a prayer and made the sign of the Cross, and immediately the mist disappeared and the spirits became visible to him. They were upon every side, multitudes of them—in the air, roaming upon the ground, some even wriggling out of the holes by the wayside with new malice in their dreadful eyes. They were of all manner of shapes, horrible to behold. Some had long skinny arms and bony claw-like fingers, some were squat and gross; here was one whose eyes flamed; there one with long pointed ears that moved like a horse's; there one whose body trailed away as if it were but a wisp of smoke; and some, most terrible of all, perpetually changed from one loathsome shape to another.

Yet they were powerless to do harm to a Christian knight if he never lost heart. And St. Andrew took new courage from his prayer. He spurred his horse, and struck at the spirits fiercely with his sword. The blade passed clean through them, and he felt as if it had met with nothing at all. Rage against these evil creatures seized him, and took away his prudence. He set his horse at those upon his right hand, and rode hither and thither

furiously, cutting and slashing at them with
his sword. Even if the sword seemed to do
them no harm, they shrank from it, and fled
before him; and he, in triumph, rode and
struck the more savagely, not seeing in his
anger that he was going farther and farther
from the path, until suddenly all the spirits
vanished, and he was alone.

He looked for the track; it was nowhere to
be seen. All around were rocks and stones
and inhospitable earth, with no sign of a path.
The light was beginning to fade, and soon was
gone altogether. St. Andrew was in a sorry
plight.

Once more the spirits began to attack him.
They pulled and pushed on every side, and
the air was full of their indistinct sounds. It
was useless to strike at them, now that they
could no longer be seen, and in which direction the true path lay St. Andrew could not
guess. Once again he murmured a prayer,
and immediately an answer came. In front
of him there suddenly glowed a small clear
light, sparkling and dancing in the air as if
inviting him to follow. He urged his steed
towards the spark, but he got no nearer to it,
for as he advanced it moved also, keeping
always at a little distance in front.

St. Andrew had heard of will-o'-the-wisps,

which lead men on till they fall into a bog, or over a precipice, or into some awful death. He did not know whether this might not be some such deadly thing. But he had faith in it, and followed it, nevertheless; and soon he was glad that he did so, for the valley seemed to grow smoother under his horse's feet, and the evil spirits grew less in number, and at last, after one great effort to drag him from his saddle, died away altogether and left him. In a little while St. Andrew felt that he was going uphill again. Stones no longer rang under his horse's hoofs, which, indeed, rustled at every tread, as if they were walking on good turf. Upwards he went, the bright light still flickering and leaping in front of him.

At last the ground grew level again. On one side he saw a growing glow in the sky; it was the moon rising. Soon she was above the horizon, lighting up the way for him. He could see that he was on a broad, clear expanse of hill, and the road gleamed white and straight in front of him. He looked for the friendly light which had led him thither; in watching the moon rise he had forgotten it. But it had vanished; its work was done.

St. Andrew rode on a little way, and came to a little clump of trees. Here he dismounted, and rested for the night. On the next day he went on with his journey, but he met no other adventure till he came to the borders of the kingdom of Thrace. Though he did not know it, he was close to the castle of Blanderon, to which, at that very time, the King of Thrace and his knights were travelling after hearing the news brought by St. Anthony and Princess Rosalind.

II

THE FIGHT WITH THE ENCHANTER

St. Andrew came in sight of Blanderon's castle about the middle of a fine morning. Like St. Anthony, he thought that in so great a castle might lie the cause of some worthy adventure, and he made haste to approach it. But when he was in an open space a mile or more from it, he saw, proceeding towards it from another direction, a great band of knights and ladies. They were, in truth, though he did not know it, the King of Thrace and his followers.

He turned out of his direct path to the castle, and made towards the new-comers. They, in their turn, had seen him, and halted and awaited him.

161

St. Andrew of Scotland

" Who are you that ride armed towards the castle of Blanderon ?" cried a Thracian knight to him, when he was within hearing.

" I am a Christian knight in search of warlike adventure," answered St. Andrew.

" A Christian ! One of our enemies !" said the King of Thrace, on hearing this. " And he seeks warlike adventure. He shall have it. He shall fight my knights, one after the other, with all due ceremony. He shall have the death of an honourable enemy. Let a herald go to him, and let my marshals draw up the lists for a tourney. Here is a fair open space that will well suit it."

A herald was instructed, and rode out to meet St. Andrew. " Sir Knight," he said, " the King of Thrace sends me to you to say that all Christians are his enemies, and you must therefore die. But the King is just and honourable, and he will grant you a knightly death. The lists shall be set, and you shall do battle with his champions. The laws of chivalry will be observed, and the King will appoint squires to attend upon you."

St. Andrew thought for a moment. He could not decline the combat, and, indeed, he was eager to uphold the Christian faith in arms; but he knew that it might be his death, for no man could fight foe after foe and not

162

The Fight with the Enchanter

in the end be conquered. "I accept your King's offer," he said at length. "Let him send whomsoever he pleases against me; I will uphold my faith against them all."

"Spoken like a gallant knight," said the herald. "Let me lead you to the lists."

He escorted St. Andrew to the place where already a great space was being barred off, and pavilions erected for the King, and for the knights at either end of the course. The champion was presented to the King, and then he was led to his pavilion, and food and drink was given him. Three squires waited upon him, and, when he had been refreshed, attended to his armour, and brought him spare weapons.

Soon the trumpets sounded. A squire told St. Andrew that it was time for him to go forth. The hangings of the pavilion were parted, and he rode out into the sunlight of the lists, his armour gleaming, a golden pennon on a small lance fluttering gaily. On the pennon were embroidered in silver letters the words: "To-day a martyr or a conqueror."

He rode to the King's pavilion, and made obeisance; then he went back to his corner of the lists, and took up his great tilting-lance, and waited while a herald proclaimed his name.

163

St. Andrew of Scotland

"Oyez! Oyez! Oyez!" cried the herald, after blowing three blasts on a silver trumpet. "The gallant knight, Sir Andrew of Scotland, is ready to do battle on behalf of the Christian faith against all who come."

Three blasts sounded from the other end of the lists. From the pavilion at that end came a knight clad all in silver armour upon a white horse. The marshal of the lists, standing near the King's pavilion, cried in a loud voice: "Set on!" And from either end the two knights thundered together. Crash! They had met. But the silver knight had not touched St. Andrew with his lance. The sound came from St. Andrew's lance, which struck his enemy full on the upper part of the helmet. His head was wrenched violently, and he fell backwards off his horse, his armour rattling about him. His horse galloped wildly on, and was secured by an attendant. But the knight lay where he had fallen. His neck was broken, and he was dead.

St. Andrew retired slowly to his pavilion. His squires made sure that his armour and weapons were still sound. The trumpets blared again, and he rode into the lists.

This time there awaited him a knight clad in golden armour. The marshal gave the word, and they rushed together. St. Andrew

The Fight with the Enchanter

was struck by the knight's lance, but only
lightly, for as they met his own lance smote
his enemy in the shoulder, and turned the
blow aside. The knight was unhorsed by the
stroke, but not greatly injured. He drew his
sword, and St. Andrew drew his in turn, and
leapt from his horse to fight on equal terms.
But this part of the combat did not last long,
for St. Andrew with one great back-handed
sweep of his sword broke through the golden
knight's defence, and clove his neck deep, so
that he died. There were murmurs of wonder
and of anger from the onlookers, who did not
like to see their champions so easily defeated.

Then again St. Andrew was tended by his
squires, and again he left his pavilion at the
sound of the trumpet. By now he was feeling
some weariness, and he was eager to see if his
new opponent would be more skilled than the
other two.

The pavilion curtains at the far end of the
lists were drawn apart, and through them
came a knight in coal-black armour, riding a
black horse. From his helmet flew a plume
black as a raven's wing, and his squire held
up as his banner a lance with a dull black
pennon.

" Who is this knight ?" asked the King of
Thrace of one of his courtiers. " I do not

know his armour, and he seems to be a stranger."

" I do not know, Sire."

But a page came to the King with a message that a knight who wished to be called the Unknown, and not to proclaim his name, was anxious to do battle with the Christian knight. He had a hatred of all Christians, he said, and he sought to serve the King of Thrace by fighting thus. He had but that moment arrived, and had come straight to the lists.

The King gave leave readily enough. It was no concern of his to limit the number of those who encountered St. Andrew, and the strange knight looked like one who could hold his own. Very huge and sinister did he seem as he towered upright on the black charger.

" Set on !" cried the marshal of the lists once more.

The knights dashed across the lists. They met with a clang and a shivering, rending noise. Each staggered a little in his saddle, but remained unhurt, and then it was seen that both their lances had been broken to atoms in the shock.

They galloped to their pavilions, and obtained fresh lances. Then they came together again. The black knight was borne clean off his horse's back, over the crupper, the horse

The Fight with the Enchanter

rearing high in the air at the blow. St. Andrew, likewise, was struck full and fair, and he leant back in his saddle till he was too far gone to stay upright, and he, too, slipped off his horse. Squires ran up and seized the horses, and quickly gave shields to each knight.

St. Andrew drew his sword; already the black knight had his out of its scabbard. They rushed at one another, and blade rang on blade as fast as the strokes of a hammer on an anvil. So fiercely did his enemy assail him that St. Andrew had to yield ground, and retreat a little. A roar of cheering came from the onlookers when they saw him hard pressed. But he was not defeated. As he gave way he watched his enemy warily. The black knight grew more eager, and came on more hastily. He aimed a tremendous blow at St. Andrew's head, striking a little wildly in his fury. St. Andrew sprang swiftly far to one side, and before the knight could recover his balance he had driven his sword down, down, clean through the black plume and the black helmet, through skull and neck to the very shoulders.

It was a wondrous stroke, and the crowd of knights and followers looking on gasped at the sight. Then they came to their senses, and knew that their third champion had been

167

St. Andrew of Scotland

defeated. They lost their tempers, and no longer could the marshal of the lists and his men keep them behind the barriers. They swarmed over them, and rushed at St. Andrew with cries of hatred and anger. " Down with the Christian ! Kill him !" they shouted. " He has bewitched our knights. Kill him !"

St. Andrew knew that he was in dire peril. He could see no hope of his life, but he resolved to sell it as dearly as he could. A great anger filled him at this treacherous onset, and instead of defending himself, he became in a moment the attacker. Whirling his sword aloft, he sprang forward with a cry of battle, and threw himself like a madman upon the mob.

Well it was for him that his armour was stout and his blade sharp ; not all the courage in the world could else have saved his life, for the Thracians were all armed. But so fierce was his fury that in a few minutes he had slain many of the crowd, and was driving the rest before him like sheep. Then he turned and strode across to the King's pavilion, aflame with wrath.

" Sir King," he cried in a great voice, " is this the way you uphold the laws of chivalry ? Your herald talked to me of honour. Is this your honour ? How do——"

"BLADE RANG ON BLADE"

The Fight with the Enchanter

" Sire, Sire, a wonder!" a voice broke in. A squire came running across the lists, with his face full of horror. " The black knight—" he cried breathlessly. " I pray you come and look."

The crowd had become silent. Strange news had come to their ears. They whispered to one another in fear, and drew back beyond the barriers, as the King and St. Andrew and certain courtiers walked to where the black knight lay.

" This was no knight," said a squire who was by the body. " It was some evil spirit in the shape of a man. Look!"

He drew back the vizor of the broken helmet, and they looked at the face of the dead man. Here were no features of a brave and powerful knight. The face was not that of a man capable of bearing arms, but of an old, old creature, wizened and shrunken. There was no hair upon the head, the eyes were sunken and full of evil (for they had remained open in death), and the teeth protruded like a dog's. Assuredly it was the face of one to whom all evil was known, and who had lived evilly all his days.

" It must have been some wizard," said St. Andrew, when he had lost his first horror, and could think more clearly. " When I

171

fought him, he was veritably a man in the prime of life, and full of strength. If he was a wizard, he could take the shape of a young knight; but when I slew him his power would vanish, and he would become as he really was, the evil thing that you see."

"By my faith, Sir Knight," said the King of Thrace, "I think that is the truth of it. Do you know why I and my knights have come hither? When we encountered you we were riding to yonder castle to see if we could discover a certain magician. It may be that this is he himself whom you have slain. If it be so, I owe you a debt that I cannot pay even with my life."

And he told him the story that the Princess Rosalind had brought to him from Blanderon's castle.

"Forgive me, good sir," he ended, "if in my zeal against Christians I used you ill. I would have treated you honourably, with all the customs of chivalry, but my knights forgot their knightly courtesy when they saw this third champion slain. You are indeed a man of might, Sir Andrew. Now I pray that you will come with us to Blanderon's castle, and we will see whether the death of this enchanter has given us help in our search. If you have delivered my six daughters from

The Fight with the Enchanter

the spell cast upon them, there is no reward that you cannot ask of me."

Attendants remained behind to break up the lists, while the King and St. Andrew and all the knights and ladies went to the castle. They came to the great gates, and opened them with the keys which St. Anthony had given the King. No sooner were they within the courtyard than there ran to meet them a host of prisoners set free from spells, and foremost among them the King's daughters, once more restored to human form, and very lovely to look upon. For what St. Andrew and the King had guessed was indeed true. The black knight was no other than the terrible enchanter, the friend of Blanderon, who had bewitched the Princesses and many other persons, and given them into the giant's charge. He had heard of Blanderon's death, and by his magic arts he knew that St. Andrew was coming thither also; and he feared that these Christian knights, by their strong faith, might prevail over his spells. He took, therefore, the shape of a knight, and tried to slay St. Andrew in the tournament. But the might of the Christian champion was too strong for him, and now he was dead, and all his enchantments void and broken.

St. Andrew of Scotland

"What shall I do to reward you, friend?" asked the King of Thrace, when all these things had become clear to him. "How can I make amends also for my treatment of you?"

"You did not use me ill, Sire," answered St. Andrew gently. "You hated Christians, and you knew that I was one. It will be enough reward for me if henceforth you do not hate knights of my faith."

"Hate!" cried the King. "I have seen Sir Anthony, and you, Sir Andrew, and I know now that there is no better faith in the world. I will become a Christian myself, if you will instruct me in the way."

They talked long and earnestly about the Christian faith, and the end of it was that the King of Thrace became a Christian, and with him many of his court. Then they set out to go back to the chief city, for the Princesses were eager to see their home and their sister Rosalind again, and Sir Andrew longed to meet Sir Anthony, his comrade, once more.

As for the castle of Blanderon, the King gave orders that it should be razed to the ground and utterly destroyed; and if you search for it now in Thrace you will not find so much as a single stone left, and no man knows where it once stood.

The Fight with the Enchanter

They came presently to the chief city. The news of their coming spread before them, and all the people assembled to welcome them, strewing flowers in the path of St. Andrew and the six Princesses, who so honoured their deliverer that they wished to be with him always.

But there was a disappointment in store for them, for they found that St. Anthony and his wife, the Princess Rosalind, hearing of the great tournament which was to be held at the court of the King of Greece, had already set out thither. St. Andrew was filled with sorrow at this news, and it was not many days before he decided to go to Greece himself also to seek his brother-in-arms and to take part in the tournament. In order not to seem discourteous and impatient, and to prevent the Princesses from trying to dissuade him, he left the King's palace secretly, only leaving word whither he had gone. After a journey of some days he came to the chief city of Greece, Athens, and there he found St. Anthony and his Princess. Right glad were they to see one another again, and many a plan for adventure in the coming tournament did they make.

But the two champions were not the only friends who were united at Athens. When they discovered St. Andrew's flight, the six Princesses of Thrace were plunged into grief. So deep was their sorrow that nothing would content them but to go secretly to Greece themselves, without thinking of their father's misery if he found them gone. They set out privately one night. But their attendants, from chance sayings and other signs, guessed whither they had gone, and told the King, who, when he first heard of their absence, had thought that another enchanter must have carried them off. But when he heard that it was only love for St. Andrew that had driven them, as it seemed to him, out of their senses, he determined that he, too, would go to Greece, and off he set in their train.

ST.
PATRICK OF IRELAND

S T. PATRICK'S road did not lead him into any such great perils as the other champions met with. He had adventures enough, and received the honour of knighthood, and wandered into many lands doing whatever deeds fell in his way; but there was no happening that need be chronicled till he came into Greece, and found himself riding through a great forest. He had heard of the tournament at the King's court at Athens—all the world of chivalry knew of it—and meant to adventure in arms at it. He was thinking, as he rode, of certain tricks of swordsmanship he had learnt from an old knight in Bohemia, when suddenly loud cries broke upon his ears. They were screams of distress, but with them were mingled strange growlings and hideous laughter. The sound came from a little way in front, and it seemed that there were many people there.

St. Patrick of Ireland

St. Patrick dismounted, so as to approach the more silently, and tethered his horse. Then he drew his sword, and crept on tiptoe through the trees. He reached a little clearing in a few moments, and then he saw the cause of the uproar. A band of satyrs, horrible creatures like those which had guarded St. George long before in Kalyb's realm, were trying to carry off with them six beautiful maidens, who wailed and struggled, but were in danger of being overcome.

St. Patrick flew out from his sheltering trees, and laid about him with his sword. In a trice three of the creatures lay dead, and a fourth was wounded. The rest fled headlong with shrill squeals of dismay.

The champion turned to the six ladies. "Oh, Sir Knight," said one of them, "you came only just in time! Why did you not come before?"

"I came as soon as I heard your cries, fair lady," answered St. Patrick courteously. "Had I known you were in peril, I would have hastened my horse. But I did not know till the sounds reached me that there was anyone in this forest. When I knew, I did all that was in my power, as a Christian knight should. You are safe now; but by your leave I will escort you on your way, lest other dangers come upon you."

"You are a Christian knight, you say?" said one of the Princesses. They had been whispering together as St. Patrick spoke. "But a Christian knight, if he be like one we know, would have found out our danger without waiting to hear our cries."

"My name is Patrick of Ireland, and I defend the Christian faith. Forgive me, fair ladies, if I think you are not just to me."

"Was not that one of them?" said a Princess to her sister. "Did not our Sir Andrew speak of Sir Patrick?"

"What is this strange talk of yours?" interrupted St. Patrick. "I have done you a trifling service, and you blame me because I could not do it more speedily. You say a Christian knight would know of dangers before they come to pass, which I take leave to doubt. And then you speak of one who is my dear comrade and brother-in-arms. What does it mean? Pray, who are you?"

For the poor knight was bewildered by their blaming him and their mention of St. Andrew. Their heads, indeed, were almost turned by the picture they had formed in their own minds of the champion of Scotland.

"Brave knight," said the eldest Princess,

181

St. Patrick of Ireland

"pardon our discourtesy and ingratitude. We are distraught by our adventure, and also our minds are full of that paragon of knighthood, Sir Andrew of Scotland, our deliverer, whom we are going to seek at the court of Greece. Tell us truly, are you that Christian knight, Sir Patrick of Ireland, who is the comrade of our Sir Andrew?"

"I did not know that he was your Sir Andrew, fair ladies. You did not tell me, and even a Christian knight cannot guess such unknown things as that. But I am indeed the brother-in-arms of Sir Andrew of Scotland. With him and five others I seek to bring the whole world into the Christian faith."

"Then we welcome you, Sir Patrick, and we thank you, moreover, as we should have thanked you already, for your valour; and we will gladly have your escort to the court of Athens, if you are going thither, as I think all Christendom is. Know that we are princesses, daughters of the King of Thrace." And she told him all the adventure of Blanderon's castle, and the doings of St. Anthony and the Princess Rosalind.

St. Patrick was overjoyed to think that he would meet two of his companions at Athens, and he gladly escorted them thither. But he

The Six Princesses

found others besides those two champions there, for St. James and the Princess Celestine, his wife, had come to the tournament, and St. Denis also, with his Princess Eglantine; so that five of the seven champions of Christendom had come together again. There also arrived in due time the King of Thrace, rejoicing to find his wandering daughters again. And still other friends were to come to that wondrous tournament.

St. David
of
Wales

I

THE ENCHANTED GARDEN

ST. DAVID took a road which, when he had crossed the sea, led him farther afield than the other champions; for he wandered, after many adventures, as far as Tartary, where he found in the capital city signs of great rejoicing, and all the people seemed to be hastening in one direction.

"Why does the city make holiday?" he asked a passer-by.

"From what distant part of Asia do you come," answered the man scornfully, "tha you do not know this is the birthday of our Emperor? A great tournament is to be held in honour of it. Thither are all the folk going, and knights from all the world have come to it. But I know who will be the best of them all, for I saw him riding out and practising tilting yesterday, and that is the Emperor's own son, the Count Palentine. Beware of him, Sir Knight, if you are one of those who will risk their lives in the tourney. He is a man of might and prowess."

" It may be that I shall test him," said St. David. "Tell me, my friend, when is the tournament to begin ?"

" This very day," said the man. "They are even now choosing those who shall take part in the last mellay, when those whom the King picks out shall do battle against the Count Palentine and his friends. The tourney ground lies yonder."

St. David asked no more questions, but hastened to the lists, and entered himself to take part in the contests which were about to begin. Such was his prowess that he overthrew all comers in that day's encounter, and was chosen to lead the King's party in the great mellay on the morrow, when the Count Palentine would himself do battle.

In due time the hour of the mellay arrived, and St. David led out his band of knights, and they fell to fighting. It was agreed that if a man were unhorsed or disarmed or at the mercy of an opponent, he should retire from the contest; the battles were not to be pressed to the bitter end of death, for there was no reason to lose so many gallant knights.

Count Palentine singled out St. David for his own foe especially, and they charged one another with a shock that seemed to shake the very earth. Fair true their lances struck. St. David reeled in his saddle and almost fell, but the Count sat as firm as a rock. They separated and drew apart, and charged again. This time the Emperor's son received St. David's lance full on his helmet. He swayed in his saddle, dropped his lance, and fell from his horse.

St. David sprang to earth to renew the combat on foot, drawing his sword; but Count Palentine lay where he had fallen, still and motionless. St. David ran to him, and knelt at his side as some squires ran up and loosened his armour, and opened the vizor of his helmet. The Count was dead; St. David had killed the Emperor's son.

A silence fell upon the onlookers, for the Count was greatly beloved. St. David went across the lists to the Emperor's pavilion, and made obeisance sadly. " Sire," he said gravely, " I have slain your son. It was in fair combat, according to the laws of chivalry. Nevertheless, I place my life in your hands; do with me as you will. I pray that you will take my sword in token of my submission."

He offered his sword to the Emperor, hilt foremost. But the Emperor refused it, saying: " Keep your sword, Sir Knight; your word is

enough. I know that my son is dead in fair
fight. Nevertheless, he was so beloved of my
people that I must needs punish you in some
way; how that shall be I will devise hereafter.
I will exact some service from you. Abide
at my court until my son is buried."

The other knights were still fighting in the
mellay. But now the marshal of the lists
threw down his staff, and they ceased at that
sign. It was proclaimed that the tournament
was stopped because Count Palentine was
slain, and all men went sorrowfully to their
homes.

A few days later the funeral of the Count
was celebrated with great pomp, amid the
lamentations of the whole people, and then
the Emperor sent for St. David and gave him
audience.

"I would desire to make amends, Sire,"
said St. David, "for this deed that I did,
though I did it without design. It was an
accident; nevertheless, I owe you reparation."

"I would not ask you to make amends,
good Sir Knight," answered the Emperor,
"if it were not that my people are enraged
against you out of their love for my son, and
they will surely kill you if it is not known
that you are offering redress. I will ask of
you, as a sign to them of your sorrow, not as

The Enchanted Garden

a punishment, for that you do not deserve, that you shall perform a great service for me. It is no light task that I shall lay upon you. Will you do as I ask you?"

"I will do whatever you ask, Sire," answered St. David, "save only that I will do nothing that is against my honour."

"That is the answer I looked for from so gallant a knight," said the Emperor. "Now, the task I charge you with is this: My kingdom has in past years and is to-day mightily oppressed by a certain notorious wizard, the foul enchanter Ormandine. This magician is the foe of all chivalry and honour, and many a wrong has he done by his arts to me and to my subjects. His home lies on the borders of my kingdom, very far to the west of this city; he dwells in an enchanted garden, weaving his spells and pondering his evil designs. I charge you to go thither and seek him out, and cut off his head."

"That is a task I will gladly do, Sire," said St. David, "if it be within my power. It is the aim of all Christian knights to slay magicians and evil-doers wherever they may be found. I have heard of the might and wickedness of this Ormandine; the world would be well rid of him. I thank you, Sire, for laying on me such an honourable quest."

191

St. David of Wales

" It is honourable, Sir David," answered the Emperor, "but it is difficult as well: Many have journeyed to Ormandine's enchanted garden, but none have returned. I would not have asked such a thing of you if I had not known how eagerly Christian knights war against enchanters and such other evil beings. If you return in safety, bringing me Ormandine's head, not only will I forgive you the death of my son, but I will make you heir to my kingdom in his place, so hard do I deem the task. Now make your preparations and go speedily, and I pray that you will fare well."

So St. David set forth upon this great quest in high hopes, and little doubting that a Christian knight would easily overcome a magician.

It was many days before he came to the western border of Tartary, and knew that he was near the enchanted garden of Ormandine. No man dwelt within many miles of that place of evil; the very air round it seemed full of ghostly powers that dulled the senses of travellers.

The garden, when St. David at length found himself approaching it, proved to be surrounded by a thick, high hedge of thorns and briars, which seemed to flame like fire, and

The Enchanted Garden

whose sharp spines burnt and stung if they pierced the flesh. But St. David, in his shining armour, did not heed them. He saw at first no way through the thorns, and began to hew a path through them with his sword; but as fast as he cut them down others grew in their place, and the hedge remained as thick as ever. Then he sought once more for a gate, and presently found one, deep in the hedge. He had to cut away the thorns once more to reach it, but here they did not grow again when he cut them, and soon he was standing close to the gate. He saw now that it was of pure beaten gold, set with rubies and diamonds. On either side it was fitted into a wall of rock that stretched away in the midst of the thorn hedge for a long distance.

St. David beat at the gate with his sword, and waited, but no answer came. He tried to force it open, but in vain. He looked about him for some means of opening it or speaking to those within the garden, and then he saw, in the rock hard by, the handle of a sword standing out as though the rest of it were buried in the rock. He looked at it more closely, and perceived that there were letters cut on the hilt in silver. They formed this rhyme:

193

St. David of Wales

" By magic art I'm firmly bound
Until a valiant knight be found
To break my spell and set me free.
Victorious knight, behold and see !"

When he read these words St. David
thought that he was the knight destined to
free the sword, and he seized the hilt and
pulled it with all his might. But no sooner
had he clutched it than a shock ran all
through him, and he fell backwards to the
ground, and lay in a deep trance. The sword
was enchanted, and none but the destined
knight could seize it unhurt.

The wizard Ormandine knew by his arts
whenever the sword was touched. He sent
four evil spirits to the gate to bring before
him whoever might be lying there. They
found St. David, and carried him to Ormandine, who looked narrowly upon him, and saw
that he was a Christian knight. He knew
that he must one day meet his death at the
hands of a Christian knight, and therefore he
rejoiced that St. David had fallen into his
power. He set upon him a yet stronger spell,
and bade his servants bind him and leave
him in a cave in the magic garden, where lay
many other unhappy prisoners.

194

"HE SET UPON HIM A YET STRONGER SPELL"

The Escape of St. George

II

THE ESCAPE OF ST. GEORGE

No less a person than St. George himself
was to deliver St. David from Ormandine's
spell and overcome the enchanter. When he
was cast back into his dungeon after killing
the lions the English champion fell into deep
despair. The wild frenzy that had given him
strength had died away, and he was weak
and weary. In that dark and noisome cell
no thoughts of hope could come to a prisoner.
Never did he see so much as a ray of daylight;
even when his gaolers thrust his food daily
through the shutter in the wall there was but
a greyness in the opening, not the bright glow
of sunlight. Loathsome reptiles splashed in
the pools on the floor of the dungeon, rats
squeaked and scuffled, and when he slept ran
over him and gnawed at his raiment. He had
no refuge but his own thoughts, and they
were not cheering; he remembered Sabra, and
he recalled that great fight with the dragon
in the blazing sun. Ah, how far off the sun
seemed now! He thought of his dear companions, and how he had delivered them from
Kalyb; and the memory of England drove
him almost to madness, so that he rushed

197

against the damp, cold walls of the cell, and beat upon them with his fetters.

But this mood of rage and hopelessness did not endure for ever. After a long time he began to grow accustomed to the darkness. He would think of the hour when they brought him food as if it were sunrise, and it pleased him to make in his mind, as it were, a map of his dungeon. Day by day he crept about it, pacing distances and feeling the hard walls, until he knew all the shape and parts of it. It was a great underground cave, it seemed, rather than a prison cell. The form of it was irregular, with uneven lines and patches in the walls, which were hewn out of the solid rock. He knew before long exactly where the barred-up door lay, and where the shutter was through which his food came, and in which direction lay the horrible pools of water. Presently he had gained such a knowledge of the cave that he could by the mere feel of the ground under his feet tell to which part of the wall he was turning.

But it was not till he had been there many weary months that he came upon the crowbar. How such a thing had been left in the dungeon he did not know. Perhaps they had needed it to prize off the fetters of some miserable captive in former days; perhaps, even, the

The Escape of St. George

craftsmen who hollowed out the cave had forgotten to take it away. Be that as it may, St. George found it one day (if day it was—day and night were alike to him) as he paced the dungeon in his weary explorations. It was in a corner that he seldom visited, where the roof sloped down to the wall, so that it was not possible to stand quite upright, and he came upon it by stumbling over it where it lay in a pool of water.

No sooner had he got possession of this weapon than he began to plan his escape from the dungeon. He found the bar still strong in spite of rust, and after he had examined the door of his cell as carefully as he could in the darkness, he determined to break out that way. But he must first be sure that he did so at an hour of the day or night when the watch upon him could be least vigilant.

He had no knowledge of the hours or of how many days had passed since he slew the lions. He had not counted the times when food was given him, nor did he know whether the shutter was opened once a day or more often.

When next he heard the shutter being opened he sprang across to it, and spoke to the guard outside. "Tell me, good gaoler, what day this is, and what hour in the day."

"I must not speak with you," answered

the man; and St. George heard another man laugh, so that he knew at least two men were stationed there.

"Have pity!" cried St. George miserably. "I cannot tell day from night in this accursed place."

"I must not answer," replied the man. But he was merciful, and he thought of a device for answering without disobeying his orders. "This Christian dog," he said to his comrade, "does not know whether it is night or day. He would not forget these things if he were like us, with a great feast to come to-night in honour of the Soldan's birthday. It is thirty years since the Soldan came to the throne, and never has there been such a festival as we shall have this night at eight of the clock. It wants but three hours of the time now. We shall not forget it. Ho! ho! A dungeon is the place for a man's memory!"

St. George dared not thank him, for fear that he might arouse suspicion. But immediately the shutter was closed he set himself to count beneath his breath, so that he might gauge the flight of time as nearly as possible. He kept his food untouched, hungry though he was; he meant to eat it a little before he started on his enterprise, so that he should have his full strength.

The Escape of St. George

Sitting there in the darkness St. George counted steadily second after second, straining his mind to check the minutes as they succeeded one another. Seconds became minutes, minutes became hours. Three hours went by; the feast must be beginning. He counted on; now it must be ten o'clock, now eleven, now midnight. He had counted for seven hours. Yet he continued for two more.

When he felt sure that it was past two o'clock in the morning he stopped. He felt his clothes all over to see that there was nothing loose or untied that might delay him unexpectedly. He ate his food slowly. Then he took up his crowbar and began his enterprise.

The crowbar was a stout one, or it would not have done its work. The door of the cell was thick and heavy. Yet he contrived to get the point of the bar into a crack at the opening, and slowly, slowly pressed upon it till the latch was free. It swung open inwards with a click; beyond were iron bars across and across, but there was space for his body to squeeze between them.

Now was the moment of danger. Would there be guards outside ? Would they have heard the faint grinding of the crowbar and the click as the door opened ? He waited for several minutes; he heard deep, regular breathing. Were they really asleep, or only feigning in order to entrap him ? He must take his chance.

There was a dim light outside as though from a small lantern. He could see that a passage ran both ways. He forced himself noiselessly through the bars, and stepped into the passage, crowbar in hand.

On the left side the passage ended a few feet away in the solid rock; on the right it ran for some distance, farther than he could see by the light of the lantern which hung on the wall just outside his cell door. Across the passage lay two guards motionless. They were fast asleep. They had had no share in the revelry, but a comrade had seen to it that food and wine in plenty were conveyed to them at their post, and now they were heavy with sleep.

St. George stepped lightly over them, and crept swiftly along the passage. He did not know whither it would lead him, except that it was away from his dungeon. After a little while the passage turned to the right, and then to the left. And now there were doors on either side at intervals—heavy iron doors, as though other dungeons lay behind them. He did not seek to open them.

The Escape of St. George

At last the passage itself ended in a door. St. George lifted the latch silently, and pulled gently; it did not open. A feeling of despair came over him. He tried it again and again; it would not open. Suddenly he laughed silently, and pressed against the door instead of pulling at it. It opened at once—the other way.

He went through and shut it quietly. The passage ran a few yards, and ended in steps; it was lit up faintly by a lantern. He walked on stealthily and up the steps; at the top was another door, which he opened easily. He was in a long, large room with great windows, through which moonlight entered. It was the chief hall of the palace. All about it lay men-at-arms asleep on the rushes, the greater part of them overcome by wine as much as by weariness.

St. George picked his way among them down to the far end of the hall; the little door by which he had entered was at the side of the dais. He went into the darkness under the minstrels' gallery; he began to remember the way from the time when he came there as the King of Egypt's envoy. He turned to the left; there should be a great door there, he recollected.

Everything was in his favour. The guards

in their feasting had forgotten to bolt and
bar this door. It swung heavily upon its well-
oiled hinges. St. George went through and
shut it noiselessly. He was in a broad passage
which led on the one hand to the stables, on
the other to the Soldan's apartments. No
one was in sight. He turned towards the
stables, and strode quickly along the passage.

His footsteps, light though they were,
seemed to echo in the silence. He turned a
corner, and almost ran into a man coming
from the opposite direction carrying a lantern.
He knew then why there was an echo; it was
no echo, but the sound of this man. Quick
as thought he swung up his crowbar, and
brought it down upon the man's head. He
fell stunned and silent; there was a jingle of
keys as he fell.

St. George stooped over him, picked up the
lantern, and looked narrowly at him. He did
not know the man's face, but by his garb he
was one in office. In truth he was the chief
warder of the palace, who was going round
the guards unexpectedly. At his belt was a
bunch of keys.

St. George took the keys, bound the warder
with his own girdle, thrust a handkerchief
into his mouth, and tied round it a strip of
linen torn from the man's robe. Now if he

The Escape of St. George

came to his senses the warder would make no noise.

The champion hastened on his way. The keys opened doors and gates and bars for him. Everywhere he found guards asleep, for the warder had but just started on his rounds when St. George met him, and had not yet roused the sleeping men. He came before long to the stables. He wished to find his good steed Bucephalus.

The horses in the stables paid little heed to him; he understood them, and they were not afraid. He left the stable-door open before he searched. At last he found Bucephalus; the good beast knew him at once, and turned round and nuzzled against him with his nose. Above the manger, to the champion's joy, hung his sword Ascalon, and a great part of his armour, which the Persians had taken from him when they cast him into the dungeon.

He put on the armour hastily, and tore some strips from his clothing, and bound them round the hoofs of Bucephalus. With his sword drawn in his hand he led the horse silently out, and locked the stable-door, as he had locked all other doors after he obtained the keys. He was in the courtyard of the palace with no more barriers between him and the city.

St. David of Wales

There was a well in the courtyard; he dropped the bunch of keys down it. Then he mounted Bucephalus and rode out. Already he began to feel sure of escape.

But when he was in the city streets, as he soon was, he was not yet free. He rode along them some little distance before he could think of a plan to get through the city gates. Suddenly he thought of one which might succeed by its very daring. He dismounted and took the rags from the horse's hoofs, mounted again, and set Bucephalus to a gallop. Straight to the main gates he thundered, and beat upon them with his sword. "Gate! Gate! Ho, within!" he cried.

A sleepy watchman came out from the gate-house in a few minutes very angry at being disturbed, for, like the men in the palace, he had been up late feasting that night.

"Wake, man!" roared St. George in anger. "Open the gates! The Christian knight, St. George, has escaped, and has come this way. He has broken out of his dungeon by some means. Let me go! I am hard upon his heels!"

The man was too dazed to wonder or to ask questions. He fumbled at the gates, muttering angrily against the Christian prisoner escaping at such a time, and at last opened them. In a moment St. George was outside. He was tempted to fly without another word. But he stopped, and spoke to the watchman first, with an air of command. " Other guards will be here in a moment. They were all as sleepy as you. I seem to be the only man to do his duty this night. When they come tell them to separate and spread out; let some go by the other gates, for we do not know whither this Christian dog went after he left the city. He climbed the wall a little way hence by the aid of a tree. And for yourself, look that if he comes this way again he does not do you a mischief. Our whole land is in peril while he is free."

The man saluted drowsily. St. George turned, and was off like the wind. He was free.

III

THE TWO RESCUES

St. George rode swiftly across the desert, not sparing Bucephalus; delay meant death. As soon as it was day, and the Persians woke from their deep sleep—sooner, perhaps, if one of them chanced to be wakeful and to see anything suspicious—they would discover that he was gone. But he had, it was likely, two or three hours' start.

St. David of Wales

Day dawned before long, and with every stride of the good horse he rode into safety. No one pursued; he met no one. And so at last he came to the frontiers of Persia, and passed them, and was indeed free.

He was not sure whither he should go. He desired to return to the King of Egypt, and claim the Princess Sabra for wife; but he was uncertain exactly in which direction Egypt might lie, except that it must be somewhere in the west. All day he rode, following the sun as nearly as he could. As night drew on he found himself near a castle standing upon a hill, and he became aware that he was very hungry. He resolved to go to the castle, and ask hospitality for the night.

It seemed to be a huge place. All the doors were of a great height; the walls towered as if they were climbing to the sky, and the windows in them were large beyond wont. Everything about it was vast; the very horn at the gate for strangers to sound to ask admittance was so heavy and hung so high on the gate-post that St. George could hardly make use of it. But he reached it by an effort, and by blowing as if he would crack his lungs sounded a faint blast upon it.

A warder presently came and unbarred the gates. " Who are you and what is your

The Two Rescues

errand ?" he asked through a spyhole in the solid oak of the gates before he opened them. This hole seemed to be set higher up than was customary.

" I am a knight-errant, and I would pay my respects to the lord of this castle, and seek a little refreshment and hospitality from him."

He thought he heard the man laugh, but he could not be sure. The gates were opened, and he rode in. The warder was a huge man, nearer seven than six feet in height.

" You may enter," he said gruffly. Yet he seemed to be smiling secretly in his heart. " My master has always room for such as you."

He blew a whistle, and attendants came; they were all taller than common men. They took Bucephalus and led him to a stable. Others showed St. George a chamber where he might set his raiment in order. When he was ready they took him to a richly decked room in which sat a beautiful lady of more than human stature. She towered above his head as she rose to greet him.

" What do you seek, Sir Knight ?" she asked. She looked upon St. George favourably, and it seemed to him that there was fear and pity in her eyes also.

" I crave refreshment and a place to rest

209

for the night," answered St. George courteously. " I have come a long journey, and I ask the hospitality of one knight to another."

" Our hospitality is strange and cold," she answered. " You will do well not to seek it."

St. George was surprised. " I am very weary, and I have not broken my fast all this day," he said. " I do but ask what chivalry enjoins a knight to give."

" If it were I alone to answer you," said the lady, " I would receive you with all due courtesy, for I see that you are a noble knight, and that you are indeed weary, as you say. But it is for your own sake that I bid you leave this castle, and hasten on your journey yet farther before you dare seek rest."

" What mean you, lady ?" asked St. George. "You speak in riddles. Who is the lord of this mighty castle ?"

" My husband is its lord, and it is against his will that I warn you. I would not have so gallant a knight come to so sorry a death as you must meet if you abide here."

" I do not understand you, fair lady. Who is your lord ? Why should I fear death ?"

" I will tell you. My husband is a giant and an eater of men. This day he has gone a-hunting, but in a little while he will return, and he will slay you and afterwards eat you."

The Two Rescues

"I do not fear a giant," said St. George. He saw now what the warden of the gate had meant by his strange greeting. "I will not stir from here till I have had food and drink. If I must die, better to die fighting than of starvation. But your giant will not kill me."

"Alas, he will!" said the giantess. "I am weary of his cruelties, but I cannot prevent them. Go, Sir Knight, I beg you."

"No," answered St. George, "that may not be. A knight may not refuse to encounter one who is the enemy of the human race. If you so pity me, give me meat, that I may have all my strength for this combat that I must undertake."

The lady tried no more to dissuade him, but bade her servants bring him meat and drink, and he feasted right well, so that his strength came back to him and his weariness fell from him.

Hardly had he finished his meal when he heard a great voice shouting rough commands. The giant had returned. In a few moments he entered the room.

"Hola! A Christian knight, they tell me!" he shouted. He was a creature as tall as two tall men, very fat and unwieldy, but nevertheless active and strong. His hair was red;

and he had a long red beard. "You are welcome, fair sir. I have had poor hunting to-day, and you will reward me for my vain chase. It is not often a man sets a snare and catches nothing, and comes home and finds the game all ready for him in the pot. Come hither, and I will cut your head off very gently; you will not know it is off, so gentle will I be."

St. George looked at him with contempt. "You are not worthy of this castle, fellow," he said. "None but a boor would offer such insults to a knight who claims hospitality."

"Knight!" said the giant with a brutal laugh. "I care nothing for knighthood. I enjoy myself, and have my own way. But no more words. You must die, and it may as well be done quietly. Come, I will not hurt you. Here is my little knife; see how sharp it is!"

And he pulled a long red hair out of his beard, and threw it into the air. While it was still in the air he snatched a huge curved scimitar, with broad blade, from where it hung on the wall, and with two quick sweeps cut the hair in half, and then each half in two again.

"I have a sword as sharp as that, and I can cut as quickly; but I will cut something more than a hair," said St. George, rising and drawing his good sword Ascalon.

" What !" roared the giant. " You will fight me, you wretched little creature ? Well, have your own way. A little sword-play will give me an appetite for you."

He rushed at St. George, and so swift was he, despite his bulk, that St. George was forced to spring aside, and put the table between them. He could not hope to live if that great scimitar touched him. His plan was to wear the giant out by movement, and seize any chance to get in a blow himself.

He had not long to wait for his chance. The giant made a furious stroke at him, and missed; the scimitar struck instead a stout oaken chair, and for a moment clove to the hard wood. He tugged at it, leaving himself unguarded. In a flash St. George wounded him deeply in the thigh, and then, as he tottered and fell, used Ascalon so well that he cut off the huge head from the shoulders in two blows.

The giantess had fled in terror from the sight of their conflict. But St. George sought her out, and told her the issue of it. If she were displeased, he said, he would go away from the castle at once; but if he had rid her of a cruel monster, he begged leave to rest there that night.

St. David of Wales

" You have saved me from great suffering, fair knight," she answered graciously. " This man whom you have slain used me very ill; I am well rid of him. Remain here this night, or as long as you please; nay, so grateful am I, and so comely do I find you, that I will take you for my husband, if you will, and you shall have all the wealth of this castle, which is great, for the dungeons are full of treasures that the giant took from his unhappy prisoners."

" I may not have you for wife," replied St. George courteously. " I am betrothed to a Princess, and I am on my way to her now. I will rest here this night, and I pray that in the morning you will set me upon the road to Egypt, for there I shall find my peerless Sabra."

" Alas, poor knight !" said the lady of the castle, " is it the Princess Sabra of Egypt to whom you are betrothed ? You will not find her in Egypt. Almidor the Moor has carried her off by violence to Morocco, and there he holds her prisoner till she will marry him. All the world has heard of this."

St. George gave a great cry, and such was his wrath and despair that he could scarcely be persuaded not to start then and there for Morocco, to rescue Sabra and slay the treach-

The Two Rescues

erous Prince. But the giantess told him that he must rest and regain his strength, for he was very weary with that day's adventures.

So he remained in the giant's castle that night, and awoke the next morning full of strength and eager for his task.

The giantess told him which way he must travel to reach Morocco, and before he went she bestowed upon him not only new armour and a store of food for his journey, but a great treasure of precious stones as well. Then she bade him God-speed, and he set out.

Now, the way to Morocco lay directly past the enchanted garden of Ormandine, and in due time St. George came to the burning hedge, and saw the gateway of gold, where St. David had cut the thorns away from it. He perceived likewise the sword, and since he was never backward in the hope of adventure, he caught the hilt and pulled it. It came out of the rock as easily as out of a scabbard. There was a great clap of thunder, and the earth trembled and rocked. In a second the hedge and the golden gate in the garden vanished, with a sound of groaning and shrieking, and immediately there appeared on all sides the victims of Ormandine's magic, the power of which had been broken for ever by St. George when he seized the enchanted sword. Among them was St. David, who rejoiced exceedingly to see his comrade. But before they could tell one another half the tale of their adventures, Ormandine himself appeared, clad in robes of mourning, and with an air of sorrow and humility.

"Great champion of England, mirror of true knighthood," he said in a solemn voice, "this day I foresaw long ago by my magic arts, though I knew not when it should come to pass. I learnt that he who slew the dragon of Egypt was the fated knight who should be able to draw out the enchanted sword from its rocky sheath, and so break all my power. By no means, human or magical, could I prevent it, and now it is fated also that I must die. But first I must tell you that I was not always a magician, that you may know that even in vile and evil things there may be hidden some good. I was once a knight even as you are. But on a day of ill-fortune I lost all my possessions, and my wife and daughter were slain, and in despair I took to the study of magic, and so gave myself up to the infernal arts that I could not lay them aside. Now farewell. You shall both of you, St. George and St. David, come to great glory, and never shall the honour of your knighthood be stained."

The Two Rescues

With that he made certain magical passes in the air, and vanished from their eyes; never was he seen by man again.

St. George and St. David told each other all that had befallen them, and St. George gave to his comrade, and also to the other prisoners who had been set free, part of the giantess's treasure to aid them in travelling to their homes. To St. David he gave as well the enchanted sword, and bade him take it to the Emperor of Tartary in lieu of Ormandine's head, as a sign that the wizard was destroyed and his power ended. He agreed with him to meet, if it were possible, at the tournament in Greece, of which also the giantess had given him tidings. Then they set out on their several ways—St. David to Tartary, and afterwards to Greece, and St. George to rescue Sabra.

The champion of England reached Morocco without further adventure, and made his way to the capital city. He wished to spy out Almidor's doings before he made any plan, for he was alone among a nation of his fierce enemies. He did not enter the city, but found a little way outside the walls the cave of a Christian hermit whom the Moors suffered to live, because he was old and thought by the Moors to be mad. No man

217

saw St. George enter the cave; he lay there
that night, and learnt from the hermit how
Sabra fared in her peril. He was told that as
yet Almidor had treated her kindly, hoping to
win her love by courteous usage. She was
given royal chambers in his palace, and a
host of servants, and she was suffered to go
and come as she pleased, save that a guard
went always with her to prevent flight.
Every morning, the good hermit said, she
passed by his cell, and often she gave him
alms, and she was wont also to give alms to
pilgrims who daily awaited her by the city
gate.

The next day St. George put on the long
robe of a pilgrim over his armour, and took
his stand by the city gates. Presently there
was a trampling of hoofs, and the Princess's
cavalcade came in sight. First rode negro
guards mounted on mules, with long whips to
drive the common people out of their way.
Then came a company of Moorish guards,
and after them the ladies of the Princess's
household, riding upon camels with scarlet
harness. In the midst was the Princess herself in a low litter covered with cloth of gold,
borne by four negroes in robes of green and
gold, with emeralds in their turbans. Beside
the litter walked Circassian slaves waving fans

"HE LEARNT FROM THE HERMIT HOW SABRA FARED"

of white peacocks' feathers. After them rode many other guards.

When the Princess saw the pilgrims (for there were many others besides St. George), she caused her litter to be halted, and all the guards and attendants halted with her. She spoke a few words of kindness to each one in turn, and gave alms. She came presently to St. George, who held out his little bowl for alms in such a way that she could not but see on his finger the ring she had given him when they were betrothed. She started a little as she saw it, but showed no other sign.

" Whence do you come, pilgrim ?" she asked in a calm voice. " Are you from Palestine like these others with whom I have spoken ? Whither do you go ?"

" Nay, Princess, from farther than that. I am newly come from Persia, and I seek to go by way of Africa to the Pillars of Hercules, and so across the narrow sea to the ancient city of Cordova." He said this so that her guards might not suspect him.

As he spoke the Princess kept her face hidden under the shade of the litter, but her eyes were fixed on his. He saw that she was moving her lips and whispering ever so faintly. He could not guess what she said. He shook his head slightly, so that none but she perceived it. She made a little movement with her fingers. Both her hands lay idle in her lap; she stirred each finger in turn gently, and the two fingers on her right hand again— twelve little movements in all. She spoke to him words of kindness and encouragement meanwhile as if he were really a pilgrim.

St. George understood it. He was to do something at twelve o'clock at night, without doubt, for it was now close upon noon. But what was he to do? How should he find out?

He leant forward with his alms bowl. "Give me alms, Princess, to help me on my journey." And he held out the bowl and rattled it.

Suddenly he put one hand to his eye, as though an insect had flown into it. As he did so he tilted his alms bowl so that some coins fell out. Then, as if in alarm, he tried to catch them, and spilt more. He had to stoop close to the Princess to pick them up. As he bent down, she whispered in a voice he just caught; " Palace garden little gate."

He knew now what he must do. He stood upright, and expressed his sorrow for his discourtesy in spilling his alms before the Princess. Then he made obeisance, and she passed on to the next pilgrim.

The Two Rescues

Long after she had gone back to the palace he stood there among other pilgrims asking alms of passers-by, lest suspicion should be roused if he went away. But when the sun began to sink in the sky he moved, and began to wander in the town, ever and again asking alms. Through many streets he wandered, striving to learn his way, that he might not lose it at night. He found Almidor's palace, and saw the latticed windows, behind which were the women's apartments; he wondered if that night he would be able to end his feud with Almidor in combat. He did not know that the Prince was absent on a hunting expedition, and would not return for three days, and that Sabra had feigned illness in order to avoid being in his company.

The champion walked all round the palace and its gardens, which stretched for many furlongs and ended in groves of orange-trees. Far down in one side of the gardens was a little door of Moorish lattice-work; all else was blank wall. It would not be hard to climb over the door. He could see through the lattice into the garden, in which bloomed all manner of flowers, and fountains played with a cool sound in marble basins.

He went back to the hermit's cave slowly, and made his plans. His horse he saddled ready for flight, and he caused the hermit to go into the city, and by a feigned tale buy another horse, which he tethered with Bucephalus in a little clump of trees. Midnight drew nigh, and he went to the palace garden walls, and found the door again. Cautiously and silently he climbed over it. In a few moments Sabra was in his arms.

But they did not lose time in embraces, deep though their longing was. The Princess had stolen a key of the garden door, and was able to open it. Locking it after them they stole through the deserted, silent city. The protection of Heaven was over them. Not a soul did they meet, but made their way safely to the horses. St. George stayed to thank the hermit for his kindness, and to give him by way of alms a great emerald worth a King's ransom. Then they fled like the wind on and on over the desert till they reached the coast of New Barbary; and there they took ship, and came at last safely to Greece, where they found all the champions united in readiness for the tournament.

THE
BROTHERHOOD
OF THE
SEVEN CHAMPIONS

I

THE CHALLENGE OF THE PAYNIMS

THERE was long and loud rejoicing when St. George and Princess Sabra reached Athens. Never had there been such a concourse of Christian knights, or of ladies so fair as Sabra, and Celestine, and Eglantine, and Rosalind, and the Princesses of Thrace. The champions came with glory even greater than that of other knights, for they had rid the world of many foul enchanters. By St. George's hand Kalyb and Ormandine were cut off, by St. Denis the Magician of the Mulberry-Tree, by St. Anthony Blanderon, by St. Andrew the Black Wizard. Few of these evil beings were now left on earth, and before long the champions were to do battle with those few.

The tournament lasted many weeks. The King of Greece's daughter was being given in marriage to a Christian knight, and in her honour they jousted for fourteen days. Then for a week they held a tourney in honour of Sabra, who so far excelled in beauty all other

The Brotherhood of Champions

Princesses as St. George excelled all other knights in valour. Then a day was set apart in honour of Princess Eglantine, and a day for Rosalind, and a day for Celestine, and a day for the six Princesses of Thrace. And then for a week the seven champions held the lists against all who came, one champion each day, St. George last; only against one another they would not fight. Day after day they jousted, and at night there was mirth and revelry, with feasting and minstrelsy and dancing. All the minstrels of the world had come to Athens to sing their old songs, and to make new ones in honour of the knightly deeds there done. Likewise there were tumblers and jugglers such as were not to be equalled in the whole earth; and scribes and learned men also came from afar to record these doings so that the tale of them might live for ever and a day.

Last of all the King of Greece decreed a mellay, in which he himself would lead one side, and St. George the other. But before that came to pass the champions spoke with one another of their own fortunes.

"My friends," said St. George, "we have to make up our minds how we shall live best in this world to fit us for the next. It is in my mind that the heathen Saracens and other

The Challenge of the Paynims

pagans have crept into Christian lands and hold them by force, which is not honourable to us. It seems to me that here, at this gathering of Christian knights, we should put in train some action against them."

"Dear comrade," said St. Denis, when they had talked of this duty to be done, "this is an enterprise worthy of champions of Christendom. But let us not enter into it hastily, lest we weaken ourselves at home while we grow strong abroad. It behoves us to set our own affairs in order, and be sure that there is good government and peace in our own lands before we turn against the enemy outside our frontiers."

"You speak justly, brother," said St. George smiling. "I myself have certain affairs of moment to carry out. I have to ask leave of the King of Egypt to wed my dear Princess, for I would not go against her father's will even if she herself would have me do so. That King sent me upon a quest to Persia, which if I fulfilled he was to give me Sabra to wife. I have fulfilled it, but he does not know it. Therefore I must find him, and get my quittance from him. Also I must go to England and claim my inheritance at Coventry, that my wife may not lack a home while I am at the wars. You also, my

The Brotherhood of Champions

brothers, have affairs in your own countries even as I have. Let us therefore, when this tourney is ended, go each to our own homes, and then by a certain time return hither and muster all the might of Christendom against these pagans."

They readily agreed to this plan, and when they had considered what powers the knighthood of Christendom could put into the field, and where they should take up arms with most advantage, they went to the mellay.

The lists were set. On one side were the King of Greece and his knights drawn up by their pavilion, on the other St. George and his party. The marshal in the midst was about to give the signal for the onset when there rang out a trumpet at a little distance.

The knights on either side waited. The trumpet sounded again, nearer. With it began to be heard the galloping of hoofs, and before long there swept into the lists a Moorish knight, attended by two negro slaves. He was fully armed, and bore himself haughtily.

"A challenge!" he cried in a loud voice. "Where is the King of this country, he who gathered here the knights of Christendom?"

"He is here, Sir Knight," said the marshal of the lists. "But what is your business with him ?   This is a tournament for Christian knights, whom the King of Greece has invited to be his guests.   I doubt that you are no Christian, and all the knights who were bidden hither are already here.   What right have you to come into these lists ?"

" The right of war and hatred," answered the Moor fiercely.   " I am no guest; I do not seek your Christian hospitality.   There can be no courtesy between Saracen and Christian. I bring war.   Show me your King."

The marshal made no more ado.   " The King is of that part," he said, pointing; " he leads his knights in the mellay.   Yonder is his pavilion."

The Moorish knight turned towards the King.   " King of Greece," he cried, " and you, Christian knights, bitter enemies of the faith of Mahomet, I bring you defiance from Almidor the Moor.   Know that the chieftains of the Saracens have gathered their powers, and purpose utterly to destroy all Christians, and to set the whole realm of Christendom under their heel. They will slay and spare not, and those that are let live shall be their slaves, and they and their children shall be in bondage for ever.   If you would seek us and make treaty for your lives, we are assembled thirty days' march from this place, hard by Constantinople. There you shall find the welcome that we give to Christians."

"You are an ambassador, pagan knight," said the King of Greece courteously. "Your person is safe, for all your bold words. We give no answer to Almidor; our swords shall write the answer on the field of battle. Is it not so, Sir George, and you, my brothers, champions of Christendom?"

"Yes," cried St. George. "And tell your chieftain, Almidor the Moor, this also, that George of England will kill him with his own hand. Once only shall they meet, and Almidor shall never meet man again."

"Marshal, let this envoy be attended suitably," said the King, "and give him safe conduct hence. Farewell, sir. You have our answer."

"King, farewell," said the Moor. "Sir George of England," he added, "Almidor charged me with this message further. You shall die by his hand; but first you shall see him wedded to your Sabra, and you shall not die easily, but slowly. These eyes of mine shall look upon your torment."

St. George clutched his sword when the Moor spoke of Sabra, but he held himself in check. "I will add this," he said calmly.

The Challenge of the Paynims

" For those words I will kill you, too, with Almidor."

The Moor departed. The tournament was ended, and the mellay was changed into a council of war. Every Christian knight in Athens was aflame to march against the pagans. St. George was chosen chief in command, and from all sides men were summoned until a great army had come together.

While these preparations were afoot St. George sent Sabra to England, that she might be the farther from danger if at first the pagans were by ill-fortune to win the day. Himself he could not go with her, but he rode by her side for many leagues of the way, and sent with her, when he parted from her, trusty attendants, with letters for the King of England. Then he returned to his task of marshalling and leading the Christian host. On his finger, night and day, was the ring Sabra had given him.

II

THE DEATH OF ALMIDOR

Before long the Christian host was ready for battle. It was divided into six armies. At the head of each was one of the champions,

The Brotherhood of Champions

and over them all, in chief command, was St. George.

They assembled in Greece. Word was brought to them that Almidor, with a horde of pagans more numerous than the stars, was awaiting them near the great city of Constantinople. They must needs march thither to encounter him if they did not wish Greece to be overrun and the land laid waste by his myriads.

It was a journey of many days, and the pagans had on their side a certain magician named Osmond, whose arts were used to throw obstacles in the way of the Christian army. This Osmond, now that Ormandine was dead, was the most powerful magician left in the whole world. By magic he caused the forces of nature to be increased against the champions. Forests grew more dense and pathless by means of his spells. Mountains were riven as if by earthquakes, so that roads ceased to be, and many men were lost through the sudden precipices where formerly there had been a safe track. Rivers flowed in torrents, and all fords were washed away. Marshes became bottomless, so that a man on horseback would be one moment on firm ground and the next vanishing in a quaking bog. Yet through all these perils the Christian

234

The Death of Almidor

knights pressed on, past the rich plains of Thessaly, over Mount Olympus, and the high lands of Thrace, till Constantinople lay not far below them, its white domes shining against the blue curved sea.

The land thereabouts was a high plain, sloping gently down to the city. All over it were scattered the pavilions of the pagan host, gay with banners. Horsemen rode hither and thither furiously. Here an Emir would be borne in a golden litter, surrounded by guards and slaves; there would be one warrior practising against another with a long lance, or a man on foot making play with a glittering scimitar, or a group watching dancers or tumblers, to the sound of barbaric music.

The Christians halted. They had long before decided that their best hope was to attack fiercely, not to await an orderly onslaught by such great numbers. They had the advantage of ground, being higher up the slope than the Saracens.

Knowing that they were near the end of their journey, they had slept long and deeply the night before, and had feasted well when they rose, so that now (for it was not quite noon) they were well fitted for battle, and full of hope. They waited only so long as to allow their ranks to close up and become

235

orderly after the march. For a few moments they knelt in prayer, and then with cries of battle and blasts of the trumpet they charged the foe.

The pagans were not taken by surprise; it had been impossible for the Christian host to approach unseen. But they had not expected battle so sudden and so rapid. The Christians came upon them like a sudden breeze over a calm sea, a little clouding and fluttering of the surface of the water afar off that becomes a great wind in a man's ears before his eyes have grown used to the sight. In a few moments the close ranks of the champions and the knights beat upon the long disorderly lines of the Saracens, and threw them into confusion.

But they were too numerous to be overwhelmed by a sudden charge. They were on all sides of the Christian knights; if a man slew all the pagans near him, others swarmed into their places.

Long and doubtfully the battle raged, the champions ever in the fiercest of the fight, doing prodigies of valour. But the issue was uncertain until it chanced that St. George found himself in a little open space, with a ring of fallen foes all round him. He paused for a moment to take breath, the good sword

The Death of Almidor

Ascalon in his hand. He was on foot now. Bucephalus had been slightly wounded, so slightly that the gallant horse could with ease have borne his master throughout the fight; but St. George cared for his beast more than for himself, and gave the steed to a squire to lead out of the battle. Bucephalus saw tended gently. Well it was for St. George, as it came to pass, that the good horse was sound and fresh when the battle was ended.

The main whirlpool of the great battle had swayed a little way from him; St. Denis at the moment was bearing the brunt. St. George stood in the little space resting. Suddenly he heard a cry from a Christian knight not far behind him. He turned swiftly, his shoulders swinging round with his movement. If he had not moved, a long thin dagger would have been buried in his back. As it was the point missed him; the enemy's hand struck his shoulder with a glancing blow, and the man stumbled forward with the force of his stroke as St. George, swinging Ascalon so quickly that the bright blade seemed but a flash of light, drove the good sword deep into the attacker's neck. The man fell dead.

St. George looked at him a little more narrowly; he seemed to recognize the figure. It was the insolent envoy who had come to the tournament at Athens. The champion had kept his word to him.

He thought sorrowfully of Greece as he regarded the dead man. Sabra had been near him then, and now she was hundreds of miles away in England, in a land strange to her, where her only welcome would be from those who knew of St. George by repute as the son of the High Steward and as a great Christian knight. Meanwhile her knight was warring for the Christian faith against her father, for it was known that King Ptolemy of Egypt was among the heathen monarchs in array against Christendom under the leadership of Almidor the Moor.

But a battlefield is no place for sad thoughts and memories. St. George saw that the wave of strife was rolling towards him again. The Christians on his left were being driven back towards him. At the head of the Saracens in that quarter rode his old foe Almidor on a great coal-black horse. Mighty deeds had Almidor done that day, and yet was unhurt.

He caught sight of St. George almost as the English champion's eyes lit on him. He spurred his charger; the great beast started and reared, and then with a bound leapt forward towards St. George, brushing aside the Christian knights between as if they had been ants.

Almidor had long before cast aside his spear; it was no weapon for such close quarters. He wielded a battle-axe. St. George had his wondrous sword Ascalon, but it seemed an unequal fight, for how could a man on foot bear up against a blow from an axe dealt from the height of a war-horse ?

Nevertheless, that day was Almidor's doom. All the wrongs he had suffered glowed in St. George's mind at sight of the Moor. With a great cry he ran forward. "Sabra and England!" he shouted, and sprang towards Almidor. No heed did he pay to the thundering hoofs of the black steed or the whirling axe of its rider; he gave no thought to defending his own body, but ran with his sword aloft, thrown far back over his shoulder almost as if it, too, were an axe, and, swerving a little to one side as the horse bore down upon him, smote upwards and down again, swinging the blade round with all his might, redoubted by his anger and hatred.

Almidor had struck at him, too, but the speed of the horse and the quickness with which St. George swayed to one side made the blow miss. He overbalanced himself a little, and his right shoulder lay open to the

The Brotherhood of Champions

champion's sword as it descended. Clean through the armour the keen blade drove, through bone and flesh, downwards and across, and out beyond his left shoulder, so that the head and shoulder and one arm were severed.

A hush of terror fell upon the pagans who saw that mighty stroke; no man, it seemed, could stand against such power and wrath. But St. George was not sated by that one victory. Shouting, he rushed like one frenzied into the fray again, striking men down as if they were but nettles beaten with a stick; and all the Christian host took fresh courage at his valour, and fought as never before. " St. George for England !" they cried; and at that cry the pagans fell or fled.

In a little while the whole paynim host was routed. Many were slain, many yielded, many fled to their tents or to Constantinople to await peacefully the coming of the conquerors in the hope of mercy, for they thought that the Christians would behave as they themselves were wont to behave after a victory, and put all the conquered to death. Many also fled farther, and took ship over into Asia, and returned to distant lands in the East, there to gather fresh forces, for even now paganism was not crushed, and the great enchanter Osmond still lived to aid it.

"CLEAN THROUGH THE ARMOUR THE KEEN BLADE DROVE"

241

The Death of Almidor

The Christian knights drove the enemy
utterly from the field, and took possession
of the tents and pavilions. Here they found
great treasure, besides armour and weapons
and other booty, and they took prisoner also
many princes and chiefs of the pagans.
Among the prisoners was Ptolemy, King of
Egypt, which when St. George heard, he
caused him to be brought into his presence.

"King Ptolemy," he said solemnly, when
the wretched man, in fear and shame, abased
himself before him, "rise and stand before me
as a man should. No longer are you a King.
I speak to you as a man. When you were a
King you used me ill; you sent me on a false
errand to Persia, whose monarch at your
bidding acted with treachery towards me. I
had saved your land from the dragon, I was a
guest at your court, and you betrayed me.
Moreover, you promised me the hand of your
daughter, the Princess Sabra, when I returned
from Persia. Well, I have done my errand,
I have returned from Persia, and I ask you
again for Sabra's hand. I will not wed her
without her father's consent, even though I
have the power and she is willing. I am
guarding her safely in England. Give me
your consent, and I will bring her to Egypt,
and we will be wedded there among her own

The Brotherhood of Champions

people. You also shall reign there if you become a Christian, and swear to observe the Christian faith in all things public and private."

"Sabra was promised to Almidor before ever you came to Egypt; I promised her secretly to him," said the miserable King.

"Almidor is dead," answered St. George sternly. "And Sabra fled with me from him, and now awaits me at my own castle in Coventry."

"Help!" cried a voice near at hand, eager and panting. "Where is Sir George of England? Tidings from England! Show me Sir George!"

A man on horseback, his raiment stained with travel, himself half falling from fatigue, had galloped up almost unheeded to the pavilion where St. George was with the prisoner. A knight checked his weary horse and helped him to alight, and led him before the champion of England.

"This is the leader of the Christian army, George of England," the man was told.

"Sir George!" he cried. falling on one knee, "forgive me. I bring bad news."

"Tell me your tidings," said Sir George gravely, and unconsciously he looked at Sabra's ring upon his finger. The stone was

The Death of Almidor

dimmed, and even as he looked three drops of blood fell from his nose. It was the sign of danger, as he knew too well.

"The lady Sabra is in peril. What day is this?" asked the man wildly. "I have come from England in such haste that I have lost count of the days."

"It is the twentieth day of April," someone answered.

"Then she is lost, Sir!" he cried wildly to St. George; "the Lady Sabra will die on the twenty-third day of June unless you are in Coventry to save her!"

"You lie!" answered St. George passionately. Then he recollected himself, and said more calmly: "I ask your pardon. I do not understand this story you tell. It seems to me impossible that the Princess Sabra should be in danger in England. Tell me what has come to pass."

"I must be brief, sir," said the messenger. "What time there is you must have without interruption. You will forgive my plain speech, sir; I would tell you the truth as clearly as is in my power. You know that the most august Princess Sabra of Egypt is very beautiful; also she is not as our English Princess to look upon." St. George bowed his head as he thought upon the dear features of his Princess. "Now, her beauty is such that many nobles of England would have sought her hand if it were not known that she is betrothed to you, Sir George. But since they are honourable and gentle, they did not seek her company. But one did—the Lord Siward, Earl of Coventry. Sir, it does not become me to speak ill of those above my station; but this Earl, sir, is of ill-repute, and I cannot hide it from you. You have been in England and in Coventry but little, Sir George, or this Earl had been known to you. He sought the Princess and bade her marry him. If she would not, he said, he would have her burnt as a witch, for—so his story ran—her foreign ways were not such as Englishmen used, and she was grievously suspected by the common people. That is not true, Sir George. In a little while after she came to Coventry, despite her foreign ways, she was beloved by all the people. Never was anyone more gentle, never any lady more beautiful, never——"

"'Tell me your story, man," said St. George. "I thank you for your courtesy to the Princess, but do you think I do not believe that all men must love her ? Tell me more !'

"I crave your pardon, sir," said the messenger. "I did but tell you my own thoughts,

The Death of Almidor

forgetting that you must know them already. This Earl of Coventry, sir, came to the Princess upon a certain day and told her what he purposed. If she would not consent to marry him, she should be burnt as a witch; he had the power to find false witnesses and a corrupt judge to condemn her. The Princess, sir, knew by then a little of the laws of England, and she thought that by chance she might summon you to her aid if she did what was in her mind. When this vile Earl came to her and made his proposal, backing it by fierce and violent gestures, she, thinking he meant to do her mischief then and there, stabbed him with a little dagger that she carried, so that he died."

" Ah !" said St. George. " To kill Almidor was nothing. I could have slain this Earl with a better will."

" The Princess, sir," continued the messenger, " when she saw that she had killed this evil man, called her maidservants and told them what she had done, and why she had done it. In due time her deed was made public, and since a judge must do what the law bids, she was found guilty of slaying him. By the law she might appeal to a knight to be her champion. Such was her faith in you, Sir George, that she declared that you would uphold her cause against all who assailed it. She believed you to be in Athens then, and did not guess how far distant you were. The judge decreed that you must appear within eighteen weeks, or her life would be forfeit without further trial. Sir George, you have eight weeks in which to save the Princess."

"What!" asked St. George, "is that the danger my ring warns me of ? I will be in Coventry, or die!"

"It is over two months' journey, Sir George," said the man. "Ten weeks have I taken to find you."

"I will go, nevertheless, and I will be in Coventry on the twenty-third day of June. By our victory over the Saracens I swear it."

He gave some orders. Quickly a council was held. St. Denis of France was chosen to lead the Christian army while St. George was absent. King Ptolemy and the other prisoners of high rank were to be kept in ward while the Saracen army was pursued, and the dominions then and afterwards conquered set in order. Any monarch who became a Christian and vowed to make his kingdom Christian was to be set free. When St. George returned he would bring Sabra with him, and they would be wedded in Egypt.

The Death of Almidor

St. George had no doubt that he would save his Princess. But it was a journey of great peril and difficulty. He had to travel fifteen hundred miles or more, and there were few roads, if he went all the way by road. The seas were infested by pirates, and the wind might not favour him. He trusted his good steed Bucephalus, but he must not press even the best of horses too hard in so great a venture. There must be no delay anywhere; it would be better to travel shorter distances without long intervals than to hasten one day, and then be unfit to go farther the next.

Bucephalus was brought. Thanks to the care bestowed on him, he was fresh and ready for any enterprise. With no more delay St. George left his comrades once more, and set out to save the Princess.

III

COVENTRY MARKET-PLACE

St. George took the road back by the north coast of the Ægean Sea, for there were towns there, and he could get food and lodging for himself and Bucephalus. Through Thrace he hastened, and then across to Epirus, and so to the north of Italy. Many a weary league did he ride every day, and never did the noble steed fail him by stumble or weariness or unwillingness. Day after day he journeyed, and the days grew into weeks. By the guidance of Heaven he kept the track aright; and such was the peace and good order that the Christian champions had brought to Europe that never once did robber or maurauder meet him. No delay befell him. On and on he pressed. In due time he came to Marseilles, and then struck north, following the way across France that has been used ever since men made habitations there. North he rode, and north by west, through Lyons and Paris; and so at last, on a Friday morning, he rode into Calais town, weary with travel (for of late the weather had been inclement and unseasonable, to add to the fatigues of his journey), but with hope and unfailing courage in his heart.

They made no ado at the gates of Calais at admitting so famous a knight; the fame of St. George of England had spread through all Christendom. But there was no lord in all the town to receive him and do him honour, for from every Christian country the flower of knighthood had flocked to the East to fight against the pagans. St. George must lodge at an inn, like any lesser man, and

must find for himself the means to be put
across the Channel. It wanted but a day to
the twenty-third of June; in little more than
twenty-four hours he must be in Coventry,
or Sabra would die.

He rode through the streets, Bucephalus'
hoofs ringing on the cobbles. The good horse
was nearly spent, but he would never give
in until his heart broke.

The streets seemed nearly empty. It appeared that all the inhabitants were within
doors. From the taverns came the sounds
of men talking and laughing. St. George
rode on till he came to the harbour. But
though there were ships there, there were few
men in charge of them, and the wind was
high, so that they did not hear his call to
them. On the quays was no one.

St. George looked round him, but saw no
man whom he could ask for help. He went
back into the main street of the town, to an
inn called the Golden Rose, and there gave
Bucephalus in charge of a stableman to be
fed and tended. Then he returned to the
harbour. The clouds of the early morning
were being blown away; the sun shone, and
far off he could descry the coast of his own
land.

But if he could see the white cliffs of England, St. George was not yet in his own country. In Calais port, it chanced, there lay but few ships at that time. There had been a storm of wind, very unusual at that season of the year, and the waves had not yet subsided. No mariner would venture out. No promise of reward would stir them from land.

It was near noon on Friday. St. George was spent with travel and hunger, for Friday was a fast day in those countries, and he had had little to eat. He had a day in which to cross the sea and ride half over England to Coventry Market-Place. Even if he were unwearied, and a swift boat were ready at his need, it was a hard task; but there was no boat.

He stood on the quay, looking at the vessels moored and deserted. All their masters and crews were on land; those he had questioned had laughed him to scorn for dreaming of venturing before the next day at least.

"If I had any skill in a ship," thought the champion, "I would embark even by myself. But to manage a boat is no part of knightly lore. Better it is to wait here; even yet help may come."

As he made this resolve in his mind a voice spoke close behind him: "It is he,

Dickon," said the voice in good homely English. "He is the English knight who has asked in vain for a ship."

Right glad was St. George to hear his own tongue again. He turned round with a friendly greeting on his lips. Two men stood before him, short, thick-set knaves in sea-faring clothes. One had a stiff, close-cropped red beard; the other was grizzled and old, but strongly built as a gnarled oak.

"Give you good-day, friends," said St. George. "It is pleasant to hear the English speech once again, after long sojourn in distant lands. Would that I could feel the English soil under my feet as I speak."

The older man laid his hand on the other's arm. "You hear him, Wat?" he said. "He is English, and by his speech he is of noble birth. It is he whom I saw in my vision."

"Be wary, Dickon," answered the other. "He is English, indeed; but if it be not the knight we seek, you will put to sea in peril of your life."

"I will ask him," said Wat. "Sir," he added to St. George, "I believe that I had a vision concerning you. I would ask you three questions, by your leave, as my vision showed me."

"Speak on, good man," answered St.

George cautiously. "If you are minded to put to sea, as your comrade says, I will answer any questions you please."

At that the man Dickon himself looked more eager, and the face of Wat lighted up. "This is my first question, Sir Knight," said Wat: "I was to ask you if you bear on your body the sign of a dragon."

"On my breast is the figure of a dragon; ever since I was born I have carried that mark," answered St. George.

"Secondly, sir, have you on your finger a ring whereby danger is foretold?"

St. George held out his hand. "Here is the ring," he said, showing the stone, now dulled and misty. "I or one dear to me is in peril, by that sign. The stone does not gleam with its natural fire. Therefore danger is at hand."

The two men were aflame with wonder and eagerness. "Lastly, this question, English knight," said Wat: "Do you seek to go to Coventry, the town where I was born?"

"I will give a great emerald, worth five thousand crowns, to any man who will set me across the narrow seas, so that I may reach Coventry by noon to-morrow."

"It is he!" cried both the men together. "Sir Knight, we will set you across the

narrow seas, and so work for you that you
shall reach Coventry by noon."

" If you can do so much," answered St.
George, " you will save the life of the Princess
whom I shall wed."

" I shall do more than that, Sir Knight: I
shall save England from a great peril," said
the man; " though how and what the peril
may be I cannot tell. Listen! I have
heard these words in a dream:

" 'To Coventry the dragon and the ring
Shall Wat the shipman and his comrade bring :
To England Wat shall carry England's knight,
And Dunsmore Heath shall witness England's plight.
In England shall he win and lose his wife ;
The dragon's lord shall end the dragon's life.'

I can make nothing of that prophecy, save
that you shall save England from a dragon,
and come to sorrow there, if you are truly he
whom I am to take by ship to my country.
You have the dragon on your breast, you
bear the ring, and you seek to go to Coventry.
So my vision showed me."

" What is all this talk of vision ?" said St.
George, growing impatient at the delay. " Do
you mean to take me to England ? If so,
set on; if not, let be, and do not affront my
ears with your talk."

255

The Brotherhood of Champions

"You speak justly, sir. Dickon, go, un-
moor the boat and bring it to the quay.
Sir Knight, we can take in our little ship only
yourself. If you have a horse, it must bide
here. I shall find you good steeds in England. It was all set forth in my vision."

The man Dickon hastened away, and took
a skiff, and rowed off to a little old battered
boat that lay moored among the rest. She
looked very frail and crank for such an enterprise on such a day. She was a thing of
small burden, not much bigger than a row-
boat. Dickon by himself could handle her,
and brought her alongside the quay. Meanwhile, at the prompting of Wat, St. George
went to his inn and gave orders for Bucephalus to be kept till he returned, and bade farewell to the good beast. Then he went back
to the quay and entered the crazy boat.

As they steered out of the harbour Wat
told him the tale of his vision. For three
nights running he had dreamed the same
thing. Terrible sounds and sights had passed
through his mind, but they were all confused,
and he could remember nothing of them.
They ceased suddenly, and he seemed to be
in great peace and calm, as it were in a
meadow of soft grass and cool airs. He lay
thus in a condition of great delight, when in a

moment, coming he knew not how or whence, a benign figure stood before him, and spoke in a clear voice: " Go to the quay on Friday at noon, and seek there an English knight, whom you shall know by the signs of a dragon and a ring that gives warning of danger. He is to go to Coventry, and you shall bear him thither. If you do this, your way shall be guarded, and you shall prosper; but if you refuse, you shall perish miserably." The figure told him also of certain provisions for the journey, and then vanished, and Wat awoke. So plain had been the vision that at first he did not know he had been to sleep. But on the first night he paid little heed to it. On the second it came again, and he was afraid, for he did not yet trust the words he heard, but thought they foretold evil to himself. But when he dreamed the same again on the third night, he doubted no more, but did as he was ordered, and found St. George to prove the truth of the vision.

By the time the telling of this dream was done, the little boat was out in the open sea, and the waves were clapping and hissing under her bows. She rose and fell, leapt and shivered with each buffet. Spray dashed over her gunwales, and ever and again her hull sank so far down in the trough of the waters that she seemed to be in a green cup or hollow channel; then she would slide upwards, her bows nosing the air, and smack!—the prow would beat the water again, with a whirl of foam.

So they fared across the Channel, in a sea where no other boat durst venture. It seemed as if Heaven smiled upon St. George, for when they were gone a good part of the way across, the wind shifted a little, dropping towards the south; and the sun shone in a clear sky, so that the waves, with their white crests, looked like ermine upon a cloth of gold, and the white cliffs, growing nearer and nearer, till St. George could see the sheep grazing upon the green slopes of the hollows, gleamed like a silver rim to the burnished waters.

Soon Dover was in sight, with its castle and the ancient light-tower standing high above the little town. The boat came alongside a little quay, in the lee of the wind, and the sails fell idle, while Wat and Dickon poled her along the quay wall to a landing-place. St. George felt great joy at the thought of the good English earth that in a moment he would be treading. The harbour seemed, as it were, home to him, and as the boat came to at some steps, he sprang ashore with a leap that sent the gunwale under water for a moment with its force.

Coventry Market=Place

" England !" he cried aloud. " Come, my good friends, on to Coventry, if you are to lead me thither. Leave your boat and set forth."

" Softly, sir," answered Wat. " I will not lose a good boat for all the prophecies and visions in the world. You cannot live by dreams ; I must have my boat to win me bread. You shall come to your journey's end in time, sir; all is prepared. Dickon, warp her to the moorings."

They took the boat along to a mooring-place and tied her up. It seemed to St. George that they would never finish the task. It was near sundown, and he had yet to go half across England—more than eight score miles—by noon on the next day. If he travelled without ceasing, he would have to go nearly ten miles every hour from that moment onwards; and he had no horse, and knew not where he could find one, or fresh ones as he went on his hasty way. Little wonder that he was anxious.

" Now, Sir Knight," said Wat, when at last he came to land with his comrade, " you will see a thing that I cannot understand, if my dream is true. And if my dream is not true, I doubt you will not see Coventry by noon to-morrow."

259

The Brotherhood of Champions

" I will show you that you can live by dreams," answered St. George bravely. " I have faith in your dream; it shall bring life to Sabra and to me—for I could not live without her. Your vision shall come true ; I know it in my heart. Now bestir you, and fulfil its commands, whatever they be."

" Trust me, sir," answered the man. " First you must eat and drink. For this I was bidden in my dream to lead you to the inn of the Roaring Lion. Dickon knows where that is; he will take you. As for me, I have to busy myself with finding you a horse. Dickon, do your part. In half an hour we must leave Dover behind us."

He turned away from them, and went along a passage leading to some old houses. St. George gazed after him anxiously; he did not understand what was to happen.

Dickon touched him on the arm. " Follow me, sir; they await you at the Roaring Lion."

St. George began to follow him, amazed. Suddenly a suspicion came into his mind. What if this Lord Siward, who had wronged Sabra, had powerful kinsmen who might avenge his death by setting spies to entrap and kill St. George if he came to England ? What if Wat and Dickon were in their pay, leading him into some deadly ambush ?

Coventry Market-Place

The champion drew his sword, and clutched Dickon roughly by the shoulder. "Look me in the face, knave!" he cried in a terrible voice. "Swear to me on your life that there is no plot against me in what you do. Who await me at this inn of the Roaring Lion? Why am I to go thither?"

Dickon looked at him fairly and squarely. "I swear on my life," he said solemnly, "and by whatever else I hold dear and sacred, that I am serving you faithfully and truly, and I know of no harm that will befall you. Kill me first if any man attacks you."

St. George believed him. "I take your word," he answered. "But I do not understand these strange doings. Why should your comrade help me because of a dream?"

"Wat is an old man," said Dickon, "and he knows much of the wisdom that is hidden from the young. He can read the stars as if they were a book written in a fair hand (for he can read writing also, which a man like me cannot do). He said to me that the knight whom he was to befriend must be under the special protection of Heaven, for the good of Christendom and England. There has been much evil in England in the past, with magicians and enchanters and the black arts; but these things are losing their power, and I think you, Sir Knight, must be one of those who war against them."

"You speak truly, my friend; all my life I have been fighting the powers of evil."

As they spoke thus they reached the inn of the Roaring Lion. The host met St. George at the door. "You are the knight who must ride to Coventry?" he asked. "I have a table set for you, sir: be pleased to come with me." And he led him to a room where there was spread a meal of good food and a flagon of wine. Hard by stood a serving-man to wait upon the guest.

"You, good fellow," said the host to Dickon, "I have a feast for you also; follow me, and leave your knight to his repast, for I am told that he has little time to waste."

They went away. St. George fell to gladly, and when he had eaten and drank, felt a new man, ready for the long, hard journey in front of him.

There was a jingling of harness and noise of hoofs outside. He rose and attired himself again for the road. Then he went down into the courtyard of the inn. There were Wat and Dickon, with three fine horses, all ready for a journey.

"This is yours, sir," said Wat, leading the finest of the horses to him. "We get fresh

" ' LOOK ME IN THE FACE, KNAVE ! ' " HE CRIED IN A TERRIBLE
VOICE "

beasts at Rochester. We must tarry here no longer. Dickon and I will go with you to London, and there we must leave you."

St. George would have paid the innkeeper, but he would take no money. So the champion gave him instead a precious jewel, and bestowed a piece of gold upon the serving-man; and so, as the setting sun began to throw the town into the long shadows of the hills, he and his two guides rode out from the inn-yard, under the archway into the London road, and clattered off at a good round gallop.

It was not very long before they came to Canterbury; but they made no halt there, but rode out by the West Gate and made all speed to Rochester. There, at an inn hard by the castle, fresh horses were in readiness, as though St. George was awaited; and in a little while they were off again on the road to London. When they came thither, Wat guided St. George to an inn in Southwark, and told him that he might wait there an hour, and rest and refresh himself. Then a new horse would be ready for him, and he must ride as best he could to Windsor. At Windsor, and again at Oxford and Banbury, there would be a fresh steed, and at Warwick, if it were not by any ill chance too late, he might rest and even sleep a little, so as to ride

265

thence to Coventry, no very long stage, with his strength as much restored as might be. At each inn where he stopped (and Wat told him the names of them), he was to give the password, "St. George for England," and he would be served faithfully by all.

Then the two good mariners bade the champion farewell; they were men of the sea, Wat said, and every man must stick to his own craft or trade. He had been bidden in his vision to go no farther than London. The champion bestowed on each a great emerald, and they departed.

St. George felt lonely when they had gone. But he busied himself with food and drink, for a long journey through the night was before him. He was not certain of his way, but there were few roads, and he could not easily go astray.

It was dark when he left Southwark and clattered over London Bridge. Whenever any guard hailed him, as at Lud Gate, when he went out of the City of London on the west side, he gave the word, "St. George for England," and immediately bars were drawn and gates flung open, and he could ride where he wished. All through the night he rode thus. Men slept soundly in those days, and did not journey by night save upon such grave errands as this. Not a soul did he meet in the hours of darkness. But at Windsor and at Oxford, which he reached near dawn, men were awake in readiness for him.

It was after he left Oxford that misfortune befell him. The road split, and he chose the wrong fork of it. So long had he been absent from England, and so little had he known of his own land, that he was not aware of his error until he passed a peasant and asked him how far away Banbury was.

"Nigh twenty mile, sir, and a bad road," answered the man. "This is the road to Stow. You must bear to your right." He told him certain landmarks to follow. It was now broad day.

St. George thanked him and rode onwards as he had been directed. But by now the strain of his journey was telling on him; he could hardly stay in his saddle. Nevertheless, he struggled onwards, and at last, half unconscious from weariness, rode into the inn yard at Banbury. He gave his horse to a serving-man, spoke the password, went into a public room of the inn, and fell asleep on a settle.

They let him sleep. But a more than mortal power was watching over him. He woke about half-past ten o'clock in the morning. He had an hour and a half left, and some twenty miles to travel, with a fresh horse awaiting him at Warwick. He ate some food quickly and galloped off.

At Warwick he waited no longer than to change his horse, but was off again in a moment. And now the sun was high in the heavens; it was near midsummer, and the rays beat down upon him mercilessly. Foam flew from his horse; the dust swirled in clouds behind him ; but onwards he pressed, ever and again putting his hand to his side to feel if his weapons were ready. Coventry came in sight. People began to appear upon the road, all hastening to the town, as though something unwonted were toward. As he came into the town itself he found it thronged with citizens, but the thunder of his horse's hoofs drove them out of his way. On, on he went, and suddenly the market-place opened before him. There, in the midst, stood a great stake on a mound, and bound to it was Sabra. There was no fear upon her face, but only a high courage and pride. Near her were bundles of faggots, and even as St. George came into the square attendants were beginning to carry these towards the stake. So mighty were the Lord Siward's kinsmen that they had prevailed upon the judge to give her the death of a witch rather than of a Princess. The chief of these kinsmen, Sir Egremort, Baron of Chester, was within the circle of guards, who kept back the great press of folk all round—a tall, black-bearded man on a dapple-grey charger. He watched Sabra with a look of cruel joy. Near him sat a judge on a throne of office, and round him were secretaries and notaries, and a herald, and divers officers of the law.

As St. George broke through the guards in his headlong gallop he loosed his sword Ascalon in its sheath. Now, if ever, it should not fail him.

The judge rose from his throne. All round the people murmured and cried, not knowing who the strange knight on the foaming horse might be. The men carrying faggots looked at the champion curiously for a moment, then went about their task again. One broached a cask of oil, and began to sprinkle it upon the wood as they piled it round the Princess.

" Hold, Sir Knight !" cried the judge. " Why do you ride thus furiously and break through our guard ?"

" Sir," replied St. George, saluting him, for he saw that the judge was in authority there, " I am told that this lady needs a champion. I will take up her cause, and approve it upon the body of any who come against me."

At that the crowd shouted, for they had grown to love the Princess Sabra in the little time she had been amongst them; and they believed that she would not have killed the Lord Siward but for a great reason. The Princess smiled gently. She knew that St. George would come. If he were by her, it was no matter what befell her.

"You deliver this challenge?" asked the judge.

"Yes," said St. George; "and if any man seeks death, sure and just and swift, let him take up my challenge." For he knew in his heart that no man there could withstand him. As he spoke he flung his gauntlet on the ground.

"I take up your challenge!" cried Sir Egremort; and he rode forward and stooped down from his horse, and picked up the glove with the point of his sword. "This woman is a witch and a murderess; she shall die!"

"Tell me your name and lineage, Sir Knight," said St. George. "I cannot fight here in my own country and among Christian men against one who is not of noble birth; and you must needs be of strange birth," he added, taunting Sir Egremort, at the very sight of whom he felt enraged, as if by instinct, " if you would take up such a cause against an innocent lady."

" I am Sir Egremort, Baron of Chester, and I am of the family of the Lord Siward, Earl of Coventry, whom this foreign woman slew. Who are you,. who take up so unworthy a cause ?"

" I am George, son of Sir Albert, formerly High Steward of England ; and this lady is the Princess Sabra, daughter of King Ptolemy of Egypt. Never a word more after this day shall you speak on this earth, base knight! Make your peace with God, and settle your worldly affairs, for I shall surely kill you—aye, and any more that follow the ways of your vile Siward !"

" Let the herald cry that a champion is come for the prisoner," said the judge. " Let him proclaim the state of these knights. Then shall the innocence of this woman be put to the proof by combat."

The herald made proclamation as he was ordered. Then the two knights stood forth to do battle. They were to fight with swords on foot.

Never did St. George take up so easy a combat. They crossed blades, and in a second, as the sparks from the first meeting of the steel were still flashing, St. George swung Ascalon crossways and struck Sir Egremort's head from his body.

There rose a great cheering from the people. The champion ran to the stake and cut the bonds that held the Princess, and took her hand in his.

" Men of Coventry !" he cried in a loud voice, " I have done battle for my lady, as the custom of chivalry bade me. Henceforth she is innocent in the eye of the law. But you know what manner of enemy she had to meet, and that she could not save herself from dishonour save as she did. You know also of what lineage I come, and how dear my father was to you. Now I proclaim to you that in due time I shall go to Egypt with the Princess Sabra, there to be married to her, since her father is King of that country. Thereafter I must needs war against the hosts of the pagans. But when the battle of Christendom is won, then shall I come to live among you here, and do you whatsoever knightly service may be needful. It may be that great need may arise; I have heard many strange prophecies."

The Marriage of St. George

IV

THE MARRIAGE OF ST. GEORGE.

There were many things that Sabra and St. George had to say to one another now that they were together again. And before he took the Princess to Egypt to wed her in her own land, according to custom, St. George had to set in order the affairs of his father's estate, which had been held in stewardship for him during all the years of his absence. This he did, and he obtained audience also of the King of England, and was by him confirmed and established in his inheritance, and given a post of honour at the court whensoever he might be in England.

But the time came soon when he must go back to the East, and he set forth duly with Sabra. No need was there now for furious haste, or for the aid of men warned by dreams. Nevertheless he was not to go without adventure. He travelled back to the East by a different road from that by which he had come with such desperate speed. He went to Calais for his good steed Bucephalus, and thence he made for the Lowlands and Germany. His way lay at first through the vast forest of the Ardennes, where in those

273

days, in the thick, dark trees, often great danger lurked for man and beast. It was near nightfall when they came thither.

The track was narrow, though clean cut and straight. So dense were the trees that they were like a wall on either side, shutting off all light and sound. The very steps of Bucephalus on the soft woodland path (for Sabra rode pillion behind St. George) echoed dully against the green barrier. There was no other sound, until suddenly Sabra cried out in fear, and shivered.

" What is it, dear lady ?" asked St. George. He had seen and heard nothing to cause terror.

" I heard a serpent hiss," she said.

" There was no sound; I heard nothing," answered St. George gently. But even as he spoke he heard a faint rustling, as of a snake in the undergrowth.

" It is there again !" cried Sabra. " Look, my lord, look ! There are fierce eyes moving there !"

She pointed to the right. In the dark green were six little points of flame, swaying quickly from side to side, and a hissing sound came from them.

As they looked they heard the same sound in front, and immediately afterwards to the left; and in a few moments all the twilit

The Marriage of St. George

wood seemed to be full of moving bright eyes peering at them. But at first they could not see any living creatures to which the eyes belonged. There was no sign of life but those swaying stars in the dark green, and a fierce, angry hissing, and the rustling of leaves, as if something were sliding stealthily along through them.

St. George looked to right and left. Then he looked down the path in front of him, and on the white, clear surface he saw a great snake gliding swiftly towards him. But it was unlike any snake yet seen by mortal eyes, for it had three heads. It was ten or twelve feet long, and dark green in colour, with a faint marking in light blue on its back. Each grisly head was set upon a neck a foot long, or more, and the six eyes gleamed with a bright flame. The jaws were open, so that the white poison fangs gleamed, and the black forked tongues flickered swiftly to and fro.

The thing came on very rapidly. St. George saw that it might strike Bucephalus before he could touch it. He slipped quickly to the ground, leaving the reins to Sabra, and drawing his sword with his left hand as he dismounted. On foot he had the advantage of the venomous creature. He shifted his sword swiftly to his right hand, and leant forward on one leg, sweeping with his blade as far as his arm could reach. The snake was well within his stretch of arm and sword, and Ascalon made light work of such a victim. The blade smote the reptile just below the place where the three necks joined to one body, and struck off all three, as it were, on one branch. The heads dropped to the ground, the mouths shutting fiercely; the long body writhed hideously for a moment, and then lay limp and still.

St. George turned swiftly to see if Sabra was safe. She was sitting on Bucephalus as if tied to the good horse, stiff and staring. On her right was another great serpent, rearing high from the ground, the three heads waving differently this way and that.

The champion gave a great cry. It seemed as if he could hardly save the Princess, so near was the monstrous reptile. But even as he shouted he sprang and swung his sword. Two heads he cleaved from the body, and the third he struck off with an upward blow as he recovered himself.

There was a great rustling in the bushes, and then silence. No longer were the gleaming eyes to be seen. The serpents had all fled.

The Marriage of St. George

" Be of good heart, dear one," said St. George. " There are no more of these gliding secret foes. We have scared them all away." There was a noise in the distance like thunder—a rumbling, roaring sound that yet seemed as though some human creature had caused it by design.

" Oh, my lord, I fear very greatly !" said Sabra. " This forest is enchanted. The earth will open and swallow us. Did you not hear its hollow call to us ?"

" No, dear lady; it was but far-off thunder," answered St. George, mounting in front of her again. She clasped him by the waist, as if he alone could make her safe.

They rode on, not speaking. The roaring sound grew louder. The path became wider, the trees less close, the light brighter. Soon they emerged into an open space. On the far side, with dense forest at the back of it, stood a great castle, huge and tall like the giant's fortress where the champion had lodged when he fled from Persia to Morocco. But the gates of this castle stood wide open. In the courtyard St. George thought he saw yet more of the three-headed snakes, and he felt in his heart that either some terrible giant or some evil wizard lived in the grim place.

He was not many minutes in doubt. As

they drew nearer to the castle, its lord stalked forth, shouting fiercely. He was a giant, twenty feet high, and he had two heads. He was the more horrible because the two faces were not alike. One had a fierce black beard that swept to the giant's chest, but the other had only a long moustache.

"Who are you?" roared the monster. "Why have you killed two of my servants?"

He carried in his hand a huge knotted club, and as he spoke he waved it threateningly. But St. George was undaunted.

"I am a peaceful knight faring through this Christian land, having the care of this Princess and her safety in my hands. I journey to the East. Let me pass without interruption upon my way. I have seen no servants of yours, except some foul snakes, of whom I slew two."

"Oho!" cried the giant. "The serpents are my servants. But tell me, are you he whom they call George of England?"

"That is my name," answered St. George. "I am a knight who does battle for Christendom according to the powers that are in me."

"Ha, Sir George!" shouted the giant triumphantly (it was the bearded mouth which spoke; the other head was silent, but its cruel eyes showed its understanding of its

The Marriage of St. George

comrade's words). "Sir George is the knight I am awaiting. Osmond the wizard gave me news of you. You will go no farther East than this castle. I shall take you and bind you, and then you shall be crushed slowly to death between two stones. Your Princess shall be my slave until the Saracens have driven all the Christians into the sea and taken possession of this land. I shall give her to them; I know not what they will do to her."

St. George felt Sabra clutch him tightly. "For that saying you die!" he said sternly. "Osmond I will kill with my own hand when I lead the army of Christendom against him."

He sprang from Bucephalus. "While I fight, dear lady," he said in a low voice to Sabra, "ride swiftly on and take refuge in the forest as soon as you can. I shall slay this villain, and will come to you; but go, lest he do you some mischief before I kill him."

He drew his sword, and advanced towards the giant on foot. "Now, monster, you shall learn not to boast," he said. And swiftly, before the giant could heave his great club up to strike, St. George ran in and smote off his left hand.

The giant howled savagely, and dashed at the champion. But St. George easily escaped his clumsy rush, and struck low and hard at his leg, and wounded him in the right ankle. The monster staggered, and fell upon one knee; and that fall was almost the undoing of the English knight, for he leapt forward to take advantage of it, and himself slipped and stumbled. In a flash the giant, recovering himself more quickly than seemed possible to so huge a creature, brought his club down. But his aim was not true; his wounds hindered him, and the club missed St. George by a hair's breadth.

Quickly the two sprang apart. As he moved, St. George saw out of the corner of his eye that Sabra had slipped past with Bucephalus, and was making for the forest beyond. The knowledge that she was safe— for a time, at any rate—gave him fresh vigour. He darted in and out at the giant, his blade flashing round him, cutting, pricking, dealing little wounds, till the monster knew not where to strike. The giant fell into a frenzy, and brandished his club wildly. His wounds began to tell upon him, and he grew more and more feeble, until at last St. George smote him deep in the side, a mortal blow. He reeled and fell, and the champion, coming close without fear, struck off first one of his ugly heads and then the other.

The Marriage of St. George

St. George went swiftly into the castle. But he found nothing there which called for his aid or strength. There were many servants, in great terror at the sight of the combat between the champion and the giant, and now afraid that the victor would put them to death. But St. George did them no harm. He asked certain questions of them, and learnt that there were no prisoners in the castle at that time. He was told also that not long before a message had come to the giant from the enchanter Osmond, warning him that an English knight would pass that way, whom he was to be sure to slay or take prisoner. St. George saw that never would Christendom or himself have peace until this wicked enchanter was dead.

Then he took fresh provisions from the giant's well-filled store, and set out to overtake Sabra. Soon enough he found her, resting on a fallen tree-trunk in the forest, with Bucephalus close at hand, cropping some sweet grass. But near her, by her side, were creatures that at first sight filled St. George with dismay. Two great lions crouched by her, one resting its head on her knee, the other lying at ease upon its side, looking up at her. They made a purring noise like a cat's, but louder and even terrible in sound.

The Brotherhood of Champions

St. George drew his sword hastily. "Do not move, Sabra," he cried. "Do not disturb them. Leave them to me."

But Sabra only laughed merrily. "Put up your sword," she answered. "These are my friends; they will do no harm to us."

St. George sheathed his sword slowly. He did not understand.

"I do not know why they came to me," continued Sabra, "nor why they are so gentle towards me. Thus it was: When I came to this fallen tree, I thought I would await you here, and I dismounted and sat down. No sooner was I seated than these brave beasts came running to me gladly like dogs, and lay down by me as you see. They did not so much as cast an eye on Bucephalus, nor did the good steed pay any heed to them."

"It is a sign from Heaven of your goodness and purity, dear lady," said St. George, laying his hand on a lion's mane. The beast did not stir. "Had you been a coward, or false to me, or a wrong-doer in any way, the high nature of these royal creatures would have been enraged at the sight of you. But they know you for what you are, all goodness and gentle thoughts and loyalty. Come, let us bid them farewell and go on our way!"

Sabra fondled the lions gently, and then

The Marriage of St. George

mounted the horse behind St. George again. The lions looked sadly upon her, as though they were loth to see her depart; and they followed behind Bucephalus, with drooping tails and downcast heads, almost to the edge of the forest, which in due time St. George reached safely. Then they stood watching till Sabra was out of their sight.

It was a journey of many weeks to the Christian host, and the way was full of hardships, but no other peril by land or sea befell the champion and his lady, and at last they came in safety to their old comrades. Great rejoicings were there in the Christian army over the return of St. George; for by now the lands conquered from the pagans were well-nigh set in order under Christian Princes, and it was time that the heathen should be attacked in the regions whither they had fled to gather fresh forces. But first there were marriages to be made, and great feasts to be held. All the champions and the leaders of the Christian army journeyed to Egypt, where King Ptolemy, now baptized a Christian, was reigning again, more justly and wisely than before. At his court St. George married Sabra, and for three months thereafter all the land was given over to rejoicings.

Then at last St. George set to work to

gather and marshal the Christian forces. The leaders of the pagans were known to be now with the enchanter Osmond, at the court of the Soldan of Persia, against whom St. George already had a heavy debt for his imprisonment long before. From every quarter of Christendom more knights came; messengers were sent into every land to summon men, and money and arms were bestowed by those who could not, for any reason, serve in person. But it was more than a year before the great army was provisioned and ready for marching.

In that time a son was borne by Sabra; the name of Guy was given him. He was to make that name famous in after years, for he became no other than the renowned Guy, Earl of Warwick. During the wars that now began Sabra followed St. George as nearly as she could with safety, and bore him two other sons, named Alexander and David.

It was long before the Christian army, mighty though it was, could make headway against the paynim hosts. They divided their forces into three. One band went by way of the isthmus from Egypt into Palestine, and drove from the Holy Land all the pagans there. Another went south to the region of Sinai and Arabia, and marched thence northwards towards Persia. The third started from Constantinople, and crossed over into Asia Minor, and pushed the Saracens back thence. Slowly the three armies advanced, growing nearer to one another with every victory, until at last they were marching upon Persia in a great half-circle, closing gradually upon the Soldan and his wild host. Narrower and narrower grew their curve, until at length the pagans came to a stand under the walls of the ancient city of Ispahan. There a great battle was fought. It lasted five days without ceasing, and at the end of it the Christians were victorious. They slew more than half the Saracen army; of the rest, some surrendered, while others fled with the Soldan and Osmond the Wizard to the strong city of Belgor, many leagues distant.

A great part of the Christian army went to Belgor and besieged the fortress. Others occupied themselves with restoring peace and prosperity to Persia, gathering the neglected crops, doing justice between the peasants who had had no part in the war, rebuilding ruined cities, setting free prisoners and succouring oppressed Persians.

Belgor held out many months. The black arts of Osmond were strong to repel attacks with all manner of strange devices. He would

cause the earth to tremble when scaling-
ladders were set against the strong walls; he
made springs dry up or become impure, so
that at one time many Christians died of
thirst; he called down lightning from the sky
upon the battering-rams and engines of the
besiegers. But all was in vain. He had
within the walls an enemy whom he could
not long hold at bay—hunger. The Saracens
at last had no food left, and they must sally
out and fight, or die of starvation.

So one morning the great gates were thrown
open, and the pagans rushed forth, mad with
despair and hunger and fury, yelling like
men possessed, their eyes glaring, their unkempt hair streaming behind them. But the
Christians were ready for them, and met
them firmly; and then began the fiercest
battle of all that long war.

It went ill with the Saracens. The Christian knights were stronger and less wearied;
they had not been shut up in a fortress with
very little food. But suddenly Osmond, in a
frenzy of despair, tried his last hope. He
knew a spell so powerful that by it he could
call up hosts of evil spirits who would do his
will. But so terrible were the words he must
utter to conjure them up, and so deep and
horrible was the enchantment, that it would

The Marriage of St. George

deprive him·of all his strength then and for ever after.

Nevertheless, he knew that unless this spell could be used, he and all the Saracens with him were doomed. Better to lose his magical power and be as other men than cease to be at all, he thought. He put on his wizard's robe, and chose certain herbs from his store. Inside the city gates he drew a large pentagram, and cast the herbs into a brazier in the midst of it. As they burnt, he rocked to and fro, crying out in a strange language. Foam came to his lips, and the herbs burnt with a green smoke that dazed the wits of all who smelt it, so that they became as drunken men. As the smoke died down and became a mere wisp, Osmond chanted yet louder and faster; and with the end of the spell he leapt swiftly from the pentagram. From the earth at every corner of it little jets of smoke began to rise, and as they swirled up to the height of a man, they took mortal shape. But there was a more than mortal light in their eyes, which burnt as with smouldering fires; and their bodies did not stay in one shape or limit, but grew big and little, thin or gross, by turns.

Osmond spoke some orders to them in an unknown tongue. With cries so shrill that they struck terror into all, the evil spirits flew against the Christians. Every moment more issued from the ground, until at length Osmond fell in a swoon from weariness at his terrible task.

The swords of the knights were of no avail against the demons; the blades passed through their bodies with a thin sound, and left no wound. The spirits, with more than human strength, caught the Christians by arm, or leg, or shoulder, and tossed them high into the air to a great height, so that they were killed or maimed by the fall. In a little time what had been a victory was like to be a disaster.

Suddenly St. George thought of a symbol that should have been ever in his mind, even in the thick of warfare. He sent a squire with a message. In a few moments a trumpet was heard, sounding a call which every Christian knight knew. They sank down upon their knees, paying no heed to the enemy, as the banner of the Cross was borne high through their midst.

Against that holy sign no evil thing could stand. With shrill cries the evil spirits vanished, and the Christians were left with only mortal enemies to fight. Aflame with new hope, they attacked again; and in a little while there was not a Saracen left free upon

"AT EVERY CORNER LITTLE JETS OF SMOKE BEGAN TO RISE."

The Marriage of St. George

the field, save those who had gained liberty by death. The wizard Osmond was slain by St. George himself. He had recovered from his swoon, and boldly enough sought to take up arms; but there was no force left in him, and St. George cut him down with one blow, thus keeping his word to the giant of the forest.

The Soldan of Persia was one of those who were captured. They brought him before St. George, and with him his chief viziers.

"Do you remember me, Soldan?" asked St. George, when the Sovereign was led in, bound strongly, for his spirit was untamed, and he did not cease to struggle even in that extremity.

"I forget no dog of a Christian who has crossed me!" roared the Soldan, his face working with passion. "If I were free, I would tear your tongue from its roots; I would pull out your eyes, and trample on you; I would torment you so subtly that you would long for even a painful death as if it were a pleasant thing! I hate you! I hate all Christians!"

And he broke into cursings and threats so horrible that the Christian knights could not bear to hear his words. St. George signed that he should be taken away. Fighting and shouting, he was led away and cast into the very dungeon in which he had once imprisoned St. George. There, in blind fury, he dashed out his brains against the stone walls.

The viziers were held to ransom, and paid many thousand pieces of gold to the conquerors, who spent the treasure in building churches and restoring the cities that the Saracens had laid waste. All through the bounds of heathendom the seven champions and their comrades went, setting up law and order where lately there had been nothing but cruelty and wrong-doing.

In due time they brought peace and justice into all Christian lands, and won many converts to the Christian faith. There still lived in many regions giants and evildoers and robbers, but they went in fear of their lives, and showed themselves but little.

When their task was at length accomplished, the seven Champions went with St. George to England; and they held a great ceremony of thanksgiving for the success of their arms, and afterwards there were public rejoicings for many weeks. When all the feasting and revelry was ended, the Champions went each to his own country, to enjoy leisure and rest awhile, until some call should come to them to take up arms afresh and sally forth together once more.

THE
SONS
OF
ST. GEORGE

I

THE DEATH OF SABRA

FOR many years St. George lived in England peacefully with Sabra, serving the King at court, doing justice among his vassals at home, caring for the poor, training his young sons in all knightly arts, that they might in their turn be worthy of their father and his honourable lineage. Nor did the champion suffer himself to become weak and idle through lack of warlike happenings. There were peaceful tournaments to be held, martial exercises to be kept up, long journeys to be taken to distant parts of England in the service of the King. Even when two score years of his life had passed, St. George was still the perfect knight, the most skilful horseman and jouster in all England, or in all the world. And not only to him did the Princess Sabra, his wife, seem the loveliest woman alive; in all men's eyes she was still the queen of beauty.

So St. George lived in all happiness and high estate, his sons growing up under his eyes in the way of truth and honour. When they were of a suitable age, he sent them abroad, that they might observe the manners and customs of other countries; and they did not return to England until Guy, the eldest, was about to come of age.

When that event began to draw near, St. George sent messengers to his six old comrades, and bade them to a great feast, not saying why they were bidden, but asking them specially to be present. In due time they came, St. Denis with Eglantine, St. James with Celestine, St. Anthony with Rosalind of Thrace. And the other champions also had taken wives. St. Andrew, St. David, and St. Patrick had each married a daughter of the King of Thrace, for the six Princesses had seen that it was in vain for all of them to love St. Andrew, and when the eldest of them had married him, two of her sisters had been prevailed upon to wed the other champions. All these were present at Coventry, and great was their joy at being together once more.

The beginning of their revelry was a great banquet. The sons of St. George were not present at it. But when it was drawing to a close, St. George stood up and spoke to his guests. " Dear friends," he said, " it is not

The Death of Sabra

only for love of you that I have bidden you
to this feast, though such friendship is between us all that I could wish you to abide
here as my guests to our lives' ends. It is
because I have also a new comrade to make
known to you. Await me here; I will return
in a little."

He left them. A few moments later a
knight came in at the entrance by which
St. George had gone out. He was the very
likeness of St. George himself, and he was
dressed like the champion. He said never a
word, but strode to the head of the table and
stood there silently. The guests waited for
him to speak.

" Well, dear brother of England," said St.
Denis at length, when no other voice was
raised, " where is this new comrade ? What
is it that you have to tell us ?"

The curtains at the end of the room parted,
and another knight entered. This also seemed
to be St. George. He advanced and stood
by the other; they were as like as two peas,
but the first-comer now looked a little more
slight in build and boyish in figure.

" *You* are our comrade," cried St. Anthony,
pointing to the second knight.

The knight smiled. " True, old friend,"
he answered. " I am St. George of England

297

The Sons of St. George

But this youth shall be another St. George, and I pray that you will be his friend, as you have been mine. He is my son Guy, and this day he has come to his twenty-first year, and is to be reckoned a man like ourselves. Soon also, I hope, his brothers will be of our company; they have but a year or two to wait." David and Alexander entered as he spoke. " Here are three champions to fill our places when we have grown old and feeble and are near our last rest."

The champions all gave hearty greeting to the three young men, and welcomed them to their brotherhood. St. Denis and St. Anthony had also sons growing to manhood, though they were not so old as St. George's, and others of the champions had young children who one day would tread in their father's footsteps.

St. George had planned a great hunt for the next day; and the day after that a tournament was to begin, in which Guy would hold his own against other knights, and, if he fared well, be made a knight himself. But that tournament was never held.

On the morrow hosts and guests prepared for the hunt. The Princess Sabra and all the other Princesses were to take part. Very gay was their attire and merry their mien.

The Death of Sabra

" It was not for peaceful errands like this
that I used to mount good Bucephalus," said
St. George to St. David, as a horse was
brought for him to mount.

" There was no horse in the world like
him," answered St. David. " When did the
good beast die ?"

" It is more than twelve years ago now,"
said St. George. " I saw that he lived at ease
to the end of his life. Good pasturage he
had, and a fair stable; and every day I
visited him, and we thought of our adventures
together, for I believe that he understood.
Many a time——"

He stopped. As he was speaking he had
put his hand to the bridle, so that the stone
in Sabra's ring, which he still wore always,
caught his eye. The gleam of its radiance
had vanished; it had grown dull. And as he
looked, three drops of blood fell from his
nose. It was the old sign of danger near at hand.

St. George paused. What sorrow was to
come into his life after these years of peace ?
Was it indeed the end of his days approaching, when his son should perforce have to step
into his place ? Or was it peril to Sabra, or
perhaps to Guy ? He could not guess.

" What is it, brother ?" asked St. David,
seeing his hesitation.

The Sons of St. George

" It is nothing," answered St. George gaily. He had made up his mind that he would not spoil their festival for the sake of an unknown danger. " I did but think with sorrow of my good horse; I am sorry that he is dead." And there he spoke truly, for never had horse served knight better than Bucephalus St. George. " Let us set out upon our hunt."

The joyous cavalcade set out, and came soon to the woods. In a little while a fine hart was started, and away they went in full chase. Foremost in the hunt was Sabra; she rode a wondrous Arabian steed that had been sent to her from Egypt. It was a beast full of fire and spirit, and yet a little dangerous also, for its mettle had not yet been trained to complete gentleness.

They flew past a copse of great thorn-trees. St. George had sent for many trees and plants from other countries, and this was a plantation of low-growing trees that bore a very long sharp thorn, and had a tough, sinewy wood which was suitable for the long-bow.

The hoofs clattered by. Sabra urged her swift steed to yet greater efforts. Suddenly a rabbit, terrified and dazed by the noise and tramplings, darted out from the copse almost under the Arab's hoofs. The horse started, swerved, and reared in the air, and Sabra, in

The Death of Sabra

the suddenness of the movement, was thrown violently into a thorn bush.

The hunters drew up. St. George leapt from his horse and ran to Sabra. "Dearest wife, are you hurt ?" he asked tenderly. "I had warning of danger. Oh, that I had stopped the hunt !"

"You cannot break the decrees of Heaven," answered Sabra gently. "I think that my time has come to die. The long thorns have pierced my heart."

And indeed she was sorely wounded. They lifted her and bore her back to the palace. Surgeons were fetched, but they found that their skill was of no avail. The thorns had wounded the Princess mortally. She had but strength to give her blessing to her sons and her husband, and then she died.

So all their rejoicings came to an end. St. George was overcome with grief, and the champions felt a sorrow hardly less deep. Long and solemn was their mourning. All the lords and people of England came to the funeral of Sabra, so dearly was she beloved, and never were such sights of woe seen at Coventry.

When all was over, St. George declared his purpose. "I am to blame," he said sadly, "because I was warned of danger, and did not heed the warning."

The Sons of St. George

"You cannot be blamed," said St. Denis. "It was fated that this should happen. You could have neither foreseen it nor prevented it."

'"Nevertheless I blame myself," answered St. George; "and as a sign of my repentance, I have it in mind to go on a pilgrimage to the holy city of Jerusalem. My sons shall stay here, and for six months they shall keep watch by the tomb of Sabra. Thus shall they learn the duty of knightly endurance, and show to all men what love they had for their mother."

"Gladly will we do so, sir," said Guy; and his brothers agreed.

"Friend of many battles," said St. Denis of France, "I cannot suffer you to go on this pilgrimage alone. Our comradeship is so close that your grief is my grief. My dear wife Eglantine would think ill of me if I could not share your sorrow. I will come with you to Jerusalem.

"And I," cried St. Andrew; and all the six champions vowed that they would go with their leader on pilgrimage to the holy city. St. George tried in vain to dissuade them; their minds were made up. They had loved Sabra dearly, and they would show their grief at her death by undergoing this hardship.

The Three Gifts

II

THE THREE GIFTS

A costly tomb was built for Sabra, and upon it was set a tablet of silver framed in precious stones. For six months Guy, David, and Alexander, watched by it, night and day, without ceasing; always one of them was on guard. So proud were they of this sad duty which they must perform that gradually they became jealous of one another. Little words, spoken with no thought of harm, would wake anger between them. If Guy, for greater comfort in the cold weather of winter, which now came upon them, were to wear a soldier's cloak over his armour, Alexander would suspect him of growing weak in his love for their mother's memory; and if Alexander, in the fulness of his zeal, watched in the thinnest of garments, that he might have no jot of cause for sleep or heedlessness, David would think that he was trying to prove himself braver and more steadfast in his affection than his brothers.

So little by little there grew up ill-feeling and enmity between the three sons of St. George. But it was not till the last day and the last hour of their watch that they quarrelled openly. It happened that it was the turn of Alexander to watch that last period (for they took watches of eight hours each, turn and turn about), and this in itself had angered his brothers, for they said among themselves that they should all three have been on guard together for the last day; but he would not give up his right to take his turn alone.

Guy and David came to the tomb as the vigil was ending. They had not started together, but met on the way, and each secretly thought that the other was going to take some advantage of him, so bitter had the suspicion between them become.

They saw Alexander standing by the tomb, very upright, his hands clasped on his drawn sword, the point of which rested on the ground.

"Who goes there?" he cried, like a strict sentinel, though he knew their footsteps well enough.

"Alexander will not let us come near our mother's tomb," said Guy to David, half in jest, half in earnest.

"He is anxious to show what a good watch he keeps," answered David, with a laugh.

They both spoke in low tones. Alexander did not hear their words exactly. But he heard David's laugh, and thought it was meant for him.

" Who goes there? " he cried again, loudly and angrily. " Stand, and give answer; you may come no nearer till I know if you be friend or foe."

He did but do his duty by such words, even though he recognised his brothers. But they were in no mood to be treated strictly.

" You know who we are, Alexander," said Guy, a little angrily. " We are your brothers."

" And we have come to relieve you of your watch," added David. " It wants but five minutes for the six months appointed to come to an end."

" You should have answered," replied Alexander sternly. " And my watch is not yet over. I see that you are friends. Now leave me to my duty; I may not speak with you while I am on guard, except to challenge you on your approach."

He told the simple truth. They could not in honour interrupt his watch. But they did not go away. Instead, they remained near, and talked in low voices to one another, and ever and again looked at their brother. He thought they were talking of him and mocking him, and his anger grew hot within him.

At last the time came to an end. Alex-

ander left the tomb, and strode towards his
brothers. "Undutiful sons!" he said fiercely,
"you came here to make a mockery of me
because I am constant in my love for our
dear mother, and will not neglect my duty.
You have no real love for her: you have but
kept the letter of your vow to guard her tomb,
and forgotten the spirit of it."

"No man shall say that to me!" cried Guy.
"No, not if he is a thousand times my brother!
My love is as strong and true as yours or
David's, and——"

"Who are you to boast, Guy?" interrupted David angrily. "I have watched as
long as you, and as honestly. And I have
not tried to make a show of my dutifulness
as Alexander has."

"I would give my life for my dear mother!"
said Alexander passionately.

"It is easy to say that when no one
requires it of you," answered Guy, sneering.

"This is idle talk," said David bitterly.
"What is the use of words? We can all vie
with one another in proud speeches. Let us
prove our love by some deed worthy of it."

"Yes," cried Guy, "let us do this: for
seven days we will take thought by ourselves,
and make our plans, and on the seventh we
will return here, bringing, as an offering to

The Three Gifts

lay on our mother's tomb, the most splendid gift we can each devise. He who brings the best gift shall be judged the most loving and dutiful, for a man gives in proportion to his true nature."

They agreed on this, and parted, each eager to think what was the most precious thing he could give out of love for Sabra.

Guy, it chanced, had heard of a famous witch, who dwelt not far from Coventry in secret; it was unlawful to practise witch-craft, and so she kept her hiding-place and her doings secret. But men often spoke of her, nevertheless, and of her dread power; and it happened that one of Guy's serving-men had spoken of her in his hearing.

Guy thought long how to obtain a gift which would certainly surpass anything his brothers might bring. By now, in his eagerness and jealousy, he had wellnigh forgotten the lessons of his mother's gentleness and love, and strove only to show himself more skilful and fuller of resource than David or Alexander. He racked his brains; he considered whether rich jewels, or the setting up of a monument even more splendid than was already built for Sabra, or some great deed of arms to be inscribed on her tomb, would be the best gift. But he could come to no decision, and at last, with much torment of mind, resolved to seek out this notorious witch. He sent for the man who had spoken of her, and obtained from him directions how to find her.

Her cave lay in a wood not far off. But it was no place of terror and mystery so far as the journey thither was concerned. All that was strange about it was the entrance, and this lay through a very old, hollow oak-tree on a sloping bank. When Guy stepped into the oak, and knocked in a certain manner upon the inside of its back, the earth beneath him sank about half the height of a man. He had then to go upon hands and knees and crawl a few yards through a little dark passage. Then he found himself in a large cave in the earth, the old entrance to which, above the ground, had long been overgrown by brambles and thick bushes.

The cavern was lit uncertainly by two flaring torches stuck in little hills of earth. Their flickering light threw strange shadows. For a moment, in the strange radiance, Guy could see nothing except moving black shapes, the shadows of curious phials and jars and implements that stood here and there upon the earthen floor. Gradually his eyes grew accustomed to the dimness, and he saw at a little distance a brazier filled with red-hot

The Three Gifts

coals, from which came a drowsy scent, sweet as burnt rosemary, but bearing sleep in its breath. By the brazier crouched a dark figure.

He advanced a step towards the figure. It did not move. But as he stood still for a moment in awe, a thin, clear, yet quavering voice came from it:

" A knightly house is sad and desolate :
A brother's love is turned by pride to hate,"

it said. It spoke in one tone, with no raising of voice or accent. Guy shivered.

" You know me, old beldam !" he said haughtily. " Doubtless you know also why I came."

" I know you, Guy, son of George," said the even, weak voice. " I know why you come hither. I know how your quest will end. I know what deeds you shall do before you die." And with that the figure stood erect, and threw something upon the coals in the brazier. Immediately a bright flame leapt up, five or six feet in height, licking the top of the low cavern with its edge. In the light the witch was revealed. She had a look of unknown age; her eyes were deep sunken, her cheek-bones stood out like white lines in her yellow, parched skin; her shrivelled lips moved upon gums that held no teeth; her hair was white and long and unkempt. She wore a robe of black, from which stretched her lean, bare arms. She looked at Guy with eyes that seemed to pierce him.

The sudden flame died down. At first Guy could see nothing after the change. But he did not wait for light. He stepped towards the brazier boldly.

"Since you know my errand, give me my answer," he said sternly.

The old woman laughed. The sound of her laughter was shrill and evil. "Why should I answer you?" she cried. "Your family has persecuted all of us who hold secret intercourse with the unseen world. Am I to show that I am grateful by doing you a service?"

"You will answer," said Guy fiercely, "or I will kill you here and now."

He drew his sword and threatened her. She shrank in terror. "I will answer," she cried, "if you will spare me. But you must swear not to reveal my hiding-place, nor to give information of me to the King's judges."

Guy vowed to do her no harm, and she continued: "You seek to do honour to the memory of your mother, the Princess Sabra; is not that true?" she asked. Guy gave a sign of assent. "I tell you that you do dishonour to yourself by this false pride and by the jealousy you show to your brothers. Nevertheless, you are wilful and must have your way. You desire that I shall give you some offering that you may take to your mother's tomb, and it must be so splendid that it will put to shame whatsoever your brothers may bring. That is true also, is it not?" Guy nodded. "You accuse yourself; you wish to shame your brothers, not to show your love. Yet through this quarrel of yours the hidden world is about to give you a warning, and I must do the bidding of the spirits I consult and bestow upon you what you desire. Now be silent; speak no word and move no limb until I give you leave, or you will be torn into a thousand pieces by forces that no man can master."

Guy was awed by her strange knowledge of his mind and the threat in her last words. He stood silent and motionless in the dim light.

The witch took up a wand, and threw some dried leaves upon the brazier. Little flames leapt up to meet the fluttering leaves, caught them in mid-air, flared with a cold blue radiance, and died, while the charred leaves sank slowly, glittering with red sparks. For a moment the whole cave was lit up by an unearthly glare, as of a flash of lightning. Guy could see the witch standing upright, facing towards the brazier, her arm with the wand in it stretched out stiff and straight, as if it were of bronze. The cavern shook and trembled; a great wind rushed and whistled through it, and Guy felt as if moths and blown leaves and gossamer were for an instant brushing his face. Then there was a dreadful stillness for the space of a minute or more.

Suddenly a faint light was seen in the air near the witch. Something frail and thin was being given to her by unseen hands. There was another flash, and when his eyes recovered, Guy could see that the witch had laid her wand down, and was busy lighting other torches. Soon the cavern was brightly lit.

"You may move," she said in a weak voice. She was trembling a little, as though from a great effort. Guy stepped towards her, half in wonder, half in fear.

She held out to him a spray of a flowering plant. "This is a flower men call Loose-strife," she said. "It may be that the name has a meaning for you. This is the gift I am to give you."

"That is worth nothing!" cried Guy angrily. "I could pluck it in any hedge or ditch in due season."

The Three Gifts

" But now is not the due season," sneered the witch. " That is why I had to have it fetched for me by my familiar spirits. If you do not take this flower as your gift, you will never find an offering more costly."

" But how shall I persuade my brothers that a country weed is worth more than silver or gold, or whatever offering they may bring ?"

" Ah !" said the witch. " That is what you must pay to learn. I have done my part in offering you this flower. If you wish it to seem wondrous to others, I must set a charm upon it, and for that I must receive a fee."

Guy thought that all her talk was but a device to make him give her a heavier reward for her enchantments; but he had come prepared for such greed, for he knew that witches were as eager for money as simpler folk. He drew from his wallet a bag of gold and a bag of precious stones.

" Either of these I will give you," he said, holding them towards her, one in each hand. " In this are a hundred nobles of gold; in that rubies and emeralds of price."

" A hundred nobles is not much," she answered cunningly; " and what should a lonely old woman like me do with rubies and emeralds of price ? I am not beautiful, to wear them, and if I sold them, men would suspect that I had stolen them. Give me both, gentle sir, and you shall have the flower, enchanted so that it will seem more precious than anything on earth. Give both the bags to a poor old woman !"

Guy had no love of bargaining. " Take them both, and let me begone," he said, thrusting the bags upon her. He knew that witches always grumbled, however great their reward.

She took them and hobbled away, and shut them into a receptacle in the wall of the cave. Then she came back, the flower in her hand. She took her wand again and waved it over the branch. Before Guy's startled eyes the flower began to grow, putting forth new shoots and new flowers, of a size and a colour and a scent more lovely than any living plant's. It grew till it was five feet in height, covered with leaves and blossoms. The blossoms were of every hue, and the leaves sparkled as if they had been silver.

" Is that a rich enough offering ?" asked the witch in triumph, giving the branch to Guy. It was as light as a feather in his hand.

" It will suffice," said Guy simply. " Now show me the way hence."

"SHE SHUT THE BAGS INTO A RECEPTACLE IN THE WALL"

The Three Gifts

She led him to a little door at the far end of the cave; a narrow passage, just the height of a man, ran thence into the darkness. " This passage is quite straight," said the witch. " Follow it, and it will lead you out into the woods two furlongs hence."

" I thank you, old woman," answered Guy. " Farewell."

But the witch had already turned away, and was going to the place where she had hidden the two bags. As Guy went to the passage, he looked back. The witch had taken out the bag of gold, and was shaking it close to her ear to hear the clinking of the metal.

Guy pushed on through the darkness of the passage, and presently found himself in the woods again. After the darkness and heavy scents of the witch's cave, it was sweet to see again the bare trees and smell the damp earth, and hear robins piping cheerfully. He hastened home with his marvellous bough, which neither air nor cold seemed to harm. He kept it tended in a private place, that his brothers might not learn his secret; and at last, on the day appointed, he bore it carefully to their mother's tomb, and laid it upon the marble. The scent from the blossoms filled all the church.

He was the first to arrive. But he had not

been there long when Alexander appeared,
bringing with him a gift which he had obtained at a great price from an old poor
man at Warwick. It was a silver lute, so
wonderfully made that it seemed almost to
be enchanted. So perfect was its form, and
so finely was it strung, that always music
came from it at the mere touch of the breeze.
Wherever it was set, and however light the
wind, the lute sounded sweetly, and its music
was like that of thin silver bells.

Alexander set this magical lute upon Sabra's
tomb, and looked at the other offering which
was already there.

" So," he said sullenly, " you have brought
a rare gift. How did you come by this
scented branch in the dead of winter ?"

" That is my business," answered Guy.
He knew he had done wrong in going to the
witch. " Where did you find that singing
lute ? But it does not matter where you
found it. My branch is a better offering."

" Better, quotha !" cried Alexander. " How
is a mere flower better than this divine music ?"

" We shall not come to agreement upon
this matter," said Guy, more peaceably.
" David shall judge between us, and I will
judge between you and him, and you shall
judge between him and me."

The Three Gifts

"And how near to agreement will that bring us?" said Alexander, laughing. "No matter. Hither comes David, strangely robed. Let us look at his gift before we quarrel again."

As he spoke, David approached. He was garbed as if for a holy festival, in a long robe of pure white silk, and he bore in his hands a silver basin and jewelled dagger.

"What is this, David?" asked Guy, half mocking. "Are you bringing these things as your gift to our mother's tomb? You have a strange fancy."

"I bring the most precious thing I have," answered David.

He set the basin down upon the tomb, and pushed his long sleeve from his forearm. Then he held his arm over the basin and pricked it deeply with the dagger, so that blood came from the wound. Thirty drops of his blood did he let fall into the basin, and as he did so he cried in a loud, firm voice: "This is the best offering that I can make at your grave, dear lady mother; nothing more precious can I give than my life's blood."

At that Guy and Alexander were amazed, for they saw how foolish they had been in choosing worldly riches and human possessions for their offerings. David had truly

319

given a more precious thing than they; he had shown that he was ready even to give up his life in memory of Sabra.

Then a kind of madness must have fallen upon them, for they drew their swords with one accord and rushed at David to cut him down. But as they raised the blades, an invisible force held their arms, and the swords flew from their hands, and fell clattering on to the marble pavement. At the same time the whole floor of the church rocked, and the tomb opened, and the spirit of Sabra appeared to them.

"Dear sons," it said in a solemn voice, "forbear to quarrel among yourselves. I taught you a better way of life than that. I do not doubt that you all love me equally, according to your natures. There is no need of such gifts as you bring to this tomb. Live in peace with one another henceforth, and join together against a common enemy. Know that your father and the six champions are in deadly peril, from which only you can save them. Go to the King, and ask his leave to quit England in search of the champions; he will readily give it. Set out to go to the Holy Land, and you will be guided to their rescue. Be worthy of St. George of England, the bravest and truest of Christian

The Three Gifts

knights. Farewell, dear sons. Love one another, and keep faith."

She vanished suddenly from their sight, and the tomb closed again. The three young knights were left staring in wonder. Then Guy spoke.

" Brothers," he said, " we have done wrong. Forgive me, David, and you, Alexander, for my pride and jealousy."

They readily forgave him, and asked his forgiveness in turn. Then they went to their household, and made preparations to set out. When they were ready, they rode first to the King, who lay at Winchester, and asked his leave to seek St. George and his comrades. The King, having questioned them narrowly, and learnt the vision of Sabra, gave them permission to quit England. He set a trusty steward over the estate of St. George in their absence; and so pleased was he by their courage and resolution in setting forth upon so perilous a quest that he gave them armour from his own armoury, and horses from his own stables, and dubbed each knight. And so, well equipped and filled with dauntless spirit, they journeyed to the coast and thence to France.

The Sons of St. George

III

THE GOLDEN FOUNTAIN

The seven champions, in the meanwhile, fared forth from England as humble pilgrims, laying aside all the power of their knighthood and the riches of their conquests, and journeying on foot in the sober robes of palmers. Slowly they wound through Europe, living sparingly and fasting often. No longer did they find it needful to watch for robbers or giants or necromancers; such violent folk took no heed of the poor, from whom neither glory nor ransom was to be won.

So the champions travelled slowly and obscurely over hill and dale, by forest and river, until at last, as the sun was setting one evening, the domes and pinnacles of Damascus shone at a great distance before them. Between them and the city lay a great plain, with a few houses scattered over it here and there.

To one of these houses they went for a lodging. A little silver bell hung upon the doorpost. They rang it, and in a short time the lord of the house himself came to greet them. He was a grave man, with a long white beard, and a look of deep sadness upon his face.

The Golden Fountain

" We are pilgrims, fair sir," said St. George courteously, " and we are bound for the holy city of Jerusalem. It was in our minds to lodge this night in Damascus, but we cannot reach the city before the gates are shut for the night. We pray that you will grant us the shelter of your roof, even if it be but a stable that covers us."

" I will entertain you more honourably than that," said the old man. " Enter, strangers; you are my guests this night. But this is a lonely house, and a house of sorrow. Come, I will lead you to a chamber where you may be rid of the stains of travel."

He went before them through the house. On every side they saw rich hangings and costly furniture. Here would be a court filled with fountains and cool, green palm-trees; there a divan with cushions and soft couches for repose; here a great hall for banquets. On the walls were devices in precious stones and rare enamels, and costly statues stood in every passage. Everywhere were signs of high estate and wealth. But everywhere, also, were signs of mourning. Instruments of music lay dumb; few servants were busy about their duties; the banqueting-hall was cold and bare.

The champions were conducted to a fair

chamber, where they washed themselves, and made their humble raiment clean. Then they were taken to a great room, where food and wine, very delicate and pleasing, were served to them; and last of all they were led to rooms in which were beds of the softest down. And there they slept in peace and comfort.

On the next day they were bidden to breakfast with their host. They saw that he seemed even more sad and weary than before. Beyond what courtesy demanded, he spoke little. But he looked narrowly upon the strong figures of the champions, as though he guessed they were no ordinary pilgrims.

When they had breakfasted, they were taken to a splendid hall with a musicians' gallery, and into the gallery came six fair youths, with lutes and harps and viols, and played and sang to them in the most exquisite manner. As they sang, the lord of the house veiled his face with his hands; and when the music died away, and the youths went from the gallery, St. George saw that their host was weeping.

" Fair sir," he cried, with kindly sorrow in his voice, " we have come to you in an hour of grief. We do not know what misfortune has befallen you, but it may be that we can

The Golden Fountain

aid you. Though we are bound upon a holy and peaceful errand, we are yet not unskilled in arms. It is our hope, before we die, to subdue all the evil things in the world—all monstrous beasts, all pagan tyrants and giants and wizards, and to win the whole earth to the Christian faith. Tell us, therefore, in what way we may serve you. Or if you have no need for our service, let us go hence without delay, and not intrude any longer upon your sorrow."

" Good sir, I will tell you all," answered the old man, "for I perceive that you are no common pilgrims. Those six youths are my sons. They are all that I have left. But formerly I had fourteen, as comely and honourable as any man could desire. We have a proverb that a man's strength is in his sons; but where is my strength when a foul giant has taken eight sons from me and stolen also my wealth ?"

" Where is this giant ?" said St. George. " Know, sir, that I am George of England, and there is no giant on earth whom I fear; aye, and my comrades, these six champions of Christendom "—and he named his companions to their host—" are no less ready to encounter any giants or wizards or other enemies of the human race. Tell us where

The Sons of St. George

this monster may be found, and we will instantly seek him out and kill him."

" That is a deed for men more than mortal," said their host. " But hear my story. I possessed formerly two palaces, this in which it gives me pleasure to entertain you, and another many miles hence, in a fruitful valley watered by a pleasant stream. Now, I have some slight skill in alchemy. Though I have not yet found the Philosopher's Stone, which turns all things into gold, yet I do not despair of that success before I die. This much did I learn from my study of the secret ways of nature: that a certain spring near my palace was possessed of alchemic properties, so that anything of base metal steeped in its waters in a certain way would, in the space of a day, be changed into pure gold. This fountain flowed copiously, and I had little fear that it would run dry. Nevertheless, I deemed it wise at first to keep my knowledge secret, lest avaricious men should drive me by force from my beauteous valley. I had in a little time as much gold as I needed for my own uses, and I was willing to tell certain of my friends, slowly, one by one, that they also might enrich themselves. But by some means, I know not how, news of the Golden Fountain crept about, and all manner of base folk

326

The Golden Fountain

flocked hither to test it, so that in the end I had to set a guard upon it, and in this work the eight oldest of my sons took a great part. At last there came this great giant, whose dwelling is in Arabia, and brave thou h they were, my sons could not withstand his terrible strength. He took them all prisoners; and if I had not been warned in time, so that I was able to flee with my young sons and some of my household, we should have been slain, every one of us. Brave knights, I beseech you, if you would bring happiness to an old man who has not many more years on earth for either joy or sorrow, rescue my sons and kill this foul giant; but I beseech you no less, if you set a value upon your own lives, do not heed my prayer."

" Sir," said St. George, " we will kill the giant and set your sons free, and give you back your Golden Fountain."

" I pray that you may," answered the old knight sorrowfully, yet with hope in his voice. " Now let me give you weapons and armour out of my store, for pilgrims do not go armed; you must be knights when you seek out the giant."

He clapped his hands, and a black slave appeared. " Bid my steward attend me," he commanded.

In a little time the steward came, and it

was not long before the champions were
armed from head to foot in good steel, with
weapons worthy of so great an adventure.
Their host gave them directions by which they
might find the giant's castle, and they set
forth, comrades in arms once again.

They came at length to the giant's castle,
and beat upon the shut gates. But a warder
appeared who told them that his lord was
absent, hunting, though he would return soon.
The champions withdrew to a little distance
to await his coming.

"It appears to me," said St. George while
they waited, "that we should win greater
honour if we attacked this monster one by
one, single-handed. I doubt not that anyone of us can overthrow him, and it will bring
the more glory to our faith and our order of
knighthood if he were slain by one man only.
Let us draw lots to see who shall assail him
first."

The other champions agreed. They found
six smooth white stones and one black one,
and each in turn drew a stone from St. George's
helmet. The black stone fell to St. Denis.
Even as they finished drawing, they heard a
noise of horns and of wild shouting, and,
looking up, saw the giant returning from his
hunt with a crew of wild huntsmen.

The Golden Fountain

They let the cavalcade get within the castle gates, which were closed upon the hunters. Then St. Denis rode boldly to the gates and summoned the warder. His comrades saw the warder speaking to him at the wicket-door and going away; then came a great shout from within, in a voice that made the air tremble, and the warder came back and opened the gates. St. Denis entered and disappeared; the gates were closed.

For a little space the champions heard no sound. Doubtless the fight was begun. Then they heard the great voice roaring again, but what the sound meant they could not tell.

They waited, and heard no more. Every moment they expected St. Denis to come forth triumphant. But the gates remained shut, and no sign of what had happened within was given. The minutes passed; half an hour, three-quarters of an hour, went to join the hours of yesterday. The champion of France did not return.

" We must draw lots again," said St. George simply at last. " If our brother has fallen into any snare, it should be no great matter for one of us to set him free."

They drew again, and this time the lot fell on St. Patrick. Once more the warder came to the gates, and disappeared, and came back

329

The Sons of St. George

and admitted him; once more they heard the first shout of the mighty voice. But no more did they hear, and St. Patrick did not return.

St. Anthony went next, and after him St. David, and then St. James. St. George and St. Andrew, left alone together, noticed that the warder no longer waited to learn the giant's will before admitting the champions, but threw open the gates as they approached.

"This giant is a greater foe than we have yet met, brother," said St. George, as they waited. "But be of good cheer. Even if he overcomes you, and me also, all is not lost. He must use some magic spell, against which knightly weapons are of no avail; but no magic can long prevail against the champions of Christendom. It is not our fate to die here in Arabia by the hand of a monster like this. Now go, friend. I think there is no need to wait longer. I will come soon if you do not return. But doubtless you will return, and our comrades with you."

St. Andrew departed, and vanished within the quickly opened gates. St. George waited, but he knew in his heart that the champion of Scotland would not return. Presently he, too, rode up to the gates, resolved to discover whatever secret lay hid behind them.

The warder laughed as he opened the gates.

The Golden Fountain

"Seven of you," he said jeeringly. "My master has not had so good a catch since he took the eight sons of the knight of the Golden Fountain. Well, I shall not see you again."

"You will see me again in half an hour's time," answered St. George sternly. "With me will be my comrades. Your lord, the monstrous giant, will be dead. You shall be beaten for insolence."

For a moment the man was abashed, with such firmness and confidence did St. George speak. Then he recovered his boldness. "You will never return, knight," he said. "And since you have made me a promise, and you will not be able to fulfil it, grant me a boon instead. Give me your sword; I would like to possess a good sword. It will be of no service to you; no sword yet forged can wound my master, as everyone knows; he has a charm against blades of steel."

"That is the secret!" thought St. George. But he did not speak the words aloud. He looked round him quickly. Across the gate stretched a great rod of iron, that fell into a socket and kept all fast barred.

"Take my sword, fellow," he said. "I can fight well enough without it. But when I come to claim it again, you shall have fifty stripes for your trouble in keeping it. Now

331

begone from my sight, lest I repent and kill you with my bare hands."

He gave his sword to the warder, who, awed by his mien, ran hastily with it into the gate-house. St. George leapt from his horse and tethered it to the gate. Then with a wrench he pulled the iron bar from its fastenings. It was twelve feet in length, and few men could have wielded it. But to the champion of England it was almost a plaything.

He passed through the archway of the gate into the courtyard of the castle. A second gate lay the other side. There was no one in the courtyard.

St. George went across and struck the second gate with his iron bar. The blow broke the bolts, and the gate flew open. A great roaring came from inside, and in a moment the giant rushed out, a long club in his hand.

" Hola !" he cried, seeing St. George awaiting him. "Another knight ! I thought I had done with you for to-day. Well, I can put seven into my dungeon as well as six, and when I take your bodies to my Golden Fountain, it will be seven gold images I shall have instead of six. Now, knight, look well at me and my castle; you have not long to

The Golden Fountain

look upon us, and we are a rare sight. You
will have eyes of gold soon, but you will not
be able to see out of them. Look! Am I
not a fine fellow? Did you ever see a greater
man?"

"Have done with your jests, monster,"
said St. George, "and use your own eyes as
long as I give you leave."

With that he swung the huge bar up, up,
and down again, so swiftly that it could hardly
be seen. Down it fell upon the giant's wrist;
there was a crack as if an oak-tree had been
riven asunder, and the monster's hand dan-
gled idly, and the club fell out of it. The
wrist was broken.

The giant made a terrible sound, half roar,
half scream, and rushed at St. George,
grasping at him with his left hand. But St.
George sprang out of his reach, and swept
the iron bar round with all his force. It
struck the giant on the knee and broke his
leg. He staggered and fell, and as he fell
the bar rose and came down once again,
smiting him on the head, so that by the time
he lay stretched on the ground he was dead.

St. George took from him his keys, which
hung at his girdle. With them he went
through the castle. In a deep dungeon he
found the six champions, bound fast, but un-

hurt. Their swords had been useless against the giant, even as the warder had said; and he had taken them alive and made them prisoners thus. Other captives also St. George found elsewhere. He set them all free; among them were the sons of the knight of the Golden Fountain.

Then the champions and the freed captives left the castle. But first St. George sought the warder of the gate, and took his sword back from him, and gave him fifty stripes, as he promised.

Very joyous was their return to their host, and great were his rejoicings at the sight of his sons. A feast was held, and then the champions donned once more their pilgrims' weeds, and set out for Jerusalem. It was not far distant, to men who had journeyed so great a way already, and in due time they came to the Holy Sepulchre, and fulfilled the vows they had made at the death of the Princess Sabra.

IV

THE ENCHANTED BED

When their vows were duly paid, the champions left Jerusalem to return to England, choosing a different way from that by which they had come. The road led them across a great wilderness, where there were no habitations of man. Beyond the wilderness lay a range of mountains.

The track through the wilderness was long and barren. The hot, dry sun gave them neither water nor kindly fruits in their season. For many days they journeyed through it (they were now habited as knights again, and riding horses, not afoot, since they had ended their pilgrimage). But their provision of food barely lasted. They ate sparingly, and divided their store up so that it might last the longer. But they grew very anxious both for themselves and for their horses, who fared even worse than they, for there was little enough grazing-land in the desert. They were glad when they suddenly saw in the distance, at the foot of the mountains, a great column of smoke going up into the sky.

"Smoke is the work of man," said St. George cheerfully. "Let us find whose dwelling lies near that smoke, and demand a resting-place and food for ourselves and our beasts."

They rode to the column of smoke, taking fresh heart and comforting their weary steeds. But when they drew near, they saw that the smoke came from a great cave in the side of

335

a hill, or from the ground in front of it, for the hill was a burning mountain or volcano, and a little outlet for the hidden fires was to be found almost at the entrance to the cave.

"What shall we do, brothers?" asked St. George, when they halted a little distance from the cave, seeing that their hopes were deceived. "Shall we see if any man—a hermit, maybe—lives in this cave, or shall we journey on, and try to find some dwelling of mankind in these rough mountains? Soon it will be night, and our horses are weary. We must rest somewhere. Shall I spur onwards and peer into this cave? If you abide here, you can in the meantime look all about to see if anywhere you can discern so much as a peasant's hut."

They agreed, and St. George rode as swiftly as his steed could bear him towards the cave. He was very near the entrance when he heard a low, rumbling sound. He halted his horse, thinking that the ground was unsafe, and might at any minute quake and burst asunder. But even as he drew near he learnt that the noise was not of the earth, but of man. A monstrous giant rushed forth, heaving himself through the column of smoke, so that it obscured his coming. He bore a huge mace in his right hand, and so suddenly and swiftly did he come that he was close upon St. George before the champion could draw his sword. But the English knight was alert. His battle-axe hung ready to hand at his saddle-bow. As the giant dashed on, St. George pulled his bridle violently, so that the horse reared up on high. The giant swerved a little to avoid the fore-hoofs; but his rush was too violent for him to stop quickly, and as he swept past St. George swung his battle-axe, and struck him on the back of his head so mighty a blow that his skull was split, and he fell dead upon the spot.

The other champions, in the eagerness to discover some mortal habitation, had not seen what had so quickly happened to St. George. But he called them at once, and together they rode past the column of smoke and into the cave. Deep in the mountain-side they found a great hollow place, which was the giant's lair. It was lit by torches, and at a great fire in the midst was half a sheep roasting on a spit. Other provisions also they found in great plenty, even fodder for their horses.

They feasted well, and lay that night in the cave at their ease. On the morrow they woke refreshed, and, taking with them as great a store of food as they could carry, set out again upon their road through the mountains, thankful to have passed the hot desert with so little misadventure.

They had not ridden very far before they descried upon the track before them a dark figure, and by it some object which sparkled in the sun like a thousand diamonds. When they came nearer, they saw that the figure was that of an old knight, in robes of deep mourning, sitting by the side of a marvellous shrine made of pure crystal. In the midst of the shrine lay a coffin of gold.

"Aged sir," said St. George courteously, when they reached the mourning knight, "have you suffered any wrong that a Christian knight may avenge ? My comrades and I are champions of the afflicted and the oppressed, and if you desire it and your cause is just, we will do you whatever service lies in our power."

"You cannot bring back the dead to life," answered the old man sadly. "That is the only service I could willingly ask of you."

"Tell us what has befallen you, sir," said St. George. "It may chance that some remedy may yet be in our power."

"I will tell you my sorrowful tale," said the old knight. "You shall judge for your-

The Enchanted Bed

selves whether you can serve me or not. In this shrine lies the body of my dear daughter. A week ago she was livihg, and beautiful as a flower. Now she is dead, foully slain by a knight false to every vow of knighthood. Know, sirs, that I am lord of these regions by right; my forbears so long as the memory of man runs have held this land, and there is no one, high or humble, in these parts by whom my daughter was not known and beloved. Now, a few years ago a knight named Leoger was granted possession of estates bordering mine, their lord having been slain in battle, leaving no heir. This Leoger was fair-spoken, and of great wealth, and seemed to be an honourable knight, and he became my friend. Woe is me that ever I admitted him to my castle ! But I think he must have secretly cast a spell upon me and all my household, for we saw nothing evil in him, though all the time (if we had but known it) he was in league with wizards and enchanters, and deep in their vile plots, being himself a magician of power. Of his wizardry I have only had news since his most wicked deed."

" We have sworn to slay all magicians," said St. George, interrupting gently. " We will take up your cause. But tell us all."

" Six months ago," continued the old

knight, his voice broken with grief, "Leoger came to me and asked me for the hand of my daughter in marriage. He told me of his great wealth and possessions (how evilly he came by them I can now guess), and promised that my daughter, as his wife, should live in the state befitting her lineage and possession. I called her to me, and learnt that she had looked on him with favour, admiring, doubtless, the graces of his person and his fair speeches, for, as I have said, he seemed to be a very comely knight. I gave my consent to his request, and allotted a great dowry to my daughter, as was seemly for one of my house. In due time, without long waiting, he married her. For a month they lived together; then, upon some slight occasion, he abused her and beat her. With one servant she fled from his castle, seeking to return to me. But Leoger pursued and caught her, and killed her then and there, seven days ago. The servant escaped and brought me word. But I could not avenge her, for Leoger, coming swiftly upon the heels of this murder, ravaged my lands suddenly, and by bribes and promises—yes, and I doubt not also by magic arts—drew away from me all but a few most faithful servants. I think that he means before long to slay me also, and claim my

340

possessions in virtue of the wife he murdered so vilely. Day by day have I sat by this shrine, weeping, and praying that Heaven would send me some aid, for I am old and weak, and hope has grown feeble within me. I think no mortal man can prevail against this wizard Leoger; but I crave for aid to escort me and this precious shrine to some place of safety, where I may end my years in peace."

"No harm shall come to you yourself, gentle sir," said St. George; "but we will do more than protect you—we will destroy this Leoger and all his tribe of necromancers. Even if he were but a knight who had been false to his vows, we would chasten him; but now we will kill him. Show us how we may approach his castle."

"The castle is distant seven leagues from here," answered the old man. "In a little while this road branches. Follow the right branch, and you will come to the castle without fail. But it is an ill place to enter by force. It is set upon a great mountain. Outside runs a mighty wall, containing but one gate. Beyond this gate is a drawbridge, across a moat which men say is bottomless. This moat must have been built by arts beyond mortal knowledge, for there is no stream so high up the mountain to fill it, and yet, so it is said, it never runs dry or becomes stagnant. Beyond it is yet another great wall, and in it only one gate, to which the drawbridge leads. When this gate is passed, there is a courtyard, and at one side of the courtyard a great staircase of marble going down into the chief hall of the castle, which is hollowed out in the very body of the mountain itself. More than that I cannot tell you, for I have visited the accursed place only once in my life. Go, brave knights, and take my blessing with you; but I pray you beware of snares and enchantments, for Leoger is strong in them, whatever your valour in arms may be. As for me, I will retire to a cave hard by that I know of, and await your return; and if it is to be that you never return, I will remain there nevertheless, for if your strength cannot aid me, no mortal help will be of use."

"Farewell, good sir," cried the champions, and took the road in joy at this high and worthy adventure. Soon they reached the place where the road branched, and turned to the right. And when they had ridden for a long time, without meeting man or woman by the way, they came in sight of Leoger's castle. It was as the knight had described it, a mighty fortress crowning a steep and barren mountain. There was but the one rough

The Enchanted Bed

winding track up to the gates of carved bronze. Grim and terrible it was, a place of emptiness and echoes, where a stone dislodged by a horse's hoof would rumble and crash as if the mountain itself were falling.

The knights rode boldly up to the shut gates. There was no watchman or sentinel on guard. They peered through the wrought bronze, and saw beyond it the vast moat, and on the other side the drawbridge, raised, so that it hid the gate in the second long, smooth wall. The waters in the moat looked black and oily and still. There was no movement in them, no ripple of a fish rising, no green leaves of lilies. No grass or weeds grew in the crevices of the stone at the moat's edges. A silence that seemed almost like an unceasing low murmur lay over all the gloomy castle.

They looked for some means to summon a warder. Fastened to the gates by a golden chain St. George spied a silver horn. He clasped it; it was rough to the touch. There were words spelt upon it in fine, small emeralds:

> "Sound me : I open gates for all who dare,
> But let the man who enters here beware."

St. George took the horn and blew it with all his might. The sound rang through the

343

stillness, and echoed as though a thousand elves were mocking him. So loud was the blast that the castle seemed to rock and sway on its very foundations. As the last note died away the gates clanged open. Slowly the drawbridge, with a grinding and screaming of its chains, lowered itself by invisible means, until the end touched the edge of the sombre moat almost at the champions' feet.

"Forward, friends!" cried St. George. "Here is a proud adventure for the knights of Christendom!"

The horses' hoofs clattered upon the drawbridge. They were across in a moment, and facing the second gate. It, too, was shut, and on it also hung a horn, which St. George sounded. Even more terrible was the blast than before. On the horn were the words:

"Be warned in time : this is no place of peace ;
Who comes within death only can release."

At the sound of the horn the gates flew open, and the champions entered. Immediately the gates clanged behind them, and the drawbridge slowly rose and shut the moat from their view. They were cut off, unless they could kill Leoger, or force him to open the gates again.

They were in a huge courtyard, such as they

The Enchanted Bed

had been told of by the old knight. In front, across the open space, lay the walls of Leoger's keep, high, massive walls of stone, with narrow windows here and there, and on the top battlements and machicolations through which stones and boiling oil could be thrown down upon besiegers. On the left the walls and the courtyard curved away out of sight. On the right a wall stretched out a little way from either side, from the keep and from the moat wall, and then ended, leaving open the way to a broad downward stairway of gleaming white marble.

There was no living thing to be seen. But from the stairway the champions thought they heard the sound of music and of laughter; it was an evil sound, as it were of wicked mirth and triumphant malice. They dismounted from their horses and left them by the gate. Drawing their swords, they went towards the stairway.

Suddenly, as they were in the middle of the courtyard, a dense blackness fell upon them. Not a foot in front of their faces could they see, and the sudden change from light to utter darkness confused them, so that they lost their feeling for direction.

But St. George kept his wits about him. " Clasp hands," he cried at once, " and say quickly your names, as soon as another grasps your hand."

"George," he cried out in a moment, as his hand touched another. "Anthony," cried a voice, and then "Patrick," and "Denis." Then for a moment there was silence, and their hearts grew anxious. At last the sound came "Andrew," and a minute later, "James." Last of all, after another silence, "David." They were joined, hand in hand. They had to sheath their swords, but it was better to be unready than alone in that evil place.

"We must find the stairway," said St. George. The voices seemed strangely distant and muffled in the dark fog.

"It is on our left," said St. Patrick.

"Our right," said St. David.

"Straight in front," said St. James.

"This is vain talk," said St. Andrew bluntly. "Let us walk until we touch some upright surface, whether it be wall or gate or keep. Then let us feel along it, and so in time we shall discover where we are. I should say that when this enchantment descended upon us we were forty paces from the stairway. If, when we find a wall to touch, we walk along it for fifty paces, and do not find either the stairway, or the gate, or the cross-

The Enchanted Bed

walls leading to the stairway, we may be certain we are going in the wrong direction, and must retrace our steps for fifty paces, and then start again in the opposite direction. So we shall find the stairway, unless this Leoger is so great a wizard that he can make it vanish altogether."

"Well said, brother," said St. George. "I think we were not so much as forty paces from the stairway; but if we walk fifty, we shall make sure of not going too far astray. Come, let us to it. Forward!"

They advanced, groping. Presently St. David, at the end of the line, gave a cry: "A wall!" and almost immediately afterwards his comrades touched it. They began to pace along it, going to the left, for they thought they were at the outer wall. Fifty paces they trod, and another ten, to make sure. But they met with no cross-wall and no gate. By that they knew that they were on the farther side of the courtyard, walking in the wrong direction. They retraced their steps. As they walked, clumsily and uncertainly in the blackness, they heard the mocking laughter more loudly. Fifty—forty—twenty—ten— they were at the starting-point. On they went: ten — twenty — thirty — thirty-one — thirty-two—and St. George cried out: "The wall

347

ends; the cross-wall is here. Loose hands and draw swords. When we reach the stairway, let each take paces to the right according to his position. I will take seven, Anthony six, and the rest in order. Now !"

They began their pacing again. In a little while St. George cried again: " The wall ends; there is nothing in front of me. The stairway is here. I shall step seven paces. Let all do their parts."

He paced off his distance, and the others after him. They felt forward with their feet, and stepped downwards in the dark. Immediately the blackness vanished, and they were in broad daylight again. The staircase lay before them. On either side it was walled. In front it curved away as though leading into the very heart of the grim keep.

And thither indeed it led. The champions went down the steps, swiftly but cautiously. In their armour they could not walk silently, but they did not wish to rush headlong into a snare.

At the foot of the stairs they found a large door of oak. They pushed against it. It swung open easily, and they found themselves in a huge hall, lit by hundreds of torches. A feast was being held. A table ran up each side of

The Enchanted Bed

the hall, and a third across, at the top, on a raised daïs. Strange and terrible were the guests at that feast. Here was a giant with three heads, there a long-bearded genie from Arabia; there a dwarf, here a monstrous creature with a bull's head and a man's body; there a shadowy thing like a wisp of smoke that changed its shape perpetually. One guest would be black, with eyes of fire; another pale and livid, long-faced and threatening. This one wore rich robes of scarlet embroidered with cabalistic signs in black; that one was covered with hair, or wrapped about in tightly-fitting black. Every face had upon it a look of wickedness. All the company were practisers of the black arts, necromancers of hateful repute.

At the middle of the table on the daïs sat one whom the champions judged to be Leoger: a swarthy man, with a lean face like a weasel's, and a long, fierce, drooping black moustache. His mouth was large, and his teeth showed white when his thin lips parted in speech.

The champions advanced between the two side-tables. "Where is the lord of this castle?" cried St. George in a loud voice. "Where is Leoger, the false knight and foul wizard?"

349

The Sons of St. George

" I am he. Call me what you please; I care not," answered Leoger, starting up. " I had news of your coming. What! seven champions against one poor knight? And all seven have come hither safely," he continued, laughing bitterly. " Well, I had hoped to separate you. But you have come through the darkness safely. You have more skill than I expected. But it is useless. You will not go hence. What say you, friends ?"

And he looked round at his terrible guests, whose evil faces scowled and grinned and mocked at the Christian knights.

" Ho, ho! Ha, ha!" they laughed horribly. " There are dungeons in the castle of Leoger!"

" We defy you!" cried St. George. " Brothers, fall on!"

And they began to lay about them with their swords. Christendom was rid of many a wizard that day. With his own hand St. George slew eight giants, and many another magician and necromancer fell before his comrades. But suddenly, as they swept in triumph up the hall towards Leoger, darkness came upon them again. And as the darkness descended, the floor of the hall vanished beneath them, and they found themselves,

The Enchanted Bed

unhurt, alone in a dungeon deep beneath the keep.

They did not know at first that they were alone, and only their voices calling to one another warned them.

" Denis, are you near me ? " asked St. George.

" Here, brother of England," answered St. Denis from, it seemed, a few paces away. But their voices sounded strangely in the darkness.

" Patrick was by me in the hall," said the voice of St. Andrew. " Are you there, Patrick ? "

No answer came. " James ! " cried St. Anthony, " I heard you stumble. Speak ! "

" I am here," answered the voice of St. James; but it spoke heavily and drowsily, as though the champion were half asleep.

" Is David with us ? " asked St. George. But again there was no answer. " Denis, was not David on your right hand as we fought the wizards ? "

But St. Denis did not answer either. " Brothers, speak ! " cried St. George loudly. " Answer, all of you, by your names ! "

All the answer he received was a faint shuffling of feet and a little jingling, as of men in armour sinking upon some soft surface gently. No voice replied to his.

The Sons of St. George

" Where am I ?   Where are my comrades ?
What witchcraft of Leoger's is this ?" said
St. George in dismay.

"Witchcraft !" said a deep, hollow voice
far away in the darkness.   " Who speaks evil
of witchcraft ?   This is the very palace of
witchcraft."

St. George looked towards the sound.   A
faint light came rapidly towards him.   A
monstrous creature, shaped like a giant, but
almost as broad as he was tall, was shuffling
along, bearing a lantern in one hand and a
clumsy axe in the other.   He had lost the
sight of one eye, but the other gleamed fiercely.
A long tooth stuck from his upper jaw over
his lip, and little snakes were writhing in his
thick hair.

" Ha ! a knight !" the figure said, holding the lantern on high so that he could see
the champion.   He growled horribly, and
slid forward stealthily, clutching the axe
threateningly.   But St. George did not wait
for him to strike.   He ran at him with sword
uplifted and smote at the ugly head.   The
blade clove the throat, and the giant fell suddenly in a heap, dead.   The lantern clattered
out of his hand, and lay, still alight, on the
ground near the champion's feet.

St. George stooped and picked up the

"A MONSTROUS CREATURE WAS SHUFFLING ALONG, BEARING A
LANTERN"

lantern, and held it up to look at the fallen monster. But the body of the giant had vanished. By that St. George knew that it was some evil spirit sent by the arts of the enchanter to terrify him.

Even as he gazed he heard a fresh sound, a roaring and blowing as of some great beast. He put the lantern on the floor quickly, and grasped his sword in readiness. Out of the darkness into the circle of faint light came a dragon breathing fire. But he who slew the dragon of Egypt was not terrified; nor was this dragon so large or powerful as that of Egypt. With a shout St. George ran at the creature, and shore off one of its wings with his sword; and immediately, with a scream like a man's, it vanished.

The dungeon fell into silence again. St. George picked up the lantern, keeping his sword drawn in the other hand. The light was not strong, but he could see a few paces away a large, low shape. He went towards it, and as the lantern was brought nearer, he saw that it was an enormous bed or couch, strewn with rich coverlets and cushions of soft down. On it lay the six champions, asleep, so still and motionless that they might have been dead.

St. George shook one of them by the shoulder. It was St. Denis. He did not wake or show signs of life. But his flesh was warm, and he breathed; he was not dead. St. George tried to wake the others, but they were fast bound in an enchanted sleep.

The champion set the lantern upon the ground and gazed at his comrades, wondering what he should do to rid them of the spell which clearly had fallen upon them. Immediately the lantern touched the ground the light went out.

A great drowsiness came over the English champion. He stooped a little, and put his hand on the couch. There was, he remembered, an empty space upon it in front of him. He felt the soft cushions with his hand. He was very weary with travelling and fighting. To rest would be good; he would wake refreshed and ready to combat Leoger with all his force.

He put his knee upon the bed. He hesitated, thinking of the slumber that had fallen upon his comrades. Then he cast himself upon the cushions at full length, and in a moment was fast asleep. So all the champions lay in a magic trance in the stillness and darkness of the dungeon under Leoger's castle.

The Princess of Normandy

V

THE PRINCESS OF NORMANDY

When the three sons of St. George crossed over into France, they landed in Provence. Thence they began to journey East. They thought it best to turn their steps towards Jerusalem, believing that there, if not before, they might have tidings of the seven champions. But they had not gone far before an adventure fell in their path. They were riding through a forest, when Alexander bade his brothers draw rein: he had heard a strange sound.

They halted and listened in silence. For a moment they heard nothing. Then there came to their ears a low moaning and sobbing.

" Draw !" cried Sir Alexander, " and press on: there is some villainy afoot here."

They drew their swords and spurred their horses. In a few moments they came to a clearing among the trees. There they saw lying on the ground a most beautiful maiden, fastened down by the hair of her head, which was tied to the stump of a tree. Her hands were bound, and she could not free herself.

Sir Guy sprang from his horse and ran

swiftly forward. He cut the bonds which bound the maiden's hands, untied her hair from the tree, and helped her to rise.

" Fair knights, I thank you," she said, when she was able to speak. " I pray you avenge me. I was left thus by six wicked Moors, who have half killed my father and have robbed me of my jewels. They have not long gone. Doubtless they heard your horses' hoofs afar off. They were carrying me off to Spain or to the coast; but when I struggled, they tied me cruelly as you found me, and galloped away. If one of you will guard me, I doubt not that the others can overtake these villains and do justice upon them."

Sir Guy and Sir David remounted, and hastened off in the direction she pointed out, leaving Sir Alexander to guard the Princess, for such by her raiment and bearing she appeared to be. While they were absent she told Sir Alexander her history.

" I am a Princess," she began.

" That I had guessed the moment my eyes fell on your loveliness," said Sir Alexander boldly.

" Your eyes are far-sighted, Sir Knight," answered the Princess. " But my eyes tell me that you also are of high lineage."

The Princess of Normandy

" I am of the blood royal of England," said Sir Alexander.

" And I of France," she replied. " My father is Duke of Normandy, but I am Princess in my own right by virtue of my mother, who was a King's daughter. But my father's palace is many leagues from here, and we may not dwell in it. Alas ! it would have pleased him mightily to entertain you and your comrades there; but I do not even know whether he is alive or dead. Nevertheless, if he cannot bid you to his palace, he would have welcomed you in the little dwelling-place that is ours. He is exiled, and he and I live alone, but for one old servant, in a little arbour of trees and wattles not far distant from here. There we subsist on what game I can kill (for I was brought up to ride and to use the bow and spear), and on the fruits of the earth, and on what we can buy from time to time with our scant means. Old retainers in Normandy send us money when they can. And so we live frugally, but content."

" Who would not be content——" began Sir Alexander, for he was dazzled by the beauty of the Princess, and had fallen head over heels in love with her.

" Nay, this is no time for idle speeches,"

said the Princess, checking him. "I pray that your comrades——"

"They are my brothers," interrupted Sir Alexander, and told her who they were, and upon what errand they were bent.

"I pray that they return soon," said she, "for I desire greatly to go back to my father and succour him. You must know that the Moors came upon us unawares and slew our servant. My father they bound roughly to a tree not far from our lodging, and me they carried off as I have said. My father is old and weak, Sir Knight, and may bear their cruelty ill. Do you think that your brothers——"

Even as she spoke there was a jingling of horses, and Sir Guy and Sir David came gaily back.

"They are dead!" cried Sir Guy triumphantly. He was young, and exulted in his prowess. "We came upon them like a whirlwind. They had halted, and it seemed as if they were quarrelling. But we did not wait for them to end their debate, but rode them down, and all six were slain in as many minutes. We rescued your jewels from them, Princess. Certain other booty which we found upon them we took also. Alexander, here is your portion." And he gave him

The Princess of Normandy

a jewelled dagger, a chain of gold, and a ring set with a ruby as large as a fourpenny-piece. " The gold we will keep in our common purse," added Sir Guy. " They must have robbed many men."

Sir Alexander told his brothers quickly part of the Princess's story, and they resolved to go at once to her father's aid. Sir Alexander set her upon his horse in front of him; and she did not take the position amiss, for the truth was that she had fallen as deeply in love with the young English knight as he with her.

They rode for a quarter of an hour or more. Then they reached a kind of arbour or shelter made of interlacing boughs and twigs, and walled in with woven wattles plastered with clay. It was large and spacious within, and furnished with rough tables and chairs. At either end a part was curtained off to make sleeping-rooms.

But they could do no more than glance at this green dwelling-place: they must search for the old Duke. They found him tied to a tree not many yards away, so tightly bound that he had swooned with the pain.

They loosed his bonds gently, and took him into the hut, and gave him a cordial water which the Princess produced from her store

The Sons of St. George

of provisions. It brought him out of his swoon, but not back to life and strength. He had been too cruelly used by the Moors. He was of a great age, and weak, and weary of the troubles of his long life. He gathered himself up to give his daughter his blessing, and then fell back dead.

The three knights withdrew for a little, and left the Princess to mourn alone. They talked among themselves as to what they should do with her. Alexander told them of his love for her, and vowed that he would return and marry her. But he did not know how to leave her in that deserted place.

They went back to her presently. She asked them to bury her father, and they dug a grave in a place where violets would bloom over him. When they had laid him to rest, they asked the Princess what she would have them do to make her safe.

"No more help do I need of you," she said bravely. "Go your ways and carry out your quest. Never shall I forget you and the help you have given me. Here in this arbour will I end my days, living alone, mourning my father and praying. If there is any danger, I will dress as a man. But no one will harm me now that you have slain these Moorish robbers, who were the plague of all

362

this region. Now farewell, young knights. May you prosper always."

She turned away. She was loth to part with Sir Alexander.

" We will go, since you wish it, Princess," said Sir Alexander. " But I will return to this place and find you. I pray that you will wear this chain in remembrance of me." And he gave her the gold chain which had been taken from the robbers.

" Thank you, Sir Knight," she answered. " Take this ring in token that I shall not forget you."

She gave him a ring from her finger. He put it upon a little chain he wore round his neck, for it was too small to go upon his strong fingers. Then the three knights remounted their horses, and the Princess, standing by her home of branches, saw them ride jingling away into the dark woods.

VI

THE QUEEN OF ARMENIA

They came after a few days to the coast, and took ship, meaning to sail to Athens, or it might be to Constantinople, to learn, if possible, some news of the champions.

The Sons of St. George

But contrary winds drove the boat out of its reckoning, and they came presently to a large and fertile island. Here, when they saw before them a little seaport, they bade the captain put them ashore, with their horses, to obtain tidings.

They made their way through the city. It was like a place of the dead. Not a soul was to be seen, nor so much as a dog or a cat. The young knights rode through the streets, to the outskirts of the town, and along a high road which, by the direction of the sun, seemed to lead east.

It was when they had gone a little way along this road that they first saw signs of life in the island. They heard a great rustling and breaking of boughs in a little copse, and a scream, and fierce bellowings. Out of the trees suddenly darted a peasant, running at the top of his speed towards the knights. He fell at their feet, talking wildly in a speech they could not understand. The crashing sound in the copse continued and grew louder.

The man looked up at the knights beseechingly. His eyes were starting out of his head with terror. He saw that they could not understand him, and his voice grew feeble and hesitating. One word he said over and over again: " Mongo ! mongo !" He looked

"THE PEASANT FELL AT THEIR FEET, TALKING WILDLY"

fearfully behind him at the copse, and then in terror at the knights again, and the poor remnants of his courage suddenly left him altogether, and he gave a cry and ran like a madman past the knights along the road to the town.

"What does the fellow mean?" began Sir Guy. But he did not finish his question, for he saw the answer to it. Out of the trees which caught it and hindered its steps, there came a terrible monster, with the head of a dragon, claws like an eagle's talons, and eyes that flamed like living fire. It had no wings, but was clad all over in hard scales, and it was ten yards long from head to tail.

It rushed towards them with a lumbering gait that yet bore it along swiftly. Sir Guy did not wait for its onset, but spurred his horse forward. The good beast was trembling in every limb. It had got wind of the monster, and its ears were laid back in anger and fear. Nevertheless, after a moment's hesitation, it sprang onward. At full speed, lance in rest, Guy met the monster. His lance struck its bony scales full and checked its rush. But the lance was shivered to atoms, and the point did not pierce the scales. Quick as thought Guy drew his sword; but the speed of his horse and the shock of meeting had

The Sons of St. George

thrown him a little off his balance. The monster turned on him clumsily but quickly, and with one great paw clutched him by the arm, dragging at him till he fell at length from the saddle. It would have gone ill with Sir Guy if by now Sir David had not come up. He smote the creature fiercely on the head, so that it was shaken and reeled unsteadily, though even yet the scales were not pierced. As he struck, Sir David unfortunately wheeled his horse into Sir Alexander's, so that it fell, and Sir Alexander with it. Immediately the monster turned on the fallen man. But Guy, now freed from its clutch, thrust with his sword at its open jaws. The blade entered the gaping mouth, and went deep down the hideous throat, wounding it mortally where alone steel could do it harm. The jaws snapped, and bit the blade in two as if it had been a thin lath of wood. But the wound was too deep. With a groan the creature rolled over and lay dead.

The three knights could hardly believe that it was dead. But when they were sure of it, they left it, well pleased at ridding the country of such a monster. They did not yet know what country they were in, nor whether it had any inhabitants living, save the man whom they had met in flight. But it was not long before they received tidings, for they passed very soon the cave of a hermit. The hermit himself was sitting outside the entrance.

He called to them. " Young sirs," he said, "ride warily. You may be in search of knightly adventure. If you are, you will have your fill of it here. But do not go unarmed or alone. No man's life is safe in this region."

" What region may it be ?" asked Sir Guy courteously. " We have come hither in a ship driven out of her course, and we do not know what land this is."

" This is the great island of Sicily, and the road you are upon leads to the famous city of Syracuse."

" What is the danger that you warn us against ?" asked Sir Alexander.

But before the old hermit could answer, a trumpet was heard. A herald in a gay tabard, on horseback, approached. He was accompanied by four pursuivants, richly dressed, but in black, as though mourning.

" Hail, sirs !" cried the herald, when he reached the English knights. They gave him a courteous greeting. " I am commanded by my lord the King," continued he, " to ride into every corner of this island, and make proclamation to all brave warriors and knights-errant whom I may meet. This I am to say, that whereas the whole land of Sicily is plagued by a dreadful monster which the common folk call the Mongo, and which has devoured many of His Majesty's subjects, high and low, rich and poor, the King will bestow on any man who kills this monster a helmet of gold set with diamonds, and will make him a peer of this realm."

"What will the King do if three men slay the monster?" asked Sir David, smiling.

"I doubt not that the King's bounty will not fail," answered the herald courteously.

"What was this monster like?" Sir Guy asked.

"No man knows exactly," replied the herald. "Those who have been near it to see have not returned to tell."

"I have seen it at a little distance," said the hermit. "It is wont to pass near my cave from time to time." And he described the creature the English knights had slain. "They say it is a sea-monster really," added the hermit. "A month or more ago it came out of the sea. Two fishermen, drawing in their nets, found it following the net to prey upon the fish. They fled at the sight of it, but it pursued and caught one of them, and ate him; since when its liking for human flesh has grown, so that men dare not abide in towns, but all have taken refuge in the high mountains or in well-hidden caves. I am old, and do not fear it, and it has not yet discovered me."

" We three brothers have killed this monster," said Sir Guy simply. " Sicily is rid of it for ever."

" What do you say, young sir ?" exclaimed the herald in amazement. " Three young knights—for you will not take it amiss that I call you that—have slain a creature that threw a whole nation into terror ?"

" Go a little way along this road," said Sir Alexander, pointing along the way he and his brothers have come, " and you will find the Mongo's body in proof of our words."

The herald and his pursuivants went, and presently returned. Meanwhile the old hermit had been discoursing with the Englishmen about knights and knight-errantry; but he could give them no news of the seven champions.

When the herald came back, he was overjoyed at the wondrous deed; and he insisted that the knights should come at once to the court of the King and receive the appointed reward. They went with him, and were welcomed by the King; and when their deed

The Sons of St. George

was told, a solemn festival was held in their honour, and a week of public rejoicing for the whole island decreed.

While they were taking part in this festival, news came to them of a further adventure awaiting them. The King of Thessaly had been driven out of his dominions by the King of Thrace—not the father of the six Princesses whom St. Andrew had rescued; he had long been dead, and at his death his country had once more gradually become pagan. The King of Thessaly was sending messengers into all Christian lands to seek aid in vanquishing the usurper, who had many giants and wizards in alliance with him. These ambassadors were nearing Sicily when they heard of the great feat performed by three Christian knights in slaying the Mongo, and they hastened to seek the knights and ask their help. They had power, if they found warriors of sufficient fame and might, to offer them all authority and command over the whole army of Thessaly.

The sons of St. George pondered this opportunity long, and at last they decided to take it. It would bring them nearer to the East, and so they might learn something of the champions, and they would gain also honour and some experience in warfare.

The Queen of Armenia

They gave their consent to the ambassadors, bade farewell to the King of Sicily, and set out. There is no need here to recount the long battles and weary journeys of the war they undertook. They achieved prodigies of valour, and in the end drove out the usurping Thracians, and killed all the enchanters and giants who aided them.

From Thessaly they set out for the Holy Land. Still they had heard nothing of St. George and his companions. But now, though they did not know it, they were near the end of their quest. Their way to Palestine led them through Constantinople and into Asia Minor, and so into Armenia. In that country they passed through a wide and lonely forest. As they rode through it, they heard a voice raised in lamentation. They could not at first catch the words, but soon they were near enough to see from whom the sound came. A little tent of black cloth lay half-hidden among the trees. At the entrance to it, on a couch, was a lady, old, but still beautiful. It was plain that she was near death. By her side, tending her, was a beautiful maiden. At her breast the maiden wore a rose of deep crimson.

The armour of the knights rattled. The two women looked round, and the younger one ran to them when she saw them. "Help, knights!" she cried. "By your vows of knighthood, do not refuse me your aid."

They hastened to the tent. "Sirs, I pray you uphold my cause," said the dying woman, "for the sake of my dear daughter."

"Lady, if your cause is just, or if you have suffered any wrong at all, however little," answered Sir Guy, "our swords and our lives shall serve you, according to our knightly vows. Tell us what you would have us do."

"Sirs, a vile knight, if knight such a man can be," she said, with sorrow and passion together in her voice, "has used me most shamefully. This Leoger—that is his name— in days past plagued me to be his wife, and at length, not knowing what manner of man he was, I consented. This child was born to us, and then Leoger seized my lands and my wealth, and drove me into this forest to die, vowing to kill me if I returned to my home. Since then he has married a dozen maidens. and got their dowry into his clutches and then killed them. Many a knight has he spirited away by magic arts, for he is a wizard. This I discovered when first he drove me forth, for at that time he brought a host of men from his own castle—necromancers without doubt, for all the valour of

my servants was of no avail against them—
and pulled down my castle, where we had
been dwelling together, about my ears, and
slew my household, and turned me into this
wilderness of a forest to starve. Since then
for nigh a score of years I have lived upon
fruits and berries, and the water of a little
stream. I have brought up my daughter,
Rosana, here alone, teaching her woodcraft,
and the use of the bow and spear, for I had
weapons when Leoger exiled me. These
many weary years have I waited and hoped
for one to come who would take vengeance
on Leoger, and win back an inheritance for
my daughter. But few have passed through
this forest; and of those who came, some
knew Leoger's evil repute, and deemed it vain
to try to overcome him, and others made the
attempt and perished miserably. I tell you
this, young knights, that you may know what
perils lie in wait for one who would serve
me thus. Nor would I ask knights so young
and so fair to suffer such perils if it were not
that I have but few minutes of life upon earth
left to me."

"Lady, we are young," said Sir Guy; "but
we have fought battles already, not without
honour. What our strength puts in our
power that will we do. If your anguish is

not too great, tell us how we may find this Leoger."

"He dwells a few leagues hence," answered the lady. "His castle is called the Black Castle, and it is surrounded by a moat and two walls." And she described narrowly the entrance to the castle in which St. George and the champions lay spell-bound. "Now Leoger," she continued, "practises the black art, as I have said. But there is to come a time when his magic power shall depart from him, and it has been prophesied fully. His spells, it has been told me, depend upon seven lanterns. So long as they burn, so long will he be invincible. How the lanterns may be extinguished I do not know. Doubtless the secret is hidden in his castle. That much I can tell you. And I can tell you this also, that Leoger shall come to his doom by a maiden's deed. Now my time is near. Know that I was once Queen of Armenia; that is the inheritance I would have you restore to my dear Rosana. Leave us now for a little, gentle knights : I would give her my dying blessing."

The English knights retired a little distance, and debated this adventure among themselves. They held that as knights they could not but undertake it; and who knew but what St. George, St. Denis, and their comrades might not have fallen, by ill chance, under the spells of this very enchanter ? By the Queen of Armenia's account, the Black Castle lay but a little distance from the chief road away from Jerusalem to the west of Europe.

They had made up their minds when they heard Rosana calling them. Her mother was dead.

They buried the Queen there. Then they told Rosana that they had resolved to take up her quest. She thanked them, and begged that she might go with them. " Remember that the spell of the lanterns is to be broken by a maiden," she said.

They were willing—nay, glad—to take her with them. She mounted behind Sir Guy, and they set out to find the Black Castle.

The forest was of great extent. Many miles they rode upon the track they were following without ever losing sight of trees or seeing bare hills or green meadows. But once, when they were near the edge of the forest, though they did not know it, they came upon a vast open space, where trees had been cut down, and the bare ground and rock showed. It was on a slope, and as the ground grew higher, the rocks grew larger, till at last they formed natural caves and shelters between one and another.

It was at the beginning of this open space that they met their first adversary in the quest. As they left the shelter of the trees, something huge and hairy dashed out of some bushes, and crouched near their path. Sir Alexander was in front. They were riding in single file, with Sir Guy and Rosana in the middle.

Alexander approached the strange shape. It sprang suddenly at him. At its full height it looked nine feet high or more, but it huddled itself up except for a moment when it leapt. Sir Alexander had his sword loose in the scabbard, for he had seen the thing run out of the undergrowth. He drew quickly and struck; but long before the blade could reach the creature it had bounded out of reach. It did not flee, but remained a few paces away, glaring at the knights. They could see now what it was—a misshapen satyr, half man, half goat, but deformed even so. Its face was a third of its height, and it was taller than the tallest man. It had but one eye, and that in the middle of its forehead.

Suddenly it sprang at Alexander's horse. If the horse, in terror, had not shied and reared up on its hind-legs, the satyr would have struck it in the neck; and so great is the strength of such creatures that probably it would have killed the horse, or torn it with its powerful hands. But the charger swerved, and as it turned aside, Sir Alexander struck it down with his sword. The blade did but just touch the satyr, but it squealed with rage, and made as if to leap upon the knight itself. Then it changed its purpose, and ran off as swiftly as a hart up the slope and vanished among the rocks.

"Let us pursue it and kill it!" cried Sir David. "These creatures are evil; they attack peaceful folk and do reat mischief."

Sir Alexander and Sir David spurred their horses. Sir Guy, having Rosana behind him, could not with safety join in the pursuit.

The two knights rode up the rocks. The great boulders lay piled this way and that. Suddenly the satyr leapt out from behind one of them, just as Sir David had passed it. It clung on to his horse's flanks, and with its sharp nails tore a long wound in the poor beast. Sir David swung his sword backwards, and the satyr dropped off hastily and darted among the stones. But this time Sir Alexander marked its retreat. He saw it leap down between two boulders, and pull, with marvellous strength, a third over the opening between them. The first two touched at the back; the satyr had made for itself a three-cornered refuge of rocks too heavy for any man to move.

Sir David dismounted and tended the wound in his horse. It was not deep. He had with him an ointment for these flesh wounds, and before long, when the blood ceased to flow, the ointment took effect, and the good steed felt little evil effect.

Sir Alexander chased the satyr to its hiding-place. He dismounted, and tried to move the stone that the creature had pulled across after it. But it was beyond his strength. It did not cover the opening exactly, and he peered within. He could see the bright fierce eye of the terrible creature. It gnashed its great white teeth at him, and threw itself against the stone in a fury. Quickly Sir Alexander thrust with his sword through the crevice between the rocks. It pierced the satyr's heart, and it fell dead in the little cave.

Thereafter the knights and Rosana continued their journey without adventure or mishap. The forest came to an end, and the way lay through stony desert ground. Presently the stones became rocks, and the rocks grew into cliffs. They were entering the mountain lands, and before long they struck into that grim, shut-in road which St. George and the champions had travelled—the road of frowning cliffs and countless echoes. And so at last they found themselves opposite the silent gates of the Black Castle.

VII

THE SPELL OF THE SEVEN LANTERNS

The horses were left outside the castle gates, and the three knights and Rosana began their attempt with high hearts. Sir Guy blew a blast upon the same trumpet as St. George had sounded. The gates opened, the drawbridge fell, just as they had for the champion of England. The second gates likewise answered to the trumpet, and again the courtyard of Leoger's castle saw strangers within it. But no darkness descended upon Rosana and her knights.

Sir Guy was the first to see the marble stairway as they stood gazing in wonder at the hugeness and strength of the castle. They went down the stairs, and found themselves in the great banqueting hall. In the minstrels' gallery, looking down on them with contempt, stood Leoger. By him were four giants, whom he had chosen for his body-guard, to stay by his side day and night.

"Uninvited guests!" cried Leoger, "you are welcome. My arts tell me that you are Christian knights. I have seven others of your kind asleep in an inner chamber. They will not wake to greet you, but, nevertheless, you will rejoice to join them."

"Caitiff!" cried Sir Guy, in deep anger. He did not know the full meaning of Leoger's words, but from the way in which the wizard knight spoke it was plain that seven Christian knights were his prisoners and under some evil spell. "Caitiff, are you that vile Leoger whom every true knight abhors? Set free your prisoners! We are come to break your power and make your spells in vain. Undo your enchantments and repent of your evil life, or we will slay you in addition."

"Repent!" sneered Leoger. "Sons of St. George"—the three knights started, they knew by this that the champions must truly be Leoger's captives—"sons of St. George, you shall lie bound for a thousand years in my dungeons, so that when my spells are lifted from you, you shall crumble into dust from old age. And as for that damsel you bring with you, whoever she may be——"

The Spell of the Seven Lanterns

" Did not your wizardry tell you who I am ?" cried Rosana. " Perhaps you cannot learn your own doom by your black arts. I am your daughter Rosana, and I have led these knights hither to take vengeance on you for my mother's sake, the Queen of Armenia, whom you used so shamefully."

Leoger turned pale at that name ; then his face darkened with fury, and he made a signal to his giants. In a moment the huge men had put their hands upon the balustrade of the gallery, and vaulted down into the hall, receiving no hurt from the distance, but alighting as gently as a feather touching the ground.

" Fall to, villains !" cried Sir Guy. " When we have slain you, we will discover the secret of the seven lanterns, and break the spells of this foul castle !"

He spoke at random, not knowing, indeed, where the seven lanterns were, or how he could break the spell. But his words struck fear into Leoger, who fled with a loud cry from the gallery, and was seen no more.

But only Rosana saw him flee, for the knights were too busily occupied with the giants to pay heed to anything else. Rosana herself, indeed, forgot Leoger in a moment, for she had to shrink back to the entrance of the hall to avoid the fierce combat that now began. It was the most perilous adventure that had befallen the young knights, for the giants were as active as lions, in spite of their great bulk, and they outnumbered the Englishmen. But this advantage they speedily lost, for Sir Alexander, ever quick and ready in the moment of need, had drawn his sword even as Leoger signed to the giants to make their attack, and had run at one of them almost as he touched the ground, and wounded him sorely in the side. Sir David, seeing this, had likewise turned swiftly upon the wounded giant, and in a moment the numbers were equal.

The battle was long and fierce. It was the youth of the knights, not their strength, which gave them the victory. They darted hither and thither like gadflies, pricking and cutting, advancing and retreating, not remaining each in combat with one giant, but leaping from one to the other unexpectedly, so that the monsters were bewildered, for all their skill and agility. At last one of them was brought to the ground and slain, and then the knights' task was light. The three of them made short work of the two other giants, and in a little while all four lay dead.

The three knights rested for a few minutes

to regain their breath. But they dared not tarry long while Leoger was still free and his magic powers unharmed. As they rested they looked round the great hall. There was another door in it besides that by which they had entered. It was under the minstrels' gallery. When they were ready they went to this and pushed against it. It swung open, and they found themselves in another huge hall as large as the banqueting hall. The high roof of it was supported by a column of pure alabaster in the midst, on which they could see a plate of silver inscribed with words. All round the hall in silver sconces against the walls tall candles burned. From the ceiling, on long chains of gold, hung seven lamps, the flames of which glowed red. There was no living creature to be seen in the hall, and no sound to be heard.

They went forward to the alabaster column. Rosana read the words of the inscription first:

"Seven lanterns burn to guard Leoger's power:
When they are quenched, the wizard's fatal hour
Is come upon him. But their living fire
Shall by one hand and means alone expire.
The Rose Princess must tread the secret path
To where the Dark Pool bubbles in its wrath.
Let her its ever-gliding waters bring
And on the flames a crystal shower fling."

The Sons of St. George

"The Rose Princess!" said Rosana. "Surely I am she!" She still wore at her breast the crimson rose which had been there when first the sons of St. George saw her in the forest of Armenia. "Look!" she said, touching it. "I am a Princess, and here is my rose, and here above us are the seven lanterns. It is as my dear mother said: Leoger's power will die with their flames."

Sir David raised his sword—all three knights now were carrying their swords drawn—and struck at the lantern hanging nearest to him. They hung low, about four feet from the ground. The sword smote the lantern full, but neither did it break nor did the flame so much as quiver; and a shock ran up Sir David's sword-arm as if he had beaten a wall of hard stone. Sir Alexander took a lantern in his mailed hand, and blew at the flame, but it did not even tremble at his breath. Sir Guy tried to extinguish the flame with his fingers, but in vain.

"They are indeed enchanted," said he. "Princess, I believe that it will be in your power to quench the flames, as this prophecy says, if we can but find this Dark Pool, whatever it may be."

"We must find it," said Sir David. "Is there any other way out of this hall?"

The Spell of the Seven Lanterns

" There is another door yonder," said Sir Alexander, pointing.

They went to the door. It was made of iron, with great bolts across it, and a large key in the lock. Sir Guy tried to turn the key; then his brothers tried. It would not move, for all their strength. Nor could they move the bolts.

" Is there no other door ?" asked Sir David.

" There might be a secret door, perhaps, hidden in the wall," said Sir Alexander.

They began to search all the walls of the chamber, feeling and pressing for unseen springs or invisible openings. They discovered nothing. But in the middle of their search they heard a cry from Rosana.

" Come, sirs !" she called to them. " I have opened the door."

They went to where she stood. The iron door was wide open: a dark passage lay beyond it.

" How did you open the door, Princess ?" asked Sir Alexander.

" I do not know," she answered. " I thought I would try the key idly, with no real hope of turning it, and behold, it turned easily in my hand, and the bolts slid back as it turned ! When they were undone, I

387

pressed the door, and it swung open as you see."

"Without doubt you are fated to break the spell, Princess," said Sir Guy. "Now let us enter this passage warily."

Sword in hand, the three knights went slowly into the passage, followed by Rosana. It was narrow and low-roofed at first, but gradually grew broader. Slowly, also, a faint light began to appear. They came at the end of it into a wide underground cellar, the end of which was beyond their sight. It was lit by one solitary great torch a little distance in front of them. Round the light of the torch writhed and swirled grey mists, making the place look like an abode of ghosts.

As they came out of the passage, a faint murmuring sound which they had already begun to hear became more distinct. It grew into a bubbling, boiling sound as of angry waters.

They went towards the torch. When they were close to it, they could see into the mists beyond. Ten paces away lay the edge of a pool, in which water rose and eddied and bubbled without ceasing. On it a little crystal bowl, curiously shaped, rocked and danced, but was never filled with the water, and came to no harm for all its tossings.

The Spell of the Seven Lanterns

"It is the Dark Pool!" cried Sir David joyfully. "Princess, take the crystal vessel and fill it with water, and hasten back to the lanterns."

Rosana started forward. But suddenly all the chamber was filled with a denser fog. It hung in the air for the space of a minute only, and then vanished. But when it had vanished, leaving only the thin mist as before, the knights saw all around them dreadful shapes : giants, hobgoblins, griffins, fiery serpents, dragons, and furies. Between them and the Dark Pool these creatures were crowded, rank on rank.

The knights did not hesitate. They fell upon the monsters with their swords; they cut and thrust, they struck and avoided blows; but they could not drive off the crowd of frightful shapes. If they slew one, his body vanished, and another creature appeared in his place. And if they forced the enemy to yield a little so that they should have drawn nearer to the Dark Pool, they found that its magic waters were no closer. The Pool withdrew itself as they advanced, and ever its edge was out of their reach.

But as they fought so valiantly, Rosana saw an opportunity. By chance a griffin knocked Sir David's shield out of his hand.

The Sons of St. George

She was close behind him, sheltered by him. She picked up the shield quickly and held it in front of her to cover her body, and thus protected she darted forward through the monsters and reached the Pool. Its waters did not retreat before her; against her Leoger's enchantments seemed void of power. She stretched out her arm over the boiling Pool, and caught the crystal vessel in her right hand. As she touched it, the bubbling ceased, and the dark surface became as still as a calm lake. She dipped the vessel in it and drew it out full of water. Then she turned to flee back to the lanterns.

Sir Guy, Sir Alexander, and Sir David were alone with her in the chamber. As she lifted the full vessel from the Pool, all the strange threatening shapes had vanished. The mist had disappeared wholly, the torch burnt clear and bright. The passage back lay open still, dark, but unguarded.

"You have saved us!" cried Sir David. "Leoger's power is broken."

"We must extinguish the lamps," said Sir Guy. "Back to the great hall!"

As quickly as they could, Rosana in their midst, they went through the passage, and out into the hall of the alabaster pillar.

Rosana stopped at a lamp. She hesitated.

"ROSANA STRETCHED OUT HER ARM OVER THE BOILING POOL."

The Spell of the Seven Lanterns

She feared at this last moment that there might be some fresh and terrible enchantment in the magic waters.

" ' On the flame a crystal shower fling !' " read Sir Guy from the silver tablet. "Hasten, Princess, lest Leoger have time to weave some new spell."

She hesitated no longer. Stretching out the crystal bowl, she spilled a few drops over the lantern. Immediately the floor of the hall rocked, and there was darkness for a moment. The flame of the lamp burst into a blazing light, and suddenly died as the darkness passed. One lantern was extinguished.

A second time Rosana threw water on a flame; a second time the flame flared and the hall rocked in darkness. Seven times in all did she sprinkle the magical drops, until all the lamps were extinguished. As the darkness fell for the seventh time, they heard a sound of thousands of harsh voices, speaking unknown words in tones of uttermost fear; and then there came a crying and screaming as of evil spirits, and a rushing noise of wind. All the enchantments and vile creatures of Leoger's castle were fleeing at that moment to their own place beyond the mortal world.

A silence descended upon them at this last

393

wonder. Then they heard the sound of gates being flung open, and the door to the banquet hall opened of its own accord, and the noise of voices came through. They hastened to the foot of the great marble stair, the door of which also lay wide open. There, coming down the stair, they saw a host of knights and ladies. From every door others followed, and in the midst were the seven champions themselves. All the prisoners of the castle were freed from their spells; every chain was loosed, every dungeon opened, when the seven lanterns lost their light.

Long and glad were the greetings that followed, and many a tale of adventure and marvel had the freed captives to tell one another. That night a joyous feast was held in Leoger's castle, for they found in it great stores of food and wine, as well as armour and horses and all things necessary alike for warfare and for peaceful living. Never had there been in that once evil place mirth and jollity so innocent and so full of happiness.

When they had feasted, they searched the castle for resting-places, and lay down to sleep. On the morrow they would go everyone to his home.

THE LAST DEEDS OF THE CHAMPIONS

I

THE ADMIRAL OF BABYLON

S T. GEORGE could not find unbroken rest in the castle of Leoger. He had a spacious chamber for his bedroom, and a bed of the finest swansdown; but he tossed and tumbled upon it as if it had been a bed of stones. He was so restless and tormented in mind that at last he did not know for certain whether he was asleep or awake.

In the midst of his tumult of thought a vision appeared to him. He saw before him a woman of surpassing beauty, clad in Eastern dress. She spoke to him in a voice sweet and clear.

"Why does a Christian knight rest when evil is abroad?" she said. "All the spells of Leoger are not broken. There remains one more powerful than all the others, which the champion of England alone can break; so it is fated. Rise, St. George, and follow me."

"Who are you, beauteous lady?" asked St. George, starting up in wonder. "What is this fresh evil you speak of?"

The Last Deeds of the Champions

"No fresh evil: an ancient wrong," she answered. "But you alone can set it right. A king lies spellbound; moreover, he is in perpetual torment. So strong was this spell of the vile Leoger, that even he cannot unbind it. Only one knight in the whole world can loose it. He must be fearless and peerless, and must have suffered and escaped from Leoger's power. You are he."

"Can you not tell me more, lady?" asked St. George. "Tell me at least who it is who bids me rise and go on an unknown errand? Might you not be some enchantment of Leoger's?"

"You know that his power has gone with the flame of the seven lanterns," replied the vision. "As for me, I was once Angelica, daughter of the Admiral of Babylon. It is the Admiral himself, the Emir of that great dominion, whom you are to free from torture. More I cannot tell you now."

"I will come with you," said St. George, putting aside his doubts. He rose and put on a shirt of chainmail and other armour, and took his bright sword naked in his hand.

The figure went out, and down staircases and through doors in the castle, and at last into the open air outside it into the courtyard, and so across the moat into the woods outside. All the gates had flown open, and the drawbridge had fallen when the lanterns had been put out. Far into the woods she led him, until they came suddenly upon a great mausoleum or tomb. A high wall stood round it, with one door in it, which was open. Inside was a lofty dome set upon four strong pillars. In the midst, under the centre of the dome, lay what appeared to be a tomb; but in reality it was a grating of marble. Above it, upon supports of marble, was stretched the figure of an old man. Through the openings in the marble grating played flames, which neither burned the marble nor consumed the raiment or person of the old man, but yet caused him the most exquisite pain, as if they were the flames of a real fire. It was an enchantment of Leoger's.

"This is my sire, the Admiral of Babylon," said the beautiful vision. "Thus only can he be released. Take your sword and smite with it with all your force upon his breast three times. Do not heed him, or anything he says. Your good blade will do him no hurt: he is enchanted. Even if you were to wound him, would not a mortal wound be better than this torment?"

St. George could not persuade himself to

do such a deed. "I cannot strike a living man defenceless as he is," he said. "This may be some enchantment, so that I may slay an innocent person."

"Strike without fear, St. George," answered the lady. "Listen: you are guarded by Heaven. There are upon earth certain deeds which you must do and you only. You alone could slay the Egyptian dragon; you alone could draw from its magical sheath the sword at the garden of Ormandine. Who but you could have put all the hosts of heathendom to flight? And for you only is waiting yet one more great deed. Do you remember the prophecy that came to you by the mouth of Wat the shipman in Calais port? Not yet has that been wholly fulfilled. Do you remember that you must save England from a dragon? I was your guardian angel in that journey to Coventry. I bid you smite this captive as I have said."

St. George heard with wonder these sayings about his past deeds and what was to come. He could not but obey. He lifted his sword, and struck down upon the breast of the man stretched upon the unceasing flames. True and full did he strike, yet no blood came from the stroke, nor was any wound made. Again he struck, and again; and at the third blow the flames ceased, and the tomb itself dissolved into a little mound of dust, and the man himself stood upright, looking around him in bewilderment.

" Where am I ?" cried the old man. " It is you who have delivered me," he added, catching sight of St. George with his drawn sword.

" Tell me first who you are," answered St. George, " that I may know this is no further device of that vile wizard Leoger."

" I am the Admiral of Babylon, as you Christians call me. Rightly my own folk call me Emir. My daughter, the Princess Angelica, was slain by a wicked wizard knight named Leoger. When I made war upon him for his wicked deed, he defeated my army by magic arts, and carried me away from Babylon by his enchantments, and put me into torment, as you found me. I warred upon him because Angelica was his wife, and he used her shamefully, and slew her, as I have said."

" Even so did he use other fair ladies shamefully," answered St. George.

" He speaks truly; this is my father," said the gracious vision. But her voice and herself were alike unrevealed to the Emir of Babylon, who marvelled that St. George

401

seemed to be listening to some sound he could not hear.

"You shall be avenged," said St. George. His words were suited equally to the Emir, to whom he now turned. "There are knights here, sire, who will restore you to your kingdom," he said. "Leoger's spells have been destroyed. This enchantment that he put upon you is the last."

"Yet Leoger himself is not slain," said the figure of the Princess Angelica. "Let Rosana seek her father in the wilderness of Arabia, whither he has fled. He will come to repentance by her aid, and never again will he have traffic with the black art."

With that she suddenly vanished from their sight, leaving St. George alone with the Admiral of Babylon.

"I have been led to you, Lord Admiral," said St. George, "by a vision of your daughter. Certain things also she told me in respect of Leoger and Rosana. Now let me conduct you to my comrades."

He went with the Admiral to the castle, and laid before the champions and other Christian knights the vision he had seen and the fate of the Admiral, and immediately they resolved to recover his kingdom for him. But when St. George told Rosana what had been prophesied about her, she would not go to Babylon with them, but was for setting out at once for the desert of Arabia to seek Leoger.

So Rosana parted from the Christian knights, and they never saw her again; for the prophecy came true, and she found Leoger alone in the wilderness, and by her gentleness won him to repentance. Many years together did they live, dwelling like hermits in that lonely place; and when at last the time came for Leoger to die, Rosana did not survive him, but died of grief, and was buried beside him by the country folk of that region.

But the champions and the Admiral went to the great and famous city of Babylon, and found, when they came there, that no great warfare would be needed, as they had feared, to restore the sovereign to his throne; for when Leoger had carried him off, the great nobles of the kingdom had fallen a-quarrelling among themselves, and had waged civil war for so long that the people were heartily weary of such misrule, and overjoyed to welcome back their rightful monarch. And in a little while the Admiral was reigning happily, as though Leoger had never done him any hurt.

At Babylon itself a public holiday was decreed to celebrate the joyful event; and during the rejoicings a tournament was held, at which the champions and St. George's sons, now admitted fully to that wondrous brotherhood, maintained themselves undefeated; and then, enriched with the spoils of Leoger's castle, they set out to return each to their own land. They journeyed together at first. They went by way of Constantinople, where another tournament was held, and they covered themselves with fresh glory, and so, travelling ever westward from those eastern lands which they were never more to see, they came at last to Rome.

II

THE END OF THE BROTHERHOOD

At Rome the brotherhood of the champions began to be broken up. Never again was that peerless band of knights to take up together the battle of Christendom against the forces of evil, of right against wrong, of chivalry against heathendom. St. Anthony of Italy had come to his own land, where he was to end his days. The champions were entertained in Rome with feasts and joustings and hunting; and it chanced one day that as they rode through a forest upon a hunt, St.

The End of the Brotherhood

Anthony perceived a little disused chapel, which out of curiosity he entered. On a stone in the wall he found these words carved:

"Rest after war ; live here in charity ;
Italy's saint shall be St. Anthony."

By that he knew that thenceforth his life was to be one of peace and good works. So, bidding a loving farewell to his comrades, he gave himself up to the service of God and mankind in that little chapel, which he caused to be restored and beautified. There he lived many years, doing deeds of holiness and charity daily; and when in the fulness of time he died, he was lamented by all Italy, and made the patron saint of his country.

The champions left Italy and journeyed on. St. James was the next to leave them, for he had to travel to his own land of Spain. But when he came thither, he found that a king reigned who was a pagan, and hostile to all Christians. St. James, however, caused a chapel to be built, and converted many of the inhabitants from their heathen faith. But the King of Spain had word brought to him of this, and sending an army, he caused the chapel to be surrounded while all the Christian folk were in it, and ordered that it should be bricked up, so that no food nor light nor air could enter it. St. James and his followers died of starvation; but in spite of their death, the chapel continued to give forth a miraculous light and a harmony of sweet sounds, as if it were lit up from within, and men were singing joyful hymns in it. Moreover, from the time when the Christians were thus martyred, the King of Spain began to pine away, and before long died; and the fame of St. James and his chapel spreading throughout the land, all the people became Christians, and St. James was made the patron saint of Spain.

St. Denis of France travelled with the champions from Britain and Ireland as far as Calais, where each was to take ship to his own country. There, with sad farewells and loving words, they parted. St. Denis went back inland to preach Christianity to his countrymen, for in the long absence of the Christian knights the people had fallen grievously from their faith. At a certain town the inhabitants, fiercer than elsewhere, set upon him and stoned him to death. But immediately those who stoned him were struck by lightning, and so great was the wonder and repentance of the people that they all became Christians, and made St. Denis their patron saint.

The End of the Brotherhood

St. David of Wales took ship from Calais to the port which lies near Caerleon-upon-Usk. But when he landed at last in his own country, he found that pagans had conquered it, and were oppressing the people; and slowly and secretly he went the length and breadth of Wales, stirring up the country folk, and presently had raised an army. He led his bands against the pagan host, and, bidding the Welsh wear in their helmets a leek, to distinguish them, gave battle, and utterly routed the heathen, and set up the Christian faith in Wales once again. Not many years after this victory he died, and was made the patron saint of Wales, which also took the leek as its emblem.

St. Patrick of Ireland was the first of the champions to die. When he landed in his own country, he felt a weakness as of old age creeping upon him, and he resolved to live as a hermit thenceforth. He shut himself up in a stone house, and caused the door to be walled up, and left only a little hole at which food could be thrust through for him. In that house he dug his own grave with his hands, and when he had done this, he passed the rest of his days by it in praying and fasting; and so, before long, died the patron saint of Ireland, and when he was buried in the grave he had

407

dug, the stone house was pulled down, and a chapel built over the place where it had stood.

St. Andrew preached Christianity in Scotland until, so strong was paganism at that time, the King declared him a foreign spy, and slew him. But when a little time had passed the Scots learnt his true nature, and repented, and became Christians; wherefore St. Andrew is to this day patron saint of Scotland.

And so only St. George was left, with three sons to carry on his great name worthily. But before he died he had yet another famous adventure.

III

THE DRAGON OF DUNSMORE HEATH

Many thoughts came to St. George as he sailed from Calais port with his three sons. The years had begun to be heavy upon him. It seemed to him long, long ago that he had tricked Kalyb into telling the secret of his birth. How many battles had he fought since then! What victories had he won against the forces of darkness! And he thought long of Sabra, and of the hardships by which he had won her. How dearly he had loved her, what high trust in his honour and might she had shown, how gentle and beloved she was !

And then he thought of how he had journeyed from Calais to England before, and of the strange prophecy of Wat the shipman to him. He was to save England, the man had been told in that vision, which in other ways had come true so wondrously. The words were wild and strange; but it seemed that he was to save England from a dragon. Ah! how should he save England now ? Many a dragon had he fought since that first monster whose death had won Sabra for him. But now he was growing old and weary; no longer could his sword strike invincibly; no longer could the swiftness of his limbs be certain of giving him the victory where strength was of no avail. Well, be the issue what it might, he would still take up with a stout heart any quest or cause that should be in his path down the highway of life.

The boat came safely to Dover. Not now were relays of horses waiting to carry the champion of England to Coventry without losing a moment. More slowly and steadily did he travel across England with his three sons. Nearer and nearer did Coventry draw. It was a town of many memories for St. George.

The Last Deeds of the Champions

They journeyed, as he had journeyed in that wild ride to save Sabra, by way of Oxford and Warwick, leaving Rugby on the right. It chanced that soon after they left Warwick St. George's horse fell lame.

"Dear sons," he said, "my horse can but hobble: I would not press the good creature unduly. Go you forward at a better pace, and acquaint the people of Coventry with my approach, and bring me a fresh horse to end my journey. I shall be safe alone; there are no enchantments in England, and no vile enemies to meet. Yet I doubt something is amiss with the people. We have met few folk; but those we have met have looked at us askance and fearfully. They fear something, I know not what. But I shall have news of this or of any other happening when I reach Coventry. Meanwhile ride on, my sons."

The three young knights rode on at his bidding. He went more slowly. But as at last he drew near to Coventry, Sir Guy came riding back to him at full speed.

"An adventure, sir!" he cried. "My brothers and I ask your leave to slay the dragon."

"The dragon!" said St. George, the old prophecy rushing at once into his mind.

The Dragon of Dunsmore Heath

"What dragon? There are no dragons in England nowadays."

"A monstrous dragon lives on Dunsmore Heath, where it has made itself a cave. It ravages all the country round here. It was not of us that the common folk were afraid, but of it. They feared it might see us in its prowlings, and attack us, for it loves horses as well as men, they say. I pray you, let us go against it and kill it."

"Nay, my son, this adventure is for me," answered St. George. "Long ago was this foretold." And he recounted the prophecy of the shipman. "I am old now," he added, "yet I shall conquer in this fight, even if it is the last battle I am to enter upon. Do you and your brothers await the issue, and be prepared to defend my people of Coventry if any misfortune befall me."

Sir Guy pleaded with him, but St. George knew that he was the person appointed to kill this dragon; and his sons saw that it was in vain to seek to change his resolution. They rode into Coventry. St. George mounted a fresh horse and set out for Dunsmore Heath. His sons and the chief men of Coventry followed him at a little distance, and watched from afar the last fight of the champion of England.

411

The Last Deeds of the Champions

He came to the great heath, a space covered with low bushes and heather. From a little hollow he saw smoke rising. The dragon, a peasant had brought word, had carried off an ox to its lair, and doubtless now was devouring it. St. George rode towards the smoke. But before he reached the hollow the dragon scented him, and rose, grim and terrible, from its prey. It was as large as the dragon of Egypt, but wingless. But it was more poisonous, for even its breath had venom in it, and would stupefy a man if it blew upon him for long, and deadly poison ran in its veins.

As it came on, fire and smoke poured out of its huge nostrils, and its bellowings shook the very earth. It ran in a kind of gallop, very swiftly. But St. George found that it could not turn swiftly, for he turned his horse aside dexterously as it was upon him, and it rushed past without touching him with its jaws or its huge talons. But its tail swung as it passed, and struck both the champion and his horse a grievous blow, so that the horse fell dead, and St. George, staggering away from the poor beast as it sank to the ground, felt as though he had been bruised by a battering ram.

He was fighting with his sword. He re-

412

"THE DRAGON ROSE, GRIM AND TERRIBLE"

covered himself quickly and ran at the dragon. It raised one great paw to strike, and he darted in and thrust swiftly at the under part of its body. The point pierced the thick hide, and poison, issuing from the wound, fell upon the champion, scorching him as if it had been liquid fire. Enraged by the pain, the monster reared up and slipped, falling on its side. In an instant St. George took advantage of the fall, and before it could regain its feet, dealt it three fierce blows, the last of them deep and mortal. Then he sprang back swiftly, but not in time to avoid the venom that came from the wounds, or the lashing of the dragon's tail as it met its death.

The champion was sorely wounded, but the dragon was slain. He cut off its head, and when his sons, seeing that the fight was over, came to him and gave him another horse, he mounted and rode it into Coventry. Word of his victory had reached the town before him, and a great crowd of people came forth to greet him joyously. Bearing the dragon's head on his sword point, he entered the town in their midst. But as he reached the market-place, where so long before he had saved Sabra, his wounds took effect on him. He reeled in his saddle and fell dead.

The Last Deeds of the Champions

So died St. George, the greatest and bravest of all the Seven Champions of Christendom.

His eldest son, Sir Guy, became Earl of Warwick, and did many famous deeds of chivalry. Sir Alexander, when the time of mourning for St. George was ended, went back to Normandy and found his Princess, and brought her to England and married her. He was appointed Captain of all the King's guards. Sir David became the King's steward and cup-bearer. And all three lived in great happiness and honour till they died.

THE END

www.ingramcontent.com/pod-product-compliance
Lightning Source LLC
Chambersburg PA
CBHW030547020726
47494CB00005B/1512